Acclaim for R

Secret Hearts "delivers exactly [...] story, sweet romance, great characters, chemistry and hot sex scenes. Radclyffe knows how to pen a good lesbian romance."
—*LezReviewBooks Blog*

Wild Shores "will hook you early. Radclyffe weaves a chance encounter into all-out steamy romance. These strong, dynamic women have great conversations, and fantastic chemistry."
—*The Romantic Reader Blog*

In **2016 RWA/OCC Book Buyers Best award winner for suspense and mystery with romantic elements** *Price of Honor* "Radclyffe is master of the action-thriller series...The old familiar characters are there, but enough new blood is introduced to give it a fresh feel and open new avenues for intrigue."—*Curve Magazine*

In *Prescription for Love* "Radclyffe populates her small town with colorful characters, among the most memorable being Flann's little sister, Margie, and Abby's 15-year-old trans son, Blake...This romantic drama has plenty of heart and soul."
—*Publishers Weekly*

2013 RWA/New England Bean Pot award winner for contemporary romance *Crossroads* "will draw the reader in and make her heart ache, willing the two main characters to find love and a life together. It's a story that lingers long after coming to 'the end.'"—*Lambda Literary*

In **2012 RWA/FTHRW Lories and RWA HODRW Aspen Gold award winner** *Firestorm* "Radclyffe brings another hot lesbian romance for her readers."—*The Lesbrary*

Foreword Review Book of the Year finalist and IPPY silver medalist *Trauma Alert* "is hard to put down and it will sizzle in the reader's hands. The characters are hot, the sex scenes explicit and explosive, and the book is moved along by an interesting plot with well drawn secondary characters. The real star of this show is the attraction between the two characters, both of whom resist and then fall head over heels."
—*Lambda Literary Reviews*

Applause for L.L. Raand's Midnight Hunters Series

The Midnight Hunt
RWA 2012 VCRW Laurel Wreath winner *Blood Hunt*
Night Hunt
The Lone Hunt

"Raand has built a complex world inhabited by werewolves, vampires, and other paranormal beings…Raand has given her readers a complex plot filled with wonderful characters as well as insight into the hierarchy of Sylvan's pack and vampire clans. There are many plot twists and turns, as well as erotic sex scenes in this riveting novel that keep the pages flying until its satisfying conclusion."—*Just About Write*

"Once again, I am amazed at the storytelling ability of L.L. Raand aka Radclyffe. In *Blood Hunt*, she mixes high levels of sheer eroticism that will leave you squirming in your seat with an impeccable multi-character storyline all streaming together to form one great read." —*Queer Magazine Online*

"*The Midnight Hunt* has a gripping story to tell, and while there are also some truly erotic sex scenes, the story always takes precedence. This is a great read which is not easily put down nor easily forgotten."—*Just About Write*

"Are you sick of the same old hetero vampire / werewolf story plastered in every bookstore and at every movie theater? Well, I've got the cure to your werewolf fever. *The Midnight Hunt* is first in, what I hope is, a long-running series of fantasy erotica for L.L. Raand (aka Radclyffe)."—*Queer Magazine Online*

"Any reader familiar with Radclyffe's writing will recognize the author's style within *The Midnight Hunt*, yet at the same time it is most definitely a new direction. The author delivers an excellent story here, one that is engrossing from the very beginning. Raand has pieced together an intricate world, and provided just enough details for the reader to become enmeshed in the new world. The action moves quickly throughout the book and it's hard to put down."—*Three Dollar Bill Reviews*

By Radclyffe

Romances

Innocent Hearts	When Dreams Tremble
Promising Hearts	The Lonely Hearts Club
Love's Melody Lost	Night Call
Love's Tender Warriors	Secrets in the Stone
Tomorrow's Promise	Desire by Starlight
Love's Masquerade	Crossroads
shadowland	Homestead
Passion's Bright Fury	The Color of Love
Fated Love	Secret Hearts
Turn Back Time	

The Provincetown Tales

Safe Harbor	Winds of Fortune
Beyond the Breakwater	Returning Tides
Distant Shores, Silent Thunder	Sheltering Dunes
Storms of Change	

Honor Series

- Above All, Honor
- Honor Bound
- Love & Honor
- Honor Guards
- Honor Reclaimed
- Honor Under Siege
- Word of Honor
- Code of Honor
- Price of Honor

Justice Series

- A Matter of Trust (prequel)
- Shield of Justice
- In Pursuit of Justice
- Justice in the Shadows
- Justice Served
- Justice for All

Rivers Community Romances

Against Doctor's Orders	Love on Call
Prescription for Love	Love After Hours

First Responders Novels

Trauma Alert	Taking Fire
Firestorm	Wild Shores
Oath of Honor	Heart Stop

Short Fiction

Collected Stories by Radclyffe
Erotic Interludes: *Change Of Pace*
Radical Encounters

Edited by Radclyffe:
Best Lesbian Romance 2009–2014

Stacia Seaman and Radclyffe, eds.:
Erotic Interludes 2: *Stolen Moments*
Erotic Interludes 3: *Lessons in Love*
Erotic Interludes 4: *Extreme Passions*
Erotic Interludes 5: *Road Games*
Romantic Interludes 1: *Discovery*
Romantic Interludes 2: *Secrets*
Breathless: *Tales of Celebration*
Women of the Dark Streets
Amor and More: Love Everafter
Myth & Magic: Queer Fairy Tales

By L.L. Raand
Midnight Hunters
The Midnight Hunt
Blood Hunt
Night Hunt
The Lone Hunt
The Magic Hunt
Shadow Hunt

Visit us at www.boldstrokesbooks.com

LOVE
AFTER HOURS

by

RADCLY*f*FE

2017

LOVE AFTER HOURS

ISBN 13: 978-1-63555-090-0

This Trade Paperback Original Is Published By
Bold Strokes Books, Inc.
P.O. Box 249
Valley Falls, NY 12185

First Edition: November 2017

Credits
Editors: Ruth Sternglantz and Stacia Seaman
Production Design: Stacia Seaman
Cover Design by Sheri (graphicartist2020@hotmail.com)

Acknowledgments

Originally I conceived of these interconnected stand-alone romances as a family saga with the Rivers family at the core. As I began building this world, I quickly recognized the characters whose stories would eventually be told were more than members of a traditional family or even a family of choice—they were part of a community bound together by shared history, sense of pride, and civic responsibility. The hospital and the village are characters too, and these stories set anywhere else would not be the same. These are romances on many levels—women finding love, finding "home," and finding hope together in a world where the past, present, and future flow in an unbroken line.

Many thanks go to: senior editor Sandy Lowe for her advice and encouragement of my author self, and her excellent publishing expertise in support of BSB's authors and operations; editor Ruth Sternglantz for treating each book as if it were the only one on her desk; editor Stacia Seaman for never overlooking a single mistake; and my first readers Paula and Eva for taking time out of their busy lives to send invaluable feedback.

And as always, thanks to Lee for before and after hours. *Amo te*.

Radclyffe 2017

To Lee, day in and day out

CHAPTER ONE

Carrie pulled her red and white Mini Cooper convertible into the farthest slot in the nearly empty staff parking lot behind the Rivers and squinted to relieve the ache in her barely focused eyeballs. Too early. Too much sun. Who the hell got up this early in the morning anyhow? Her idea of morning started around eight, not five thirty. She grabbed her bag, locked the car, and hurried toward the side entrance to the administrative wing, navigating the gracefully meandering flagstone paths between flower beds and towering trees mostly by memory, refusing to be seduced into a cheery mood by the ridiculous beauty of the place. She lost that battle halfway across the green. Assaulted by the scent of fresh-mown grass and Sweet Williams, she stopped, took a deep breath, and surrendered to the pleasure of being in the place she loved most in the world.

And really, who wouldn't fall in love with the stately old red brick hospital, with its sweeping lawns, lush gardens, and imperious perch above the quaint village nestled below it. Usually she loved coming to work, as long as it wasn't in the middle of the damn night! Today was a special case, though, and she picked up her pace. She needed an hour at least to get the weekend's accumulated emergencies taken care of if she was going to make it to pre-op by seven. Mondays always sucked, but with everything going on, this one was already shaping up to be worse than usual.

Never mind—handling the tough stuff was her job, after all. Once she triaged whatever emergent problems had been directed toward Presley's attention after the end of the workday on Friday, she could safely ignore anything else until at least noon. Flann had said she'd be done well before that.

The wide marble-floored hall leading down the center of the administrative wing was empty. All the sane people were home in bed. She ducked into the coffee room to put on a pot and have her second cup of the day. Maybe this would get her brain working. Why did anyone think it was a good idea to come in this early? Bad enough Presley always started before the sun came up, and Carrie *had* to be in by seven thirty or feel guilty all day that the boss was working three times as hard as her.

Not that she regretted the decision this morning. She'd volunteered to go through the mail, because if she didn't, Presley would, and Presley needed to be with Abby right now. They all did. That's what friends did, offered moral support during times like this. Presley would never ask her to come in this early, but someone had to, and that's why she was the admin, after all. She was the wall, the immovable object that kept all the daily traumas and dramas away from Presley so Presley could do whatever it was CEOs did. Not that she didn't know what Presley did every day—she logged Presley's correspondence and handled follow-up phone calls and, more often than not, took over projects once Presley had all the necessary moving parts moving the way they should. Presley had to focus on the big picture—the one where the hospital stayed open and the community had accessible health care and the town didn't dwindle away and die like so many other rural towns. Presley had dragged the Rivers back from the edge of extinction and probable demolition in the last half year but was still juggling finances, staff issues, insurance contracts, and new hires simultaneously. That's why she'd finally been able to talk Presley into letting her spearhead the renovation of the emergency room and the expanded trauma area and MRI suite. Really, how hard could it be to handle a bunch of construction workers? She wrangled a team full of guys into line three times a week from the pitcher's mound—mostly they were like a bunch of puppies, rambunctious and tending toward chewing on the furniture, but a swat on the butt usually brought them into order.

She smiled thinking about the upcoming interleague tournament as she hunkered down at her desk and powered up her computer in the alcove framed by tall white arched columns adjacent to Presley's office. The only thing she loved more than her job was pitching for the hospital softball team, especially when they were in first place. As long as Blake's surgery went well, she'd be playing tonight.

Her stomach tightened. Okay, so she was really nervous, even if she didn't have any reason to be. The anxiety was normal, right? Even if she did work in a hospital surrounded by constant emergencies. Even if she lived with a doctor who was called out in the middle of the night almost every night of the week for some emergency. Sort of lived with, although not so much anymore, and not for much longer.

But this was different. This was family. How quickly they had all become family—Presley and Harper, Flann and Abby, Blake and Margie. All the Rivers family, and the ones they loved and who loved them. Blake would be fine. Flann was an exceptional surgeon and Glenn would be with her, steady, solid Glenn, who was everyone's strength, especially Flann's and Abby's right now. And her cousin Mari. She smiled to herself. The cousin she didn't know she'd had until just a few months before, now as much family as the one she'd grown up with.

"Is the boss in?" a husky, irritated voice demanded, jerking Carrie's attention up from her screen.

A woman in khaki canvas pants cinched by a wide, worn brown leather belt, work boots, and a faded blue T-shirt with the sleeves torn off stood in front of her, dark eyes snapping, her equally dark hair ruffled and sweat slick even at this hour of the morning. A thick black lock dragged across her forehead, almost falling into her right eye. Her arms were tanned and muscled, her hands long fingered and, at this moment, hooked over the waistband of her pants. Her long lean legs were spread wide, her expression impatient. A hard hat rested in the crook of her arm, clamped against her side as if it was simply another appendage.

"No, she isn't," Carrie said with her office voice, calm and collected and friendly. "She's not expected until this afternoon."

"Well, I have to talk to her." The woman wasn't making a request. She stared back at Carrie, as if Carrie could conjure Presley from her top desk drawer.

Carrie kept her smile in place. "I'm very sorry, but she's unavailable. Perhaps I can help—"

"Nope, you can't. Look, miss, here's the situation—I've got six guys, a heavy excavator, a dump truck full of crushed stone, and a front loader idling in your parking lot—"

"It's Ms.," Carrie said, feeling the smile slip and not particularly caring. Really, it must be the job and not the hormones that made some of these hard-hat types just plain hardheaded. "And what parking lot are you talking about? We don't have security scheduled to reroute traffic, and if you're blocking—"

"We wouldn't be blocking anyone, if we had—"

"So you *are* blocking access? What parking lot? Tell me it's not the emergency room."

The woman blew out an exasperated breath. "Do you want an extension to the emergency room or not? Because if you do, I have to bring my equipment across the parking lot to get to the excavation site."

"And exactly when did you inform us you would be starting this morning?"

"I called and left a message on Friday afternoon."

"With whom?" Carrie felt her eyebrow rise. "I didn't take a call from you, Ms.—"

The dark brows drew down. "Somebody by the name of…Phillips, maybe? Some guy in resources."

"How on earth did you end up with Stan Phillips?"

"What does it matter? I'm wasting fuel and man-hours chatting with you. Under other circumstances, that might be pleasant, but right now, I don't have time for this. I need you to get Worth on the line for me."

Carrie snorted. As if there'd ever be a time when a conversation, let alone a *chat*, with this woman would be on her must-do list. She'd lost count of the times she'd been interrupted. Way too many times to worry about making a professional impression. "That is *Ms.* Worth, and who might you be exactly?"

"Gina Antonelli. The contractor who's going to build your new wing if I can actually ever get to work."

Damn it. That project was a priority, and her baby to boot. Carrie sighed. "Okay, let's start at the beginning."

"Let's not. Just get me the boss."

Would snarling *I am the boss* carry any weight at all? Carrie's jaws tightened and her back molars began to throb. Not a good sign. Not the morning to try her patience. Definitely not anytime, any day to pull a strong-arm act on her. Good looks—okay, fabulous looks—could only get you so far, and in this circumstance, no mileage at all.

"Let me speak slowly so you understand me," Carrie said, very carefully and very precisely. "Ms. Worth is not available and will not be available until later today, at the earliest." She held up a finger to forestall the interruption she saw coming. "And…if you have a problem, now or in the future, you will need to explain it to me, and I will be able to assist you. Now, which part is not clear?"

"I understood all of that, quite well, actually." Antonelli scowled. "My turn. I can't start work because the necessary permits are not posted. That suggests to me that the inspector has not approved the project. You and your absentee boss are wasting my time and money and, by the way, your own." She smiled, a smile that suggested, under other circumstances, she might be drop-dead gorgeous, but right now she only reminded Carrie of a very dangerous wild animal.

"Now that," Carrie said dryly, "is something I might be able to help you with. Where can I reach you? No one is going to be in the municipal offices until at least eight thirty, if we're lucky."

"And what am I supposed to do until then? Tell my guys to sit on their hands?"

Carrie gritted her teeth and avoided the response she might have made if she'd been on the field in the midst of a heated game. "If you can't begin work without the permits, then I don't see that you have any choice."

"I hope you people are a little bit better at your job where the sick people are concerned," Antonelli muttered through clenched teeth. She tossed a business card onto the desk. "You can reach me at that number. *Miss.*"

Before Carrie could respond, the woman spun on her heel and stalked away. Carrie watched her go, aware her mouth was open. What the hell? Gina Antonelli elevated rude to an art form. She absently noted Antonelli's stiff-legged gate, as if her left leg didn't quite bend at the knee, although her ability to stomp didn't seem impaired. The thought was fleeting as Carrie quickly turned back to her computer and pulled up the contracts for the ER expansion plans. She was going to have to wake some people up. She couldn't wait for the town supervisor to get to the office, not if she was going to get to the OR in time to see Blake.

❖

Gina slapped on her hard hat and strode through the ER toward the exit into the parking lot. The very same parking lot, currently filled with cars, she planned to turn into a twenty-foot-deep quarter-acre pit, Lord willing and the creek didn't rise. At least she *would* be tearing it up if the hospital administrators ever got their butts out of bed and filed the necessary permits. And why the hell was she surprised anyhow? She'd been doing this for going on seven years now. Nothing new about this FUBAR. Dealing with bureaucrats was always a pain in the butt. She should've told her father to put Vince in charge of this project. Her brother-in-law could be cooling his heels in the eighty-five-degree sun, and *she* could be building a NAPA Auto Parts store right now, throwing up rebar and laying down asphalt with no one to bother her. Big enterprises like NAPA knew how to get things done fast. But these private places, especially something as rinky-dink as this hospital, just couldn't get their acts together. Really, what the blazes? The boss didn't come in until noon? No wonder they weren't on top of the project, and now her crew would be behind before they even put backhoe to stone. And of course they were looking at rain in another day or so. So who would hear about it when they came in over schedule and over budget?

"Not the freaking desk jockeys, that's for sure," she muttered, skirting a wheelchair someone had double-parked across from the reception area. She glanced in by reflex and a chill ran down her spine. A man and a woman huddled in the corner, his arm around her shaking shoulders, tears streaking both their faces. Gina jerked her gaze away. The road to memory lane was barricaded and long closed to traffic.

"Hey, who pi…sprinkled in your Cheerios this morning?" a boisterous voice called.

Gina slowed and looked over her shoulder at her brother. "Long story. Why are you so freaking jolly?"

Joe Antonelli spread his hands and gave her a bright-eyed, happy-as-a-hog-in-mud grin. "I'm about to go off call in an hour, I had an easy night, and I've got a hot date tonight. What's not to be happy about?"

Gina stepped out of the way of an orderly pushing an elderly woman on a stretcher and leaned her shoulder against the tan-tiled wall. Her temper still simmered, but Joe always had a way of taking the heat out of her fury, even when they were kids. Maybe because he was the oldest, and the only boy in the immediate family. Everyone pretty much worshipped him, even her, in secret at least. People said they looked alike but she didn't see it—he was movie-star handsome in a rough-and-tumble kind of way, big shoulders, broad chest. Swoonworthy, apparently, if the number of girls hanging around him since he was twelve was any indication. She scowled at him. "How about the dimwits in administration don't have the paperwork in order, and I can't start the job until they get things sorted out."

"The new MRI wing?"

"Yeah. Only the biggest job this summer."

He winced. "That sucks. Man, we're all waiting on that to get done. I was so pumped when I heard the old man got the bid. He must have done some fancy dealing, because I heard that O'Brien Construction was pushing hard to get the contract."

"He's not gonna be real pleased if he sees us all sitting around on our butts." Gina thumped her boot against the wall. "I don't even have anyone to chew out, and it's giving me heartburn."

"That doesn't sound like you. Don't hold it in, you'll hurt yourself."

Gina grinned wryly. Okay, maybe she'd chewed out the CEO's receptionist a bit, but she'd managed not to curse, and that was saying a lot considering the runaround. Not that she made a habit of cursing, especially not in front of women. Hell, if her mother got wind of her using bad language in front of a lady she'd skin her, and somehow Ma had a way of knowing everything. Plus, the receptionist was the one throwing up roadblocks—man, talk about immoveable force. And icy cool.

Gina said, "I was the picture of control."

"That'll be the day." Joe smiled. "I'd help you out if I could, but that's all above my pay grade. I steer clear of the east wing at all costs."

Gina sighed. She knew when she was beat, temporarily at least. "So, you still seeing that respiratory therapist? The one you brought to Sunday dinner a couple weeks ago. Wendy?"

"Oh, we're just friends."

Gina shook her head. "How do you do that, run through so many so fast and still end up being friends with almost all of them?"

"It's my winning smile."

"Uh-huh. Along with the BS line you've perfected."

"Some call that charm." He lifted a thick black brow. "So what about you?"

"Nothing about me." Joe was the only one in the family who ever bugged her about her private life. Her father had finally come to terms with her being a lesbian but didn't talk to her about it. She figured that was his right. Her mother mostly addressed it by bemoaning the fact Gina wouldn't be providing grandchildren. But they loved her and she knew it. Sometimes that's as good as it got.

Joe gave her a long look, the kind of contemplative look he gave her when he was trying to judge how she really felt. Luckily, she'd learned to keep the shade pulled down even to him. After a few seconds, he sighed and his expression relaxed. He had the good sense not to push any harder. The last time he'd declared six years ought to be long enough, she'd punched him in the gut, and considering he'd been a battle-ready Marine then, she'd hurt her hand more than she'd hurt him. But he'd gotten the message all the same. *Don't go there.*

"So listen," Gina said, pushing away the old ache that still plagued her when she let it, which wasn't often any longer, "I gotta go give the guys an update. And then I gotta start rattling as many trees as I can find."

"Good luck with that." Joe squeezed her shoulder. "Might all get sorted out before long anyhow. There's a new administration, and scuttlebutt says they're pretty decent. Hopefully they'll get you what you need."

Gina snorted. "Believe me, if the one I talked to up there is any example, I'm not so sure. Je—" She caught herself as a woman in scrubs walked by. "Jeez, Joe, nobody in authority is available during working hours?"

Joe laughed. "It's not exactly working hours for the office types, sis."

Gina glanced at the wall clock. Six thirty. "Okay, but somebody ought to be able to answer a damn phone."

"Why don't you go grab another cup of coffee and a doughnut. Maybe it'll improve your mood."

"Not likely. Catch me before you go if you get a chance, unless by some miracle I'm actually working." She gave him a wave and stormed toward the exit, practically slamming into the automatic doors that were way too slow to open. Was everything about this place going to be a pain in the behind? Maybe the pretty redheaded receptionist would actually be able to get something done in time for her to save some of her day. Miracles did happen now and then, right? Her mother believed it, so it must be true.

Chapter Two

Blake wondered if anyone really believed the flimsy striped curtains in the pre-op area actually made anyone feel private. He was pretty certain everyone around him in the logjam of stretchers lined up along one wall could hear his nervous breathing. Not that he was scared, because he wasn't. He'd been waiting for this moment for what seemed like forever. Still, the next few hours would be weird. He was going to go to sleep, and while he was asleep, everything about him was going to change. When he woke up, his body would be even more different than it had become in the last few years. He'd be closer to looking in the mirror and seeing the reflection of who he knew himself to be. Mostly, he was happy. Only a little bit of him was afraid of the unknown, or if it would hurt a lot or look bad or whether anyone would ever really believe he was who he said he was.

"You scared?" Margie whispered, leaning over the stupid side rail that separated Blake from everyone, taking his hand.

He studied her face, her ocean-blue eyes that were always just a little bit serious, her crazy tangle of wild blond hair, the little hint of a smile that always made him feel like he was special. He threaded his fingers through hers. "Not scared so much. Just, you know, nervous."

Margie nodded, still serious. "Yeah, I get that. It would be a lot better if you could be awake and watch."

He laughed. Margie never tried to talk him into feeling differently about anything, but she always had her own ideas, good ones most of the time. This time, he'd pass. "Maybe *you'd* want to do that. You'd probably figure out a way to talk Flann into letting you too."

Her smile widened, her eyes brightened, and she laughed lightly. "Well, yeah. She's my big sister, after all. I usually can." She tilted her head as if a thought suddenly caught her attention. "And since she's, you know, your stepparent now, you ought to have an in."

"No thanks. I pretty much know what's going to happen anyhow," Blake said, trying to sound nonchalant. "You know, from the YouTube videos."

"True, they were cool," Margie said.

She'd watched them with him, not saying anything until the very end. He'd waited, holding his breath almost, wondering if she would think it was crazy. Or that the way the guys looked after it was done was a turnoff. He should've known better than that.

"That was amazing," Margie said as soon as he'd paused the video. "It makes such a huge difference. In the way they look, sure. But even more in how they feel about themselves. I can see why you want to do it."

The terrible tension that had been squeezing his insides snapped like a rubber band. She'd said exactly what he needed to hear. She understood. But then, she'd always understood him. Nobody had ever understood him that easily, that deeply. Well, except his mom. He knew he was lucky, really lucky.

"Plus, I've got the best surgeon ever," Blake said. He wasn't just saying that because Flann was family now, either. He hung around the hospital enough to hear people talk, and when he was volunteering in the ER he'd seen Flann in action. Flann was the best.

"Also true," Margie said. "Plus, you have all of us."

"You don't have to wait, you know," Blake said. "Mom will call you when I'm done, or somebody will."

Margie shook her head. "No way. I'm staying here to make sure your mom is okay. You know how mothers are."

He grinned. "Yeah, I know. Even when they're doctors."

"Even when they've raised a whole family of them." Margie rolled her eyes. "If it was me having surgery, my mom would be in there with Flann."

Blake snorted. "I'm glad my mom hasn't tried that with Flann. I'd feel weird with her—"

The curtain parted and Flann stepped in, already in navy scrubs, a surgical mask hanging around her neck. She had sandy hair and brown eyes, but the same penetrating and intense gaze as Margie. The same set to her jaw—confident and sure. "Did I hear my name mentioned?"

Blake half sat up, balancing on his elbows. "Hey."

Flann paused at the foot of the stretcher, shuffled through some of the papers there, and dropped them after a quick look. "Hey, yourself. How you doing?"

"Good. Great."

Flann held Blake's gaze, steady and calm. "You ready?"

Blake wasn't bothered by the question. He got it. Flann wasn't testing him or trying to get him to prove he knew what he was doing; she was letting him be in charge, letting him call the shots the way his mom had done every step so far. "I'm totally ready."

"Good. Listen," Flann said, glancing at Margie, "I'm going to need you to sit up so I can make a few marks on your chest. You good with that?"

Margie squeezed Blake's hand and let go. "I'll wait outside."

"Thanks," Blake said quietly. If and when Margie ever saw him with his shirt off, he only wanted her to see him. The way he should be. Not now.

Margie slipped through the divider in the curtain, and Flann looked over her shoulder after her until the barrier fell completely closed. She let down the side of the stretcher and motioned for Blake to sit up. When he did, Flann reached behind him, untied the gown at his neck, and let it fall into his lap. Blake knew he was blushing but just stared straight ahead. No one else had seen him naked since he was twelve and his body'd really started to change and it was all wrong. It'd taken him two horrible years to finally tell his mom, and then their whole life changed too.

Blake blinked, glad Flann didn't say anything about him shaking.

Flann pulled a pen, a purple one, out of her shirt pocket and put a hand on his shoulder. "Remember what I told you? About where the incisions will be?"

Blake nodded. "Yeah, half a circle underneath, right?"

"That's right." Flann bent and drew on his chest with the purple pen. The lines were bright purple too.

He laughed when he looked down. "I hope that comes off."

"In a month or two." Flann grinned and touched a spot at the outer corner of each half circle on either side of his chest. "This is where the drains will come out. You'll probably just have them overnight, maybe a day or two at most. It depends on how much they drain."

"Right. And they'll be attached to those little suction cup things. And I'll have to empty them."

Flann smiled. "Well, maybe your mother or I will do that for you."

Blake lifted his chin. "I can do it."

"I'm sure."

"Will I wake up with the…you know, the chest corset on?"

Flann laughed. "We call it a compression garment. Where'd you get chest corset from?"

"YouTube." Blake grinned.

"Of course. I should've known." Flann paused. "I checked out some of those videos, you know. They're pretty accurate, and the results are realistic. Just remember everyone is different. You may or may not look like any of those guys."

"I know."

Flann capped the pen and slipped it into her pocket. "Any last-minute questions for me?"

"Nope. I'm good."

"Me too. And remember, Glenn will be there, so with the two of us keeping an eye on things, nothing's going to go wrong."

"I know." Blake glanced toward the curtains and lowered his voice. "You'll make sure Mom is okay, right?"

Flann cupped Blake's cheek. "Always. That's a promise."

"Thanks."

"I'm going to open the curtains, okay? There's a bunch of people that want to see you. We'll be ready to go in about fifteen minutes."

"Yeah, sure. Give me a sec." Hurriedly, Blake pulled the gown back up, tied it behind his neck, and slid his bare legs under the sheets. He patted them down around his body and sat up straight. "Ready."

Flann opened the curtains at the end of the stretcher. Carrie waited with Margie, and when Carrie saw Blake, she gave him a bright smile. "Hey, you. I just wanted to say hi before you got started."

"Hey," Blake said. He spent almost as much time at Harper and Presley's house as he did at his own. Carrie'd lived with them until just recently when she'd started staying at Harper's old place that was going to be hers soon. She was funny and easy to talk to and never treated him like a kid. She'd also never once looked at him like he was strange, and some people did, even the ones being nice to him. "You didn't have to get up so early. I'll be home after lunch."

Carrie reached out and squeezed his foot through the sheets. "Oh, phooey on that. I'm not missing the start of your big day. Besides, this way I get a morning off from work."

"Everybody's here," Blake said softly. He'd already seen Harper and Presley, and his mom, and Glenn, and Mari Mateo, his and Margie's supervisor in the ER and Glenn's new girlfriend. He'd never imagined so many people would understand.

He hadn't wanted to move up here—he'd figured he'd never fit in. Now he had more family than he had ever had, and he'd never felt so accepted. He swallowed hard. "I'm glad you're here."

Carrie pushed up along the side of the stretcher, leaned over, and kissed him on the forehead. "You're already the best-looking guy in town. And don't you forget it."

The lump in his throat eased. Blake cocked his head. "You know, I'll be eighteen in a couple of years. If you wanted to wait around…"

Carrie laughed and ruffled his hair. "Sweetheart, if I weren't playing for the other team, I might just take you up on it." She nodded to Margie. "I'll let you two talk. I'm going to go find the rest of the family."

"Can you see if my mom is still out there?" Blake asked, suddenly wanting to see her just to make sure she was okay. He'd been a little anxious on his way to the hospital, and he could tell she knew.

"I'll find her." Carrie waved and disappeared.

Margie poked his arm. "Did you just try to make a move on Carrie?"

"I was just fooling."

Margie grinned. "Can't say as I blame you."

Blake shot her a look. "Oh yeah?"

"Well, she is hot."

He rolled his eyes. They never really talked about how they identified—it didn't really seem necessary. Every now and then he'd comment on some hot guy or girl or Margie would do the same. When it came right down to it, he'd rather spend his time with her than anyone else. She seemed pretty happy hanging with him too. Maybe that's all that really mattered.

"She's too old for you," he said.

"I'm not looking for a girlfriend," Margie said. "Or boyfriend, really. Not right now."

"So what are you looking for?" Blake asked, wondering when *not right now* would be *now* and how to tell.

"I already got what I want." She smiled and reached over the side rail to take his hand again. "I got you."

Happy with that answer, Blake leaned back and closed his eyes to wait for the next big change in his life. Not worried, not scared. Not even nervous anymore.

❖

Carrie stepped outside into the hall to look for Abby and saw her talking on a wall phone a few feet away.

"All right," Abby said, eyes closed and her fingers pressed to the bridge of her nose. Her voice was tight, strained. Her blond hair was drawn back with a loose tie at her nape, accentuating the sculpted angles of her high cheeks and tapering jaw. "I'll be down as soon as I can. See if you can get Mari to stay until I get there. Yes, that's great. Thank you." With a sigh, she hung up the phone and, when she saw Carrie, gave her a weary smile. "Morning."

"Hi. Blake asked me to find you." At Abby's quick look of concern, she added quickly, "He seems fine, but Flann just left and I think they're starting soon."

"Give me a minute to see him, and I'll buy you a cup of coffee," Abby said. "I won't stay long or else he's going to complain I'm hovering."

"I'm pretty sure he likes it when you hover." Carrie waved a hand. "Go ahead. Take your time. I am so ready for another cup of coffee. I don't know how any of you get started so early."

"I understand Pres always starts before sunup."

"True," Carrie said, "and as far as I'm concerned, I do too." She laughed. "Only sunrise for me is usually a few hours later."

Abby chuckled. "Hold on. And I'll get you that second—or is it third?—cup of coffee."

When Abby returned, they walked downstairs to the cafeteria, went through the line, and grabbed coffee and doughnuts.

"I heard you on the phone," Carrie said. "You're not getting called in, are you?"

She hadn't known Abby all that long, but she'd spent so much time with Abby, Presley, her cousin Mari, and Carson Rivers, the fourth Rivers sister, planning Presley and Harper's wedding, she felt as if she and Abby had been friends for much longer. Abby had taken over as head of the emergency room in the midst of the private hospital's purchase by SunView Health Consortium, and not everyone at the Rivers had been behind that change. Somehow, Abby had managed to set up a PA training program and push through approval for an ER residency training program in record time. All that while moving her son from the city to a small rural community in the midst of Blake's transition. Abby'd been at the Rivers for less than a year, but already she was a focal part of the hospital staff, and she and Blake were part of the community. Of course, Abby's romance with Flannery Rivers, the hospital's most notorious bachelor, had made her something of a celebrity. Despite Abby's professional dedication, Carrie knew she wouldn't want to work while Blake was in surgery.

"Well," Abby said ruefully, "I wasn't planning to be available, but Mike Carrera just called and his wife went into labor two weeks early. He'd volunteered to trade shifts with me, but I can't exactly ask him to cover for me under these circumstances."

"Surely there's someone else who can do it."

"Not until this afternoon. I'll wait until Blake's anesthetized and Flann starts the procedure. At that point, there isn't likely to be a problem Flann and Glenn can't handle." She sighed and shook her head. "It's not as if I can do anything from out here anyhow."

"I can only imagine it's tough for anyone waiting while someone they love is in the OR, but being a doctor probably doesn't help."

"You're right. Everyone thinks it makes it easier, but believe me, it doesn't." Abby glanced toward the pre-op area, her green eyes clouding as if she could see Blake, waiting beyond the closed doors. "Thanks for coming by. I know Blake appreciated it."

"He's really a sweetie, and I feel like with him being part of Harper and Presley's family, he's part of mine too." Carrie smiled, wondering if she sounded strange, but somehow knowing Abby understood. "I feel as if all of us living together makes us a family."

"I think it does." Abby broke her jelly doughnut in half and started in on the jelly side. "You're going to move into Harper's old place on the farm pretty soon, though, aren't you?"

"I'm already pretty much staying there full-time now, although it needs some serious renovation. Like a bathroom big enough to turn around in."

Abby laughed. "You mean an upgrade from bachelor's quarters?"

"Totally." Carrie snorted. "I was hoping we'd get the demolition started by now, but it seems like every contractor we've contacted is tied up until fall."

"I know. I've talked to most of them about the new project in the ER, and I know you and Pres have too. I can't believe how difficult it is to actually get them to agree to any kind of start time. Thank God we're finally getting under way."

Under the circumstances, Carrie decided not to mention the slight snafu with the contractors. "I know Presley is trying to get someone for Harper's place, so with any luck, I'll have a bathroom and kitchen from this century before Labor Day." Carrie sighed. "The old farmhouse is gorgeous, but antiquated. All the same, I'm sticking it out. Really, it's been fun living with Harper and Presley, and I adore them both, but now that they're newlyweds, I'd really rather not be sharing their space quite so intimately."

Abby laughed. "We're looking for workers for our new place too. If I hear of anything, I'll let you know."

"I appreciate it." Carrie polished off the last of her sugar doughnut and sipped her coffee. "So you're doing okay? You know, about today?"

"The usual nerves. I'm not really worried, but I'll feel a lot better when he's in the recovery room. Actually, I'll feel a lot better when he's healed and happy."

"I think the happy part is pretty much a given."

Abby nodded. "It's what he wants, and that's the most important thing."

Carrie hesitated, not sure where the boundaries were, especially since Abby rarely talked about her own feelings regarding Blake's transition, only Blake's. Carefully, she said, "I hope you don't mind me saying so, but I think you're a fabulous mother. Exactly who he needs."

Abby pressed her lips together and, after a moment, said softly, "Thank you. Believe me, I haven't always known the right thing to say or do. It's all been instinct. Mostly, I've tried to listen to him." She laughed and shook her head. "And he has always been much surer and much clearer than me."

"I imagine he would've had to be for you to be so supportive."

"It's a difficult line sometimes, knowing how to be supportive and still keep him safe. But he's never wavered."

"I'd be frightened if I was the parent, I think. I hope I'd be as supportive as you."

"You know," Abby said, "I remind myself sometimes, when I worry about the surgery or what's going to come in the future, if he were in an accident and needed surgery to save his life, the only thing I'd be concerned about is that he got well. I would accept the necessary pain as part of healing and a small price to pay for recovery. This isn't any different. He needs this to be well."

Carrie swallowed around the tightness in her throat. "That's what I mean—you're exactly who he needs."

"Well, we're pretty lucky since he's exactly who I need too," Abby said with quiet certainty. After a second, she glanced at her watch and rose. "Flann should be starting about now. She promised to have the nurses call when they got under way. I'll head on down to the ER."

"Thanks for the coffee." Carrie stood. "I ought to go find Presley."

"She and Harper came by earlier to see Blake. She's probably in the family waiting area. As soon as I get things settled in the ER, I'll be there."

"I'll see you later, then," Carrie said. Hopefully she wouldn't have to tell Abby the ER construction project was delayed. She looked forward to that almost as much as she did breaking the bad news to Gina Antonelli.

CHAPTER THREE

Carrie found Presley in the family waiting area down the hall from the OR. Presley stood at the windows in what for her was casual wear, dark green slim-cut cotton pants, brown flats, and a muted rose shirt. The waiting area was empty except for a young woman reading a magazine in the corner. The inevitable television was mercifully blank. Carrie joined Presley and took in the panorama unfolding outside, barely able to absorb the beauty of acres of grass and flowering shrubs bordering the long front drive and a vista of distant mountains towering above the church steeples and rooftops of the village below. She still couldn't get over the abundance of windows in the 110-year-old hospital. She'd never been in the operating rooms, but she understood that many of them overlooked gardens where azaleas and rhododendrons bloomed in the spring. The ambience was so different from the blank institutional walls and featureless hallways she was used to in modern hospitals. The light filling the interior spaces alone made everything about the Rivers seem more hopeful and more personal.

"I love this place," Carrie murmured. "How could anyone even think of letting it die?"

"We won't," Presley said, continuing to gaze outside.

Carrie flushed. "Sorry. I didn't even ask. How are you doing?"

Presley turned, her blue eyes clear and calm. "I was just thinking how glad I am Blake is having his surgery here, surrounded by people who love him. We're all very lucky to have this place in our lives."

"We're all pretty damn lucky you're here to save it for us."

Presley laughed and threaded an arm around Carrie's waist. "I can't take all the credit there. That's a family affair—and that includes you too."

"Thanks—I'm pretty attached to everyone and everything here." Actually, she couldn't imagine being anywhere else. If Presley suddenly decided to move back to Phoenix and take her rightful place as the head of SunView, Carrie would stay here even if giving up her job and seeing her best friend move far away would hurt her heart. "I'm glad the Rivers family is rooted in this place. I don't have to worry about you leaving."

"No chance of that." Presley scanned the room. "Have you seen Abby? I thought she'd be down here by now. There isn't a problem in the OR, is there?"

"No," Carrie said quickly. "I just left her. She had to put out a fire in the emergency room. Her stand-in couldn't make it. He's about to become a new father."

"That's bad timing," Presley said with a sigh. "Good for him, though. Is she okay?"

"Other than being understandably nervous, I think so."

"Eight fifteen," Presley said. "They were due to start at eight, and knowing Flann, they did."

Carrie laughed. "I'm sure of that. Abby said if there'd been any problems, she would've heard by now, so I guess we just wait." She rolled her shoulders. The stiffness didn't yield much. What a morning. "Boy, it sure is a lot harder than I realized."

"First time waiting?"

"Yeah. I'm the oldest, so no babies to wait on yet, and thank heavens no one in my family has ever been seriously ill."

"I'm glad." Presley smiled. "Everything will be fine. Harper was even going to suit up and drop in to the OR once they got started. Blake is in good hands—lots of them."

"I'm sure everything will be fine, but it will still be good to have it over." Carrie hesitated. "I know everyone says the procedure is straightforward, but it seems so…monumental. Does that even make sense?"

"It does," Abby said from just behind them. "Psychologically, it's a major hurdle, and for Blake, and I think a lot of trans boys, this is the first huge step toward a sense of completion."

Nodding, Carrie said, "That must be what I'm sensing."

"That's also why it means so much to him—and me—that you're all here," Abby said quietly.

Presley snorted and gave Abby a look. "Where else would we be?"

Abby crossed her arms and feigned looking perplexed. "Oh, I don't know—at your desk, where you can usually be found anytime, day or night."

"That's not true!" Presley pointed a finger. "I've even been resisting checking my email, although I suppose I should look at it."

"No need," Carrie said quickly. "I've been through everything, and there's nothing urgent. You'll have some phone calls to return this afternoon, but they can wait."

"You didn't have to come in early," Presley said. "I know your love for early morning."

"Actually," Carrie said archly, "I was here in the middle of the night."

Presley laughed. "Let me guess. Six?"

"Five thirty, I'll have you know."

Abby added, "I am truly impressed, and I'll mention your dedication to your boss."

"So noted," Presley said playfully. "One merit badge coming up."

Carrie laughed. Presley was her boss, and she was also her best friend. Somehow they made it work, probably because Carrie loved her job, and on the rare occasions when Presley was fraught or just having a bad day and directed her mood at Carrie, she never took it personally. She was pretty good at compartmentalizing and wasn't prone to hurt feelings too often. The only thing that ever really bothered her was if she screwed up. Then she was harder on herself than Presley could possibly be.

"Today, I think I might've earned it," Carrie murmured, picturing Gina Antonelli glowering at her before she'd even finished her second cup of coffee. No wonder she hadn't dispatched the verging-on-surly Antonelli with her usual scalpel-like precision. She hadn't yet had a good warm-up, and Antonelli was a little off-putting. In a distracting, too-attractive, and mysterious way. "Yeah, right."

"Something you're not telling me?" Presley asked, studying Carrie intently.

"It can wait."

Presley quirked a brow. "Take my mind off things. What's going on?"

"Have you ever met Gina Antonelli?" Carrie experienced a conflicting surge of annoyance and interest just mentioning the short-tempered, mildly abrasive contractor. The woman was definitely maddening, but intriguing too. Usually Carrie liked hard-charging women—just look at all her best friends—but none of them came with a healthy dose of entitlement and arrogance. All the same, Antonelli had definitely made an impression. "The contractor in charge of the ER project?"

"No, we dealt with Thomas Antonelli when bids went out, and after that, the hospital attorneys handled the rest."

"I guess that explains why she didn't seem to know who you were. Considering her attitude that everyone jump to do her bidding, I would have expected her to be more on top of the facts." Carrie shook her head.

"Something's gotten you fired up," Presley said. "What's going on?"

"Someone in the business office or legal dropped a ball or two. Gina Antonelli, the daughter and project manager for the expansion, showed up at your office in a storm this morning about six. They can't get started until some of the permits are straightened out."

"You're kidding," Abby said.

Presley snapped, "Are we on it?"

Carrie returned the arched eyebrow. "Really? You have to ask?"

Presley chuckled. "Sorry, I forgot who I was dealing with. Is there anything you need me to do?"

"No, I'll take care of it." Carrie checked her watch. "In fact, it's almost time for me to start making phone calls. I'm going to do that because I suspect if I don't, Antonelli will be in here chewing up the furniture before long."

"That personable, huh?" Abby said.

"Let's just say her table manners aren't the best."

Her friends laughed as Carrie left to make calls. She had a feeling no one would be laughing if she had to tell Gina Antonelli there'd be no work today. Oddly enough, she wasn't bothered by the possibility of Antonelli's temper. What she didn't want to do was disappoint her. Why, she didn't know.

❖

"Hey, Coach," Arnie Cohen called, hiking a hip up onto the low stone wall next to Gina, "how long do you think it's gonna take the paper pushers to get this straightened out?"

Gina snorted. Nine a.m. So far, they'd lost three hours of work time. The clock was running and so was the bill. She didn't have much faith that anything was going to get done until the boss showed up from her morning golf game or wherever else she was off to. After all, how much could the receptionist really do? Make a few phone calls— maybe. Expecting the help to handle a major FUBAR would be like her expecting one of the summer grunts to do her job. Chance of success, zero to none. "Not likely."

"Figured," Arnie said.

"I'd lay odds we don't work today." Gina gripped the edge of the wall and glared into the morning sun, aimlessly watching ambulances pull up to the emergency room, most of them going pretty slow, but now and then one careened in with lights flashing. She'd counted six in the last hour, which she guessed was a good thing in a backhanded kind of way. A lot of people depended on the hospital for a living and to stay alive, and right now, so did she. At least the make-a-living part. This was one of the biggest projects their company had landed all year. With the housing market around here in the dump, new construction was limited and plenty of builders were skating the edge of going under. Her father hadn't said anything, but she could do the numbers easy enough. They needed this job to come in on time and on budget. She owed it to her crew and her family to make that happen. So far, the hospital bureaucracy wasn't helping.

Arnie pulled a hunk of beef jerky from his shirt pocket, folded it up, and shoved it in his mouth. "How long do you think the old— sorry—the big boss is going to keep us out here?"

"We'll give it a while longer," Gina said evasively. She hadn't called her father yet. He already seemed strained to the max. She could tell her mother was worried about him, even though he'd never complain. "It's not like we got much else to do, not with all our heavy equipment already here. We could move it, but that'll be costly, especially if we're going to start tomorrow."

"You know, it's damn…darn…boring when we're not working."

"You're usually complaining you're working too hard."

He grinned and scratched at the stubble on his chin. He was her foreman, twice her age, having come up through the ranks from unskilled grunt to master carpenter. He never turned a hair when her father put her in charge of her first project two years before, just watched her for the first few weeks until she'd proven she knew what she was doing. "Yeah, well, I'd rather be complaining about work than complaining about nothing to do."

"You and me both." If it was up to her, she'd work seven days a week, and she knew some of the other guys on the crew would too. They needed the money, she needed to fill her time. When she wasn't working, options were few. The few things she liked on TV hardly used up a few hours a week, and she'd given up drinking except on Friday night with the crew or after a game, when it was pretty much tradition, and even then she only had one. She couldn't hang around with the family any more than she already did. She loved them all, and she never missed a Sunday dinner if she could help it, but too much family often led to too many questions. Once everybody got talking about their boyfriends or girlfriends or children, glances inevitably shot in her direction, the questions unspoken but crystal clear. *What about you, Gina? When are you going to settle down and start a family?*

No one would like or believe her answer. *Not in the game plan.* Even after all this time, the bruise on her heart still hurt, and she wouldn't sell anyone short by getting involved when her heart wasn't in it. So work it was. There wasn't much that pounding a nail or shifting a mountain of rubble couldn't cure—restlessness, the vague feeling of hollowness that followed her everywhere, the loneliness that caught up to her when she wasn't paying attention, and the simmering sexual need she recognized but couldn't figure out a good way to satisfy. She had options there, none of them good ones. She recognized the looks from some of the guys who didn't know her well enough to realize they hadn't a chance in hell, and from the women who picked up on something she didn't even know she was telegraphing. She'd tried accepting those invitations a couple of times when she'd been too weary to resist, and she still flushed with embarrassment thinking about it. She hadn't made the experience very good for them. She couldn't have been less connected if she'd been sleepwalking. That's what bothered her most.

Nope, she knew what she needed. Watching a building go up, something she'd made, seeing her crew working together, bitching all the time as crews usually did but stopping at the end of the day with the feeling of shared accomplishment, was a reward she could hold on to.

"This day is going to pretty much be a loss," Gina said.

"Maybe so," Arnie muttered, "but my morning just got a whole lot better."

Gina followed his gaze and sat up straighter. The receptionist, whose name she hadn't gotten, was marching across the parking lot, a slim leather folder tucked under her arm. In the sunlight, her red hair gleamed like fire and her lithe body, in tailored black pants and a pale, shimmery shirt, looked tight and strong and curvy in all the right places. Gina's mouth suddenly went dry. She swallowed a couple of times before she spoke.

"Maybe I was wrong. Maybe we'll be getting to work sooner than I thought." She pushed off the wall and strode to meet the receptionist. "I hope you've got good news for me."

Carrie shielded her eyes with one hand and glanced up a few inches to meet Gina Antonelli's hot, dark gaze. She was scowling. No surprise there. Was the woman always in a temper? A light sheen of sweat dotted her brow, but she didn't seem to notice it or care. Her dark hair lifted a little in the breeze, what there was of it cresting the hill and floating over the expanse of grass and the asphalt parking lot. Some generous few might've considered Antonelli's jaw strong, but right now it was leaning more toward rock. A muscle bunched at the angle. Her T-shirt, navy blue with an emblem of a truck over the chest pocket with the words *Antonelli Construction* underneath, hugged her shoulders and chest. Her body looked as hard as her jawline.

Antonelli jammed her hands on her slim hips. "Well?"

Oh, this wasn't going to be pleasant. Carrie smiled, doubting it would do a bit of good. But after all, *she* was the professional here. "That would be a yes and a no."

Antonelli squinted at her. "I don't think I like the way that sounds."

"We're finally in agreement on something," Carrie said. "I've just talked to the town supervisor and I'm waiting to hear from our legal department, but it appears that this particular township, of all the towns in the county, requires state verification of your insurance coverage and workers' compensation plan and payments." She paused. Might as well deliver all the good news. "For this fiscal year."

"Son of a…gun." Gina gritted her teeth. "We're just finding this out? What incompetent is in charge of this fiasco?"

Carrie sucked in a breath at the insult. *Be the big person. Be the big person.* That was going to become her mantra dealing with this unreasonable walking ego. "Believe me, I'm no happier about this than you are. We've been waiting more than a month to get started until your crew was available, remember?"

Gina snorted. "Really? A whole month? And I suppose you think we've all just been sitting around doing our nails because we don't have anything to do? We had to shift other project commitments to get this started because your boss twisted some…arms. And being civic minded, we appreciate how important this is to the community."

"You're right," Carrie said, holding her temper in. After all, as far as she could tell, Antonelli's company hadn't been in the wrong here. As with most snags like this, no one was really at fault. Just a long line of miscommunications. Which didn't help a damn bit right now. "Maybe we can agree we're on the same side."

"There isn't any side," Antonelli said flatly. "There's a job to do, and I'm here ready to do it and so is my crew. How long is it going to take your boss to get this straightened out?"

"I'm working on it now—"

"Uh-uh. I think this is a little above your pay grade. When can I talk to the boss?"

Heat climbed up Carrie's spine. "Above my pay grade?"

Antonelli ran a hand through her hair. "Look, I'm sure you're a super receptionist. You tracked down the paper trail really quickly. Good for you. Now we need someone who is capable of twisting arms and anything else that needs twisting. So you need to hand this off to your boss."

"I do?" Carrie wished for all the world she was on the pitcher's mound and Gina Antonelli was at bat. The unbelievably insulting contractor would be getting a brushback pitch that trimmed the sexy lock of hair falling in her eyes. "Because I'm just a pretty face?"

"Come on." Antonelli sighed dramatically. "That's a no-win for me. If I say yes, I'm probably being a chauvinist pig. And if I say no—well, you never say no to something like that."

"Oh, you don't. And you're an expert on what women like to hear, I guess."

Antonelli's expression darkened—not with temper, but something else that moved through her eyes like a slow-burning shadow. "No, I'm definitely not."

"I'm in charge of this project," Carrie said quietly. "I've already talked to legal—"

"Hold it." Antonelli's voice dropped. "Run that by me again? You're in charge of this? Your boss doesn't think it's important enough for her to waste time on? Worth, right?"

"Yes, Presley Worth."

"Well, presumably your boss is not just a pretty face, either. So maybe you could drag her off the golf course or out of bed or wherever she is—"

"Okay, I can see we are not going to be on the same side here." Carrie opened the folder. "And I'm wasting time trying to have a conversation with someone whose head is harder than concrete. So"—she held out a stack of forms—"your company will need to file these with the township after the state confirms various payments, license numbers, and other details."

Gina glanced down at the stack of papers and shoved her hands in her pockets. She wanted to take them about as much as she wanted to grab a live snake. Or even a dead one. She detested snakes. It was about the only thing, other than some dreams that took her unawares, that gave her nightmares. "What the hell am I supposed to do with them?"

Carrie let out an exasperated breath and shook them in the air as a ring of men moved behind Gina, all of them close enough to hear what was going on. Wonderful. In a town this size, you couldn't change the color of your mailbox without someone commenting on it and everyone in town knowing about it. By the end of the day this conversation might as well have been recorded. At least then there'd be an accurate rendition as it made the rounds in the bars and hardware store and gas station. Lovely. She lowered her voice. "I need you to take them back to your corporate headquarters—"

"My corporate headquarters." Gina made an elaborate eye roll. Some male voice guffawed behind them.

"Office?" Carrie said bitingly. "Do you think you could look up the term *cooperation* at some point?"

"And then what?"

"Have your boss get them completed and filed with the town supervisor. Copy our attorneys. Once that's done, hopefully we'll be able to get you all to work."

Gina's gut twisted into a knot. "That could take a month!"

"We'll do everything we can to expedite from this end," Carrie said. "We have every bit as much invested in this project as you do, probably more. We need these facilities as a requirement for our training programs and for our level one trauma certification. And we want to move on with our plans for the helipad."

Gina glanced up at the top of the hospital. "You're going to put a heliport up there. I heard that rumor. That's going to be a pretty project."

"It is, and"—Carrie smiled sweetly—"we're opening up for bids very soon."

"I heard that too," Gina said. And they needed to land that project, which meant she probably ought to try sweet-talking the receptionist and her boss.

"Then you can see why we are very anxious to get this project going."

Gina took the damn papers, folded them in half, and shoved them into her back pocket. "We'll get on it. About your boss—"

"Ms. Antonelli—"

More laughter from the gallery.

"Gina," Gina said. "It's Gina or Antonelli, not Ms."

"Sorry. I should've known that."

Gina grinned in spite of herself.

"Just to set the record straight, I'm not the receptionist. I'm the executive administrative assistant to Presley Worth. And I'm in charge of this project. If you have problems, you bring them to me."

"Hey," Gina called as the ticked-off redhead walked away. "I didn't get your name."

"You may call me *Ms.* Longmire," Carrie called without looking back.

Gina's grin widened as the guys behind her whistled.

CHAPTER FOUR

The guys were waiting behind her—she could feel their presence like a heavy weight in the air. Looking to her for answers. They were probably all looking in the same direction as her too. Watching the hospital's executive administrative assistant clip across the parking lot, her low heels tapping out an impatient tattoo on the macadam. Gina waited a few more seconds after the redhead disappeared through the ER entrance, then rewound the conversation and winced a few times. She'd whiffed a few plays from the beginning. *Ms.* Longmire was not the receptionist, but the CEO's majordomo. Dumb of her to make the assumption she was something else.

Gina shook her head. So she hadn't gotten off to a good start, but heck, who could blame her for being a little PO'd? This was a major snafu. And worst of all, there wasn't much she could do about it except urge the paper pushers to push the paper. At least on her end she'd have her sister Angie lighting a fire under whoever needed to be lit up. Thank God she had ended up on the right end of a hammer and not in the business office, but then, Angie's experience as a quartermaster in the Army had prepared her well. There wasn't anything she couldn't find, beg, borrow, or steal—figuratively, of course—at a better price than anyone else around. And she'd come home sound in body and mind, and that counted for even more.

Gina didn't have any of those qualifications, not like everyone else in the family. The parking lot faded a little in her vision as she thought back to watching first Angie, then Joe, and finally her baby sister Sophie don uniforms and head out to serve. Just the way she'd been destined to do before everything went sideways. She still had the

West Point acceptance letter crumpled up somewhere along with the rest of her dreams. As if any of that mattered now.

"So what's the word," Arnie said, his raspy voice loud in her ear, chasing away the shadows and bringing the world back into hyperfocus.

Gina cleared her expression of everything except the annoyance he'd expect to see. Her reality was right here, right now. "Somebody forgot to dot a few *i*'s and cross a few *t*'s. Paperwork's not in order. I'll have to call the front office and figure out where everybody's going to report while we get ready to go here."

"Can't say I'm surprised, but the situation stinks. Everybody's been geared up for the start of this job since the beginning of summer."

"Them and me both."

Arnie pulled another length of jerky. "I'll tell them all to take an early lunch. Call me with the new game plan and I'll make sure they get the word."

"Right."

Chewing on the dried beef bit, Arnie sighed and glanced around at their idle machines, like prehistoric monsters grazing in the noonday sun. "It's a shame."

"And then some." Gina rejoined the crew. "That's it, guys. No start here today."

The men straggled away amidst grumbles and curses, and Gina walked toward the far end of the lot where she'd left her pickup truck. Joe's red Mustang was tucked into an out-of-the-way corner where it had a lower chance of getting dinged. She thought he would've been gone a couple hours ago. Fully admitting she was avoiding an unpleasant task, she turned on her heel and headed back toward the ER. Inside, the halls were bustling with patients and personnel, and the waiting room was half-full. When she peered into the clinical area, she counted six cubicles with curtains pulled from her vantage point.

A small African American woman in blue jeans, white sneakers, and a light green polo shirt with a hospital ID clipped to her collar paused, gave her a long look as if she knew her but couldn't quite place her, and changed course to head her way. "Can I help you?"

"Sorry," Gina said. "I was just looking for my brother. I don't want to take up your time. I can see you're busy."

The woman, five or ten years older than Gina, smiled, her brown eyes sparkling with amusement. "That's why you look so familiar. Joe Antonelli, right?"

"That's right. I'm Gina. The—"

"Good-looking one?"

Gina flushed. "Uh, no. Well, yes." The woman laughed. "But I was going to say contractor working on the new wing."

The woman held out her hand. "I'm Pam Wendel. I'm the charge nurse this shift. Joe is just finishing. If you wait a minute, I'll tell him you're out here."

"No, that's okay, it's not that important."

"We've got the flood under control now," Pam said, her voice light and friendly.

"Looks like you got a rush there a while ago."

"Typical Monday. Everyone puts off the aches and pains and nagging problems all weekend, because hey, who wants to ruin their time off, right? But come Monday morning, missing work or school doesn't seem like such a bad idea."

Gina laughed. "I did notice the traffic in the ER lot picked up right around eight."

Pam nodded. "Regular as clockwork. And we're tight on space down here in the best of circumstances. You're going to be a very welcome sight around here." She grinned. "For lots of reasons."

"I hope so," Gina muttered. When Pam's brow rose, she added quickly, "I'm looking forward to the project."

And boy, did that sound lame. Rusty did not begin to describe her nonexistent social skills. Mercifully, Joe turned the corner, spied her, and ambled toward them. On his way, he dropped a form into a plastic bin on the chest-high counter. "The guy with low back pain in three has a script for Naprosyn and a follow-up appointment with ortho, Pam. He's the last one for me."

"Great. Thanks for staying, Joe."

"No problem." He grinned at Gina. "I thought you'd be tearing up the parking lot by now. Too hot out there for you?"

"No such luck," Gina said. "Nice meeting you, Pam."

"Gina, right?" Pam asked.

"That's right."

"I hope I'll see you around. Have a good one, Joe."

Joe waited until Pam reached the desk and murmured, "Pam's single."

"Uh-huh. That's nice."

"And, you know, likes variety."

Gina narrowed her eyes. "Variety?"

"Yeah, you know. Guys and girls." He leaned closer. "I could get you her number."

"You could mind your own business too."

"Yeah. True." Unperturbed by her cranky tone, he shrugged. "Come on, I want to get out of here before we get hit with another rush."

"You were already done, right?"

"Almost out the door when the place filled up."

"Nice of you to stay."

He lifted a shoulder. "It happens sometimes. The ER chief's kid is having surgery, so everything's a little sideways down here."

"That's too bad."

"No, I think it's probably one of the rare times when surgery is a good thing. He's a trans kid having his first top surgery."

"Wow. That's something. You know him?"

"A little. He volunteers down here. He's always willing to work. Really nice kid."

"I hope he does okay."

"I heard he's on his way to the recovery room, so sounds like everything's good." He stopped at the door marked *Staff* and held it open. "Come on in while I get my stuff, and I'll walk out with you." Gina followed him in and waited while he opened his locker, pulled out a duffel, and packed clean scrubs he pulled from a nearby shelf. He looked right at home, and he'd only been in the clinical part of his PA training a few months. She envied him a little and instantly felt small for begrudging him his dreams come true. He'd put his life on the line, after all.

"So, how's it going with you?" Gina asked.

He zipped up his duffel. "Great. This is a really good place to work."

"I'm glad," she said, and she meant it. "Keep an eye on Dad for me, will you?"

Joe hefted his duffel, studied her intently. "What's wrong with him?"

Gina shoved her hands in her pockets. "Nothing that I know of, but he's been looking a little stressed out lately. And I think Ma's worried about him." She blew out a breath. Discussing things her father would never admit felt a little traitorous. "Business has been up and down the last year or so."

"Bad?"

"Who can tell? You know he never talks about that kind of stuff. But I think more down than up."

"Damn," Joe muttered. "I didn't know that. Is there anything I can do?"

"Hey, you're doing it. You're home, you're making Ma and Dad happy as can be." She shrugged. "You could get married and start a family. That would definitely help. Take some of the pressure off me."

"No way. Angie already gave them one grandkid. Besides, I think the girls should, you know, provide the kids."

"Soph is still active duty, and it's not happening with me."

"Don't know why not. My chief is a lesbian, and she's got a kid. Lots do."

"Well, I'm not lots," Gina said tightly.

Joe shot her a look. "You know, Gina, if things had been different, you might—"

"Things aren't different," she snapped. "They can't be different. Emmy is dead. Remember?"

He let out a breath. "Yeah, I remember. We all remember. But you're not." He poked her in the chest. "Even if you want to pretend you are."

She grabbed his finger and resisted the urge to twist it. He was her brother, the closest to her in age, in everything. They'd done everything together as kids. Learned to play ball, learned to play war, planned to be soldiers together. Only that hadn't worked out for her. "I'm not pretending anything. I just like things the way they are, okay? It's not about me."

"Why don't I believe you?"

"Because you're thickheaded, and you think because you've got a dick you know everything."

He burst out laughing. "Oh yeah. Like you believe that makes any difference."

She grinned. "Okay, maybe not. Maybe it's just that you're a Marine."

"Oorah." Giving up the argument, he threw his arm around her shoulders. "I'm telling you, Gina, one of these days, it's going to happen whether you like it or not."

She saw no reason to argue with him. He was wrong, but what did it matter. He was still her brother. "You playing tonight?"

"Of course. Four more days till the tourney," he said as they walked through the hall toward the exit. "I'm looking forward to kicking some contractor ass then."

"Butt. That's contractor *butt* to you," Gina said, striding into the sunlight and blinking as if she'd just stepped into a different universe, "and I don't think it's *our* butts that are going to get kicked. We ought to be able to handle a bunch of soft hospital types without any problem at all."

"We'll see come Friday night, babe," he said heading for his muscle car.

"I don't have to wait to see," she called after him. "I already know."

Her team had a comfortable lead at the top of their division, and although this was the first time the county had organized interdivision tourneys, she wasn't worried. They'd kick butt in the best of five coming up. It probably wouldn't hurt to check out the competition. Just to get her game plan ready. First, though, she had to make the call.

She slid into her truck and pulled out her phone. She couldn't put off the bad news any longer. She dialed and waited.

"Hey, Dad. It's Gina. Listen, we've got a bit of a problem."

❖

Carrie almost bumped into Flann in the hall when she hurried out of the elevator. "Hey, you're all done."

"Just finished."

Flann's surgical mask still hung around her neck and she hadn't bothered to put on a cover gown the way she usually did when she left the OR suite. She must've gone straight to the family waiting area to talk to Abby and the others. She looked relaxed and confident, though, and Carrie's spirits soared. "Everything went good, huh?"

"Everything went great. He's awake and he looks terrific." Flann's voice held an unmistakable note of happiness.

"Oh, that's wonderful. Where is he now?"

Flann tipped her chin toward the OR. "In recovery. As soon as he's a little more awake, we'll get his mother in there to sit with him."

"Do Presley and Harper know?"

"Yeah, Harper came in when we were about half done and hung out until we finished. She let Presley know. I think Presley's still with Abby."

"You're okay, right?"

Flann frowned. "Yeah, why wouldn't I be?"

"Oh, I don't know. I thought maybe you might be a little stressed or anxious, considering, you know, it was Blake."

"I guess it may seem weird, but this is what I do. I wouldn't do it, any of it, if I didn't know I could." Flann shook her head. "Anyone else wouldn't hesitate to help their kid with a problem if they had the expertise to fix something. Mine just happens to be surgical, and that's what he needed. Part of what he needed anyhow."

Carrie nodded. "I get that. I feel the same way. Does that seem weird?"

"Not to me." Flann smiled. "If you see Abby, tell her I'll be down to check him again in a half hour. I need to see my next patient first."

"Sure. Hey, will you be at the game tonight?" Carrie didn't want to push, but she hated to lose their star hitter.

"You bet. I'm not even on call. As long as Blake is doing okay, I'll be there."

"Good, because it's Houlihan's, remember."

Flann snorted. "They're hanging on to second place by a thread. After tonight, they won't be a problem."

"Well, just keep your batting arm ready."

Flann winked. "I'm always ready."

Carrie rolled her eyes. "Just forget it, Flann. Everybody knows you're Abby's toy now."

Flann threw back her head and laughed. "I don't think she's heard that one yet. I dare you to tell her."

Carrie grinned. "Not me."

"See you tonight, hotshot."

Hotshot. Carrie secretly liked the nickname, even though she was mostly just lucky to be blessed with good eye-hand coordination. Although she *did* have the fastest arm in the league. Four years of college softball had stuck with her. When she was on the mound and on her game, she felt like she imagined Flann did in the OR. Unbeatable. On top of the world. She couldn't wait for the next game, the next chance to test herself and give her best for the team.

All she had to do now was get through an afternoon of thrashing with various state and city bureaucracies over this whole construction thing. Because she'd be damned if she'd let Gina Antonelli get in the last word. She'd make it happen ahead of Antonelli's prediction if she had to drive to Albany herself.

CHAPTER FIVE

Carrie ran into Abby and Margie just outside the family waiting area. The lines of tension around Abby's eyes and mouth had disappeared, and her step was brisk and eager.

"I just saw Flann," Carrie said. "Everything came out great, huh?"

"Surgery went without a hitch, and Flann said he woke up saying he was hungry." Abby's smile widened. "That means he's pretty much normal. I'm just on my way in to post-op to see him now."

"Tell him I said hi." Carrie glanced at Margie, who hovered by Abby's side. Blake was important to her, maybe more so than to anyone other than Abby and Flann, and Blake clearly was emotionally connected to her. Whatever the exact nature of their relationship, they loved each other, and what else really mattered? "How are you doing, sweetie?"

"I'm cool," Margie said. "I'm going to go down to the ER and help out for a while."

"You don't have to do that," Abby said, squeezing Margie's shoulder. "You've been here for hours already. You should go home."

Margie shrugged. "That was personal. This is work."

Abby regarded her fondly. "Your stint in the ER is not supposed to be work, actually. It's called volunteering for a reason. You don't have to put in forty hours a week, you know."

"Yeah, but if I go home, I'll have chores. This is way more fun."

"I'm going to pretend I didn't hear that," Abby said. "And I promise, your mother will never know you're escaping your duties by spending extra time here."

Margie rolled her eyes. "My mother always knows. I'm a Rivers, after all. We all end up here eventually."

Laughing, Abby surrendered. "I can't possibly argue the truth of that. All right, but don't stay all afternoon. I'm going to call down and make sure you get out of there in a couple of hours."

"So," Margie said, the playful note in her voice gone, "do you think he'll be up and ready to leave soon? Because maybe I can see him before he goes home."

Realization dawned in Abby's eyes. "Tell you what. If he's feeling up to it, and I bet he will be, you can ride home with us."

"Really?"

Abby hugged her. "Totally. He'll like that."

"Thanks," Margie said.

"Talk to you soon, then," Abby said and hurried off.

Carrie walked with Margie to the stairs. "See you tonight at the game?"

"Oh yeah," Margie said. "I'll be there. I can't wait to see us kick Houlihan's butt."

"I think Flann has the same idea."

"Don't you?"

Carrie grinned. "Totally."

"Later!" Margie called when they reached the first floor.

"See you tonight." Carrie headed the opposite way, thinking of the half day left to her and the dragons she still needed to slay. Presley was for sure already in the office, busy juggling budgets, soothing demanding department heads who always needed more personnel and more of pretty much everything, and wading through the reams of red tape that needed to be cut through for the new programs. Carrie could sort out one little tangle of antiquated documentation requirements to get the ER expansion under way. She didn't need to get the CEO involved.

Not yet, anyhow.

And if handling the problem on her own just happened to show Gina Antonelli exactly how misguided her judgment of her had been, well, that was just a bonus.

❖

Waiting for her father to get back from his daily sweep of the job sites, Gina parked her truck behind the steps of the renovated trailer he used as an office in the corner of the chain-link-fenced lot where their equipment and building supplies were stored. He should be back at four thirty, just like every day for the last twenty-five years she'd been around, and probably a lot longer than that. She'd always liked hanging out around the lot when she was a kid. When she wasn't kicking a soccer ball around the enclosure, she'd been climbing on the trucks and excavators, playing hide-and-seek with Joe and Angie and Sophie behind the piles of stone and pallets of rock and wood. Of course, then she'd been playing soldier. She hadn't envisioned herself working here. Soccer was going to be her ticket to a scholarship, the key to her future. The lot hadn't changed much in the last fifteen years, but she had.

Gina leaned back against the metal siding, watching the trucks pull in at the end of their shifts, the heat of the sheet metal penetrating through her T-shirt. Soccer and a military career were part of those distant memories. Funny, it'd taken her a few years, but she'd gotten to like the work she'd been forced into by default. She liked running crews, she liked watching buildings rise out of pits in the ground. She had no medals to show for her labors, but she hoped she made her father a little bit proud all the same.

She wasn't about to make him happy today, though.

He pulled through the chain-link fence in his battered black Ford pickup truck, the one he'd been driving for a decade at least. He parked beside the trailer, climbed out slowly, and rubbed his face with both hands. He looked much the same as he had all the years of her growing up, but she'd just begun to notice his hair was gray now instead of black, his step was a little slower, and the lines around his mouth a little deeper. The realization that time moved on tightened her stomach.

Tom Antonelli narrowed his eyes and lasered in on her.

"Hey, Dad."

"Gina," he said briskly, straightening up and striding toward her. "Read me in on the details."

She smiled to herself. Once a Marine sergeant, always a Marine sergeant. Growing up, she and the other kids had heard all about his time in the military, before he'd mustered out to raise a family and start a business. He'd never been unfairly hard on them, but he'd demanded their best, and they'd all wanted to give it. They all still did. She straightened and only just resisted standing at attention.

He stopped in front of her and planted his big hands on his hips, his gaze sharp and not the least tired looking now.

"The short and sweet of it," Gina said, "is we don't have the permits to start the job at the Rivers. The fine print for the township requires we get documentation from the state about some of our labor coverage."

His mouth pressed into a thin line. "Our fault?"

"No, sir," she said, covering Angie's butt, not because Angie had done anything wrong, but someone had to be responsible and it shouldn't be her. "It's not the norm, and the hospital signed off on all the paperwork. Nobody over there followed up on permits, and we had no reason to."

"Did you put a boot to someone's butt over there?"

Gina briefly thought of Ms. Longmire's shapely butt and almost smiled. A boot was the last thing that image conjured in her mind. "Yes, sir. We've got someone working on it in administration—talking to their legal people—and I've already filled Angie in. We'll be coming at it from both flanks."

He nodded. "What about the boys in your crew? You have them redeployed?"

"I talked to Vince, and he can use all of them over at the NAPA site. Hopefully, it won't be that long a wait." Gina shrugged. "I'll fill in for Vince when he's off-site."

Her father shook his head. "You're gonna be wasted over there."

"Maybe so, but I figure I can make myself useful—"

"I've got an idea to keep you busy for a few days. Something your brother mentioned to me."

Gina froze. Her father didn't have ideas, he had orders. "Sir?"

"You know, there's another big contract in the wind for the hospital."

"Yes, sir, I'm aware of that. A helipad."

"Yeah, and everyone wants in on that one." Tom put a work boot up on the corrugated metal stair and leaned an arm on his knee, almost as if standing up straight was an effort. "Apparently one of the people over there who will be reviewing the bids is friends with Joe's boss down in the ER."

"I'm not following," Gina said carefully.

"A little goodwill tour to buy us some positive PR when it comes bid time."

PR? Goodwill? What the hell? The hair on the back of Gina's neck bristled. Whatever this was couldn't be good.

❖

Margie stopped outside room 520 and tapped on the open door.

"Hello?" Blake answered quietly.

"It's me," Margie said without stepping inside. She didn't want to make him uncomfortable if he wasn't ready to see her yet.

"Hey, come on in."

Blake sat on the edge of his bed in navy sweatpants and a zip-up gray sweatshirt open partly down his chest. A swath of beige bandage showed just below his collarbones. He was pale, but he was smiling.

Relief flooding her, Margie stopped a few feet away and, not knowing what to do with her hands, slid them into the back pockets of her jeans. "Your mom texted me and said you were ready to go. She said I could come up."

"I told her to find you," Blake said. "You could've come up sooner, but I was kinda out of it for a while, and I didn't really want you to see me while I was drooling."

Margie laughed. "Um, I've seen you drool before, you know. You always fall asleep when we watch movies, remember?"

"Yeah, but I never drool."

"Maybe I just don't tell you about it."

He laughed and stopped abruptly. "Ouch."

"What?" Margie's heart raced. "Should I get your mom?"

He shook his head. "No. It's just if I move too quickly or take a really deep breath, it hurts."

"Is it bad?"

"Not really. My chest mostly feels numb, but a couple places burn, you know, like when you get road rash from falling off your bike."

Margie grimaced at the thought of road rash on her chest. Her leg was bad enough. "That sounds nasty."

Blake shrugged in slow motion. "Honestly, it's about what I expected. I mean, it's hard to define pain, you know? So I wasn't really sure what it would be like, but it's not so bad."

"I'm glad." Margie swayed from side to side a little, hesitating over getting too personal. That was weird. They talked about everything, but everyone had their private places. She did too. They were best friends because they were careful with those places. "So, has Flann been in since surgery?"

"She stopped by to see me and Mom just a little while ago."

"Ah. That's good. I saw her too, right after surgery." Margie paused, then settled for, "She said you did good."

Blake's smile returned, brighter and wider. "She told us it went even better than she hoped. That my chest contour looks really good after surgery."

Margie let out a long breath. "That's great. I'm glad it's going to be what you want."

Blake searched her face. "You're still cool with it, right?"

"Totally," Margie said instantly. He didn't look quite convinced. "I know you, and you'll be you no matter what kind of body you're in, but I totally understand wanting to feel like everything matches the way it should. It's about who you are when you're alone with yourself, right?"

Blake visibly relaxed and Margie sighed inwardly.

"For the longest time," Blake said quietly, "I didn't want to be alone with myself. I felt like I was living with a stranger. Since I started transitioning, that's been a lot better. And you know what's really helped almost as much as all the physical stuff?"

"What?"

"You."

Margie tugged on her lip, waiting until she was sure her voice wouldn't shake. "Well, I think you're special. Even when you drool."

Blake laughed. "Yeah? Well, same goes."

Relieved the hard stuff was out of the way, Margie said, "So, are you going to have to stay in the house for a while?"

"Flann says I can walk around tomorrow as much as I want, as long as I'm not lifting anything. No driving, either."

"Bummer on the no driving."

"Really," Blake said.

Abby said from the doorway, "You'll just have to suck it up for a week, buddy. Flann will have your head if you undo all her great work."

"Oh, don't worry," Blake said. "I'm going to be the model patient."

"Uh-huh," Abby said. "I give you twenty-four hours before you start moaning about being bored."

"How can I be bored if Margie keeps me company every day?"

Margie laughed. "I promise to be as entertaining as possible."

Blake carefully slid off the side of the bed and didn't even resist when Abby pressed a hand to the small of his back.

"You okay?" Abby murmured.

"Yeah. Mostly super tired."

"The car's down front," Abby said. "I just have to sign some papers with the nurses. You two go ahead."

Blake walked slowly with Margie at his side. "I don't really expect you to hang out with me. There's no point in both of us being bored."

"Well, I'm going to be by every day," Margie said. "If you can walk around tomorrow, we can at least go out for something to eat. I'll drive."

Blake grinned. "Oh yeah, you're on."

Margie hurried ahead and pushed the button for the elevator, making sure the door stayed open while Blake stepped inside. She stood protectively between him and the rest of the people in the car as they descended.

When the doors opened, she whispered, "Okay? You want me to get a wheelchair or something?"

"I'd really like it if you pushed me around the parking lot in a wheelchair." Blake grinned. "But I don't need one. I'm okay as long as we go slow."

Margie figured they'd already crossed all of the sensitive lines and asked the next big question. "So when are you going to let me see?"

"You want to?"

"Well, yeah." Margie rolled her eyes at him.

"How about after all the stitches and stuff are out?"

"Sure, whenever you're ready." Margie held open the door.

"I don't think I'm going to be one of those guys who documents every day on YouTube. I'm really glad some of them did, but…I don't know…I guess I'm just not the get-naked-in-front-of-people kinda guy."

Margie laughed. "No kidding. I won't mind if you're not broadcasting everything to the world at large, anyhow."

"Okay then." Blake grinned. "I'm good with that."

"Yeah," Margie said, "me too."

Abby came up behind them and unlocked the car. "Blake, you ride in front. Margie—you coming with us?"

Margie shook her head. "I have to get home and help out with supper. There's a game tonight, and Mama will want to go too."

"I don't know how I forgot that," Abby said. "Flann said to tell everyone she's heading over to the field after she finishes rounds."

"You can go too, Mom," Blake said, sliding gingerly into the front seat. "I don't need a babysitter."

Abby ruffled his hair and did up his seat belt for him. "Good thing, since I'm no babysitter. But I think I'll stay home anyhow."

Blake leaned his head back and smiled at Margie. "Tell Flann to kick a—butt."

"I'll call later and tell you all about it." Margie waved as Abby drove away and sprinted around to the visitors' lot for the truck she'd inherited from Flann. Heading for home, she put the windows down and turned the radio on. The retro songs were staticky, but she sang along. Blake was fine and the big game was two hours away. The day was turning out to be perfect.

CHAPTER SIX

I want to talk to you. Where are you?" Gina sat in her truck in the narrow pathway between her house and the neighboring pasture fence with the engine idling, one leg out the open door on the running board, wondering if the steam coming out of her ears would fog up the windshield. Considering it was ninety outside, maybe not. Might set something on fire, though. "And if you're getting ready for your hot date, you'll just have to wait a little longer to get—"

"Whoa, Firecracker." Joe laughed. "My *date* is for after my game tonight. What's got your fuse lit?"

Gina wasn't amused by the childhood nickname or her brother's attempt to dampen her irritation with teasing. She'd been looking for a target for her frustration all day, and he'd painted a big old bull's-eye right in the middle of his own forehead. "How about that half-baked job you talked Dad into palming off on me, for starters? PR, my aching ass."

"Ooh, swear words now. I was just getting ready to head over to the field. How about I give you a call tomorrow?"

Joe chuckled, his good humor amping up her temperature. She was seriously PO'd and wanted to be taken seriously. "How about I meet you over there and twist off some body parts."

"What exactly are you in a snit about?"

"I'm not in the Marines," Gina said, stating the painfully obvious, "and for that matter, neither are you anymore. You can't *volunteer* me for jobs."

"I didn't exactly volunteer you," he said. "I just suggested it would get us some goodwill, you know, professionally speaking, if we used some of our downtime to help out the people we wanted to impress. You know, for future contracts."

"Impress." Gina slammed her door, shifted into reverse, and backed out into the lane that passed in front of her house and circled the very edge of town before joining a bigger county road and heading east. The two-story white clapboard house with its wide porch and gabled roof had been her mother's mother's family home, and Gina had played in the broad front yard and surrounding fields as a child. She hadn't hesitated to move in when she'd learned the house had come to her in lieu of any other inheritance. Home meant more to her than money. She still qualified to be in the same zip code as the village, and she could walk the mile and a half to the center of town or pretty much anywhere else in the village with a little more effort. "Who exactly are we supposed to be impressing? And don't tell me it's some girl you're trying to get to go out with you."

"I don't need any help in that department." His car engine revved in the background. "But my boss's friend needs a helping hand, and the two of them pull a lot of weight around the place."

Gina set her phone in the hands-free holder and pulled out behind the school bus making the last run of the day. She squinted in the glare of the slanting sun and ground her teeth. "Maybe you should stick to medicine and leave the building business to the rest of us."

"If I say yes, will you forgive me?"

"Verdict's out till I see the job." Gina shook her head, trying not to smile. "I'll see you at the field."

"Coming to check out the competition, huh?"

"That was my plan originally. Now I'm coming to hurt you."

He laughed again. "Dream on."

"Stop talking and drive. Idiot." Gina disconnected to the sound of Joe laughing and switched off her phone. Sometimes, Joe's devil-may-care attitude grated on her. Especially when his easygoing ideas had an impact on her life. Not that anything she said to him was going to change anything now, not once her father had decided on a course of action. The deal was done, so she might as well accept it.

A night of watching a good softball game while checking out the competition would be the highlight of her day. Joe had just joined the hospital team a few weeks earlier when his rotation in the ER started, so she hadn't seen what kind of team he really had. He'd asked her to come pretty much every game, but she knew what that would mean. Joe introducing her to his friends and trying to get her to go out with everyone after the game. He wasn't very subtle about his matchmaking, either, and occasionally embarrassed her.

She didn't need more friends. And she didn't need her brother setting up dates for her, either. But this was softball, and softball was serious business. To hear him talk, his team was unbeatable. But then, her team was in a different league and she knew *they* were unbeatable.

Gina reached the big grassy plateau in ten minutes and parked at one end of the cleared lot next to a long line of SUVs, pickup trucks, and the occasional muscle car. She climbed out, locked up, and headed over to the field. Houlihan's was in the field taking batting practice. Houlihan's Tavern was a popular place for burgers and beers on a nearby lake, and their team had played in their league until five years ago when they switched to a different division. They had a rep for being super hard-core and prided themselves on being willing to risk body parts to steal a base or beat a throw to home. They were usually at the top of the leaderboard, but she'd heard they'd recently lost one of their two best pitchers when he'd moved downstate, and they were struggling because of it.

Hitting and fielding were always important, but pitching was key. If you didn't have a pitcher who could put it across the plate, you were going to be in deep trouble.

She sauntered over to the fence behind the backstop and hooked a finger through the wire, watching Houlihan's starting pitcher, a heavy-lifter-looking guy with curly black hair down to his shoulders and arms corded with muscle, lob easy balls to his teammates, who took casual swings and smacked the floaters into the outfield. Fielders in green shirts with *Houlihan's* scripted across the front in white ambled to get them and tossed them back in. The whole team looked relaxed, but she suspected that was all just an act.

The Rivers team congregated on the bench to her left, waiting for their turn to warm up. This year's uniform consisted of maroon shirts with *The Rivers* blocked on the front in navy, numbers on the back, and black baseball pants. She searched for Joe although she didn't plan on accosting him about his meddling in her life until after the game. Warm-up time was sacrosanct. Time to focus and get into the zone. The hospital team looked roughly evenly divided between men and women, about like her team. According to Joe, they fielded the strongest hitters and the best pitchers in the league. Of course, her team wasn't in this league, so she didn't bother to argue with him.

Houlihan's streamed off the field and the Rivers ran out.

Gina stiffened. The pitcher settling in on the mound was unexpectedly familiar. Her heart jumped in a weird and worrying way. She frowned. What the heck was that all about? Since when did a little surprise make her breath short?

Joe hadn't said much about his teammates when discussing the games with her. Not much reason to, really, since she didn't know the hospital personnel. But she knew the pitcher. Ms. Longmire, executive admin, had pulled her red hair back into a ponytail and threaded it through a navy blue baseball cap with the number 1 on the front. Her tight black pants ended midcalf, and her baseball-cut maroon jersey with three-quarter-length sleeves fit her the way a sports shirt should, roomy enough to move around in, but not so big as to get in her way. Not so loose that it didn't showcase her figure, either. Gina's breathing got a little more uneven and she hooked the other hand in the fence, losing sight of everyone else on the field as she watched Longmire wind up to throw. She was fluid and graceful and looked like she'd been reigning on the mound for a lifetime.

Longmire lobbed an easy pitch across home plate to the catcher, who threw it back. She snagged it out of the air with a quick flip of her wrist, looked over her shoulder toward first, and threw it arrow straight and lighting fast into the waiting first baseman's mitt. The ball made the bases in a familiar warm-up routine and then back to the pitcher. Longmire turned toward home, paused, and frowned in Gina's direction. With a slow smile and the barest tilt of her chin that might have been a hello or just a quick move to chase the errant strands of hair away from her eyes, she rocketed a bullet across the plate. Gina involuntarily jerked at the smack of fastball on leather.

Well then. Gina reckoned she'd been noticed, and it looked like the game was on.

❖

The last person Carrie expected to see watching her from behind the backstop was Gina Antonelli. Even less expected was her reaction to seeing the builder staring at her. Sure, she noticed good-looking women, she was alive and breathing after all, and noticed them looking back, but those casual glances from strangers were a nice ego boost, something to smile at inwardly as she walked on by, but nothing to get her pulse racing. Gina provoked something entirely different. A fast shot of adrenaline mixed with something that felt suspiciously like lust coursed through her the instant she saw her. Not only was that weird, it was really disconcerting. She hadn't had that kind of hormonal jolt since puberty. Maybe not even then. Not that she minded a good old healthy dose of arousal, but she really wished it wasn't indiscriminate. And indiscriminate was the only word to describe any reaction to Gina Antonelli. Given her druthers, she'd pick almost any other woman than the just-on-the-edge-of-surly thorn in her side to get the hots over. But there she was, leaning insolently up against the chain-link, fingers foolishly linked through the fence, and annoyingly inciting hotness.

How did Antonelli know she wasn't going to throw a wild pitch and slam into her fingers? She had a vision of those long tapering fingers curled over Antonelli's work belt that morning, cocky and sure like the rest of her. She definitely would not want to damage them. And in the next instant, she was firing a speedball during warm-up, registering the surprise on Harper's face an instant later as she caught the rocket. Antonelli gave a satisfying jerk from behind the fence and then shot her an impudent grin as if she'd been reading her mind.

Really. The woman was beyond annoying. Carrie wasn't going to give her another thought. She had a game to win and wasn't going to be bothered by a spectator. An inconsequential one at that. She dialed down her arm a little and finished her warm-up at a more reasonable pace, testing the corners of the plate, judging her curveball, working on the slider. She didn't have to worry about her fastball. No one had clocked her in this league—there was really no need to. She was easily twenty miles an hour faster than anyone else, but she'd had four years of intense pitching coaching at Stanford. Some things came back quickly, and her arm was almost as good as it had been then.

When Harper called an end to warm-up, she jogged over to the bench, studiously ignoring Gina, who sauntered back toward the bleachers directly behind them. At least she hadn't come to watch Houlihan's. That might be the final straw, if she was rooting for their competition. Flann sprinted across the field from the parking lot just as

Harper was going over the starting roster. Harper was Flann's mirror opposite in looks, in temperament too. Dark hair to Flann's sandy blond, blue eyes to Flann's brown. She was cool and steady while Flann burned hot and fast, but at the heart, they were carved from the same stock. Solid, strong, family-oriented, and loyal. Not to mention the hotness factor, which Carrie ignored, seeing as they were both married, or about to be, to her best friends. She didn't begrudge Presley and Abby their perfect matches, since she knew she'd be looking for the same thing one day. Someone to count on, someone who wanted to build a life with her, someone who looked at her as if she was the only woman in the world. There had to be at least a few more woman left like that, and she was in no hurry.

"Sorry I'm late," Flann said, dropping her duffel onto the ground and her butt onto the bench. She leaned over and pulled out her cleats. "I wanted to stop home to see Blake first."

"No problem," Harper said. "How is he?"

"He's good. He's tough."

Everyone murmured some version of *awesome* and turned their attention back to Harper, who continued reading out the expected starting lineup. Carrie was on the mound, Harper was catching, and Glenn was at first base. They had the field first, so Carrie would have first shot at striking out Houlihan's leadoff hitters. She liked the chance to make her mark first.

"Remember to shift right for Beecher," Harper said to the infielders. "She always pulls to that side, and she'll take the first pitch that's anywhere close." Harper glanced at Carrie. "Give her something low. She swings high."

"Right," Carrie said, although she didn't need the advice. She knew how Houlihan's big hitters hit. She'd done her own scouting at their games a couple times in the last few weeks, watching for weaknesses in their hitters. Overkill maybe, but she liked to be prepared. She found that being prepared cut down on unwelcome surprises. She wasn't big on surprises. She liked knowing what was coming down the pike, she liked preparing for all contingencies. Almost against her will, she glanced behind her at the bleachers. Maybe that's why Gina's presence was like a little nagging spur in the back of her mind. She didn't have any plans in place to deal with the unsettling force of her personality blowing into her day and disrupting her evening. She sure as hell wasn't prepared for her own completely out of left field response to Antonelli showing up at the game. She couldn't seem to forget that Antonelli was sprawled on the top bleacher, her lean legs in tight dark jeans propped on the bench below her, her arms stretched out across the top rail behind her. The picture of relaxation and, damn it, hotness.

Presley, Margie, and Ida Rivers waved as they came around the corner of the bleachers and climbed up to the midsection, Margie carrying a cooler. Carrie's cousin Mari followed a few seconds later, a bag of what looked like sandwiches under one arm. Glenn waved and Mari sent her a brilliant smile.

Everyone's girlfriends or spouses were there and none of *them* were distracted. Of course, she wasn't, either. Resolutely, she turned her back to the bleachers and Gina Antonelli.

"Something bothering you?" Flann asked quietly, walking over to join her as everyone grabbed their gloves.

Carrie jumped. "No, why?"

"I don't know, you seem a little…distracted."

Carrie bristled. "Not at all. I'm totally ready."

Watching Carrie talking to the blond jock, Gina took in the swift dismissal as Carrie pointedly turned away. Carrie, as she'd learned from listening to the players call to their pitcher, had very clearly sent a physical message. *You are not worth a second look.* She would've believed it too, if she hadn't already *gotten* a second look. Actually, she'd gotten a couple more looks than that. Carrie had checked her out a few times, even if she had been scowling while she did it. Gina smiled, remembering the double take when Carrie had first seen her standing behind the backstop. Oh yeah, she'd gotten a look. Good thing bullets hadn't come with it. Knowing she'd stirred her up a little gave her a little charge.

Being checked out wasn't completely out of the ordinary for her. She worked jobs all over the county, and she met women now and then who would give her a look or two. Most of the time she let the silent questions pass right by her. She wasn't interested in any kind of looks or any of the unspoken messages that went along with them. For some reason, though, she enjoyed knowing she'd gotten Carrie Longmire's attention.

That was different, but it made sense. She wanted to be on Carrie's radar, especially if it would get the work orders out sooner. Funny, though, that Joe had never mentioned her before. It wasn't like him not to bring up any eligible woman in a fifty-mile radius.

A tight knot twisted in Gina's stomach. Maybe Joe never mentioned her because she wasn't available. A woman like her—smart, sexy, beautiful—would catch the attention of any unattached man or woman. For some reason, that idea didn't sit very well, although it shouldn't matter to her if Carrie was single or married or living with three lovers. All that mattered was that Carrie straightened out the mess that was keeping her from doing her job.

Satisfied she'd sorted through the reasons for the unexpected jolt of heat she'd gotten when Longmire—*Carrie*—had turned and locked eyes with her in the bleachers, she settled back to watch the game. Just like any other night.

CHAPTER SEVEN

Carrie planned to pitch the first two batters a little on the slow side, playing with the zone, keeping them just a little off balance with the changeup and then, just when they thought they had a good read on the ball, sliding one past them low and hard. The first batter struck out, and she could hear him mutter an oath all the way out on the mound. The second grounded to short, a whiff of a slapshot with nothing behind it. Mindy McIntyre, a neonatal specialist by day and a superjock by night, fielded it easily and tossed it to Glenn at first for the out with almost casual nonchalance. Her husband cheered from the sidelines, and Mindy grinned as if to say, *Nothing to it, baby.*

Carrie smiled at the attitude. The team was feeling good about this game. The third batter, a power hitter, came to the plate. Rachel Beecher, a lefty, co-owned Houlihan's along with Howie Murphy. Carrie'd heard rumors the two had been hooked up when they opened the bar, had parted less than friends, and barely spoke to each other when they weren't on the field. Classic story of business and pleasure definitely not mixing. Not a cocktail Carrie ever intended to sample.

She felt the team shift right behind her even without looking. Rachel pulled right like most lefties, and as sure as Harper had predicted, Rachel jumped on Carrie's first pitch. She swung even earlier than Carrie had expected, though. The sharp crack of a well-hit ball careening off a strong bat had her pivoting, watching the ball loft into the outfield way to the left of where the right fielder had set up.

Crap. That was going to drop in for a double. Joe Antonelli sprinted out of center field while the right fielder made a mad dash for the ball. Joe was faster, or maybe just more determined, and called off the right fielder before they had a head-on collision. Just as the ball arced down toward the ground, Joe made a full stretch dive, his glove hitting the ground just under the ball. He landed hard, bounced, and somehow came up on his feet in one fluid motion, waving his glove with the ball firmly in hand.

"Out!" the ump in the field called.

Three up, three down. Just the way Carrie liked it.

"Nice catch," she called to Joe as he jogged by on his way in to the bench.

He grinned, grass staining the front of his jersey and a streak of dirt on his chin. "Nice pitching."

"You landed pretty hard—you okay?"

"Oorah."

Carrie laughed and followed him to the sidelines. Before she could catch herself, she glanced up at the bleachers. Skimming past the middle section where her friends and her cousin Mari congregated, she focused in on the top row. Gina leaned forward, elbows on her knees and hands laced beneath her chin, watching her. Carrie tried to tell herself she was imagining it, but Gina's gaze never wavered, even when their eyes locked. Carrie flushed.

Look away, idiot!

Gina nodded and mouthed, "Good inning."

Carrie blushed. Wonderful. How many other ways could she be uncool?

Before Gina had a chance to read her pleasure, Carrie turned away. She wasn't exactly comfortable having no control over her reactions and no good reason to explain why Gina's approval pleased her so much. Or why she felt just a little bit like showing off. Gina's attention had absolutely nothing to do with it.

Carrie plunked down on the bench as Glenn got up to bat, and studied her with a little twinge of worry for any sign she was stiff or sore. The chief ER physician assistant—and her cousin Mari's new love—had been hospitalized not that long ago after a car accident. What could have been a major injury thankfully had been only bruises and bumps, but the scare still lingered. Glenn, rangy and lean, settled in at the plate and looked out at the pitcher with almost Zen-like calm. The Houlihan's pitcher twitched at his shirt, his hat pulled down low over his face, his hand tucked into his glove. With an abrupt, abbreviated windup, he whipped a fastball toward the plate. The ball was high and headed straight at Glenn's head. Glenn jerked back from the plate, nearly stumbling, and went down on one knee in the dirt. Every person on the Rivers team was on their feet, yelling and waving their arms in protest.

The Houlihan's pitcher glanced over at them and smirked.

Harper took an angry stride toward the field, but Flann caught her by the back of the jersey.

"She's okay, Harp," Flann said. "We don't need you getting tossed this early."

"Come on, that was intentional!" Harper, usually the controlled one of the pair, strained in her sister's grip. "He ought to get tossed, not me!"

Carrie flanked Harper on the other side. "The ump's going to give him that one, Harp. Sometimes the ball gets away from you. Or he'll say Glenn was crowding the plate, and he was just trying to establish his strike zone. You gotta let this one go."

The ump took his time brushing off the plate while Glenn got to her feet. Waiting for the uproar to die down, he glanced at Harper, whose neck strained with the tension of staying quiet. With a quick nod, he called, "Play ball."

Carrie'd said what needed to be said to keep Harper from exploding. Sometimes the ball *did* get away from you. And sometimes if a batter was crowding the plate, messing with the strike zone, making it difficult to get the ball where you needed to get it, then you pitched in close and pushed them back. No one wanted to hurt anyone. That wasn't what had happened with Glenn. The butthead on the mound was trying to intimidate them. Steaming inwardly, she stayed standing, as did most members of the team. Daring him to try it again.

His second pitch was way outside and Glenn let it go. On his third pitch, Glenn contacted solidly and smacked a ground ball between third base and shortstop and made it easily to first. Harper batted next, waited the pitcher out for the ball she wanted, and advanced Glenn to second on a sacrifice fly. That put Flann and Joe up next, their place and power hitters. Flann hit into a double play and, just like that, the inning was over.

Houlihan's was good, but so were they, and going into the last inning, Carrie's team had a slim one-run lead. Carrie was still pitching, and Harper stopped her on her way out to the field.

"How's your arm?"

"Fine," Carrie said instantly.

"We've got the tournament this weekend. We'll have another crack at these guys before the season's over, but I want you to be able to pitch at least parts of three of the tourney games."

"I'm fine." Carrie knew herself well enough to judge. She had a little soreness in her shoulder, but her elbow and forearm were pain free. "I can pitch another inning, and I'll have plenty of rest by Friday. Besides, I don't want to wait to beat these dicks."

Harper grinned. "Neither do I. How's your fastball feeling?"

"Fast."

"Then give them everything you've got so we can get out of here."

"You got it."

She threw the first batter out on strikes, and the second popped-up in the infield. One more out and they had the win. Carrie didn't let herself think about winning. She just thought about throwing the pitch she wanted, every time.

The pitcher came up to the plate. A lot of pitchers, her included, were only average hitters. This guy was big and strong, and she'd seen him hit. He settled himself in the batter's box, adjusted his various parts, and stared at her as if to tell her she didn't have anything to challenge him.

Carrie didn't bother to smile. She didn't have anything to prove. She added a little extra spin on her first pitch, and it dove under the bat as he swung hard. Behind the plate, Harper caught it cleanly, threw it back, and signaled for a fastball high and away. Carrie put it right where Harper called for, and the batter stood watching it. Two strikes—one more was all she needed. She put the fastball down at his knees, but he was a good hitter and he must have read it coming out of her glove.

The ball came straight at her, so fast she couldn't even see it.

She was falling away before she'd even registered the sound of the bat contacting the ball. She hit the ground on her left side, her cheek landing in the dirt at the edge of the pitcher's mound. She heard people yelling, a few cursing. She rolled onto her back, opened her eyes, and decided that all of her parts were in working order. She held her glove up into the air and smiled at the ball set firmly in the web.

The angry protests from her teammates turned to cheers, and she slowly got to her feet, wiping the dirt from her face against her sleeve. Harper ran out to her.

"You okay?"

"I'm good."

"That moron put it right at your head," Harper said, glancing over her shoulder at the Houlihan's pitcher, who tossed his bat onto the ground and stalked back to the Houlihan's bench.

"It happens," Carrie said.

"Yeah, but it shouldn't."

"Hey, we won," Carrie said, smiling. "So no harm, no foul."

Joe jogged over from center field as the rest of the team crowded around, congratulating her and each other. "Man, that looked like a rocket. I can't believe you got your glove on that."

"Instinct," Carrie said. "Really, I didn't even see it coming."

"That guy is a dick," Joe muttered.

"Won't argue." Carrie dusted herself off as they all headed for the bench. Everyone in the stands was on their feet too, and she couldn't see Gina. Realizing she was searching for her, she quickly looked away.

Harper called, "Everybody up for pizza and beer?"

"Sounds good to me," Carrie said, riding high from the victory. That had to explain the way her whole system seemed to buzz with anticipation.

Mari jumped down from the bleachers and ran over. "Hey! That was an amazing game. Are you okay? You fell awfully hard."

"I'm fine," Carrie said for what felt like the hundredth time. "I'm great."

Mari gripped her chin and turned her face, frowning. "You're going to have a bruise on your cheek. I don't see any break in the skin, though. You were lucky. If that had hit you…"

Carrie threaded her arm around Mari's waist. She hadn't even known about her cousin until a short time before, when Mari joined the ER as a PA. Now she was as close to Mari as to her own sisters. "Don't worry. I've got good reflexes."

"That much is obvious."

"How's Glenn?" Carrie asked quietly.

Mari looked over to where Glenn sat on the bench, methodically and quietly packing up her gear like the soldier she still was, inside.

"According to her, she's never been better. Her knee is bothering her a little bit in the morning, but I think that's just temporary stiffness. No postconcussive symptoms, thankfully."

"Good," Carrie said. "Are you going out with us?"

"Not tonight. Glenn has the night shift, so we're going to head home for a few hours before she has to go in."

"Okay. I'll catch up to you soon, then."

"Don't forget, we have to start in on our next wedding planning."

"How could I forget!" Carrie shook her head. Flann and Abby were just waiting until Blake was recovered from his surgery before they set a date, but it was never too soon—in fact, it was already too late in the game—to start serious planning. They were going to have to do a lot on the fly. "This weekend, right?"

"Uh-huh. I'll confirm with Abby and Presley." Mari was a natural organizer and, now that she had settled in at the hospital and with Glenn, was rapidly becoming the moving force of their social gatherings. She'd left her family behind in California, and she was making a new one here.

"I'll be there." Waving as Mari hurried off to join Glenn, Carrie turned and almost bumped into Gina Antonelli. "Oh. Hi."

She mentally rolled her eyes. That was brilliant.

"Nice game," Gina said.

"Thanks."

"Sweet catch there at the end." Gina glanced over at the Houlihan's bench where some of the team still remained. Her expression darkened as she scanned the bruise on Carrie's cheek. "You okay?"

"It's a little sore," Carrie admitted. "But hey, the ball didn't hit me, so I'm not complaining."

"Yeah, I could see you'd been there before. You pitched the pants off them. Where'd you play?"

"What do you mean?"

"College, I'm guessing Division I. Notre Dame?"

"Please," Carrie said, feigning disdain.

"No," Gina mused. "Too conventional. Somewhere a little more free-spirited, but hard-core competitive."

Carrie laughed. "Right."

"Stanford," Gina said as if it were truth.

Which it was. Carrie bent down to stick her mitt in her bag and give herself time to figure out exactly how she was going to handle this. Gina had been watching her. Really watching her, if she could tell that much about her from one game, and Carrie wasn't sure how she felt about that. She wasn't used to being read quite so effortlessly, and to make it worse, Gina was not only *hard* to read but irritatingly attractive. Carrie straightened, her duffel in her hand. "You're right about the school. But don't be so sure about the rest."

Gina grinned. "What rest?"

"Never mind," Carrie said abruptly. Whenever the two of them talked, she ended up not being sure just what they were talking about, and that was beyond annoying. "I've got to get going. Hope you enjoyed the game."

Lame, lame, and lamer. Carrie hurried away before she could come up with anything more lame.

"So you'll call me?" Gina called.

Carrie flushed and turned. "Sorry?"

Gina grinned. "About the permits. You're working on them, right?"

Carrie narrowed her eyes. So that's what all the friendliness was about. Antonelli obviously didn't care about anything except work, and her charm routine was just a way of getting a foot in the door. Not that she was in the least bit charming. "You'll hear from me when I have something to tell you."

"Soon, right?" Gina smiled, watching Carrie's shoulders stiffen and her stride lengthen. Why she should find a woman who was constantly irritated at her so mesmerizing she had no idea.

"What's going on?" Joe asked, sliding up next to her.

Gina quickly smothered her smile. "Nothing."

"That's the longest I've seen you talk to a woman in five years."

"Business," Gina said, tracking Carrie out of the corner of her eye as she disappeared into the parking lot.

"Is that what you call it."

Gina shot him a look. "She's the CEO's executive admin, did you know that?"

Joe shrugged. "Sure, I knew she was management. It doesn't matter much out here."

"Well, it matters plenty now. We're stalled on the ER project until we get the permits, and she's the gatekeeper."

"Ha. So you're hoping your winning personality will speed things along?" Joe play-punched her in the arm "Because I gotta tell you, sis, that's probably not gonna work out too well."

"Just building a little goodwill," Gina said.

She'd only intended to congratulate Carrie on the game when she'd climbed out of the bleachers, but that had turned into something else when their conversation had stirred the fire in Carrie's eyes and brought a little bit of flush to her throat. She still felt some of the heat.

"So where are you headed for beer?" Gina asked.

"Why, you suddenly feeling friendly?" Joe asked.

"Just thirsty," Gina said softly.

CHAPTER EIGHT

Bottoms Up was already packed by the time Gina walked in. The one big room took up most of the first floor of a plain-faced red brick building. Two double windows on either side of the front door faced the street. The bar ran down one side with tables filling the rest of the space and a kitchen in the back. Two ceiling fans beat impotently against the July night air, stirring a lackluster breeze smelling of yeast and cooked beef. The hazy half-light in the bar tinged everyone with a patina of silver, like barroom players in an old daguerreotype. About half of the Houlihan's team had shown up, which was odd as their sponsors ran a tavern, but maybe this was the closest place to start nursing their wounds. Plus, plenty of townies played on Houlihan's team, even if they were based ten miles up the road, and this was their regular hangout. Pretty much all of the Rivers team along with their fans had migrated over, and she picked out jerseys from two or three other teams as well. Joe waved to her from a row of square four-top tables that had been pushed together in the middle of the room, surrounded by a jumble of chairs and at least a dozen people. She shook her head and tilted her chin toward the bar. She wanted the excuse of grabbing a drink to give her a minute to get the lay of the land. She wasn't quite ready to jump into the mash of Joe's teammates right away.

"What can I get ya?" The middle-aged bartender wore khaki pants and a T-shirt that read *Ace Hardware*.

"Whatever dark you've got on draft."

"Coming up."

"Thanks." She didn't recognize him, and for a place like this in a town this small, that was unusual. The last time she'd been in, the owner, Frank Durkin, had been pulling the taps. Come to think of it, though, she hadn't been in Bottoms Up or much of anywhere else for six months, maybe more now, and she might have gotten a little out of touch. Joe would say she was more than a little out of touch.

She put a five down and collected her draft when the bartender slid it in front of her. After a long pull, she edged sideways to the bar so she could scan the faces at Joe's table. She recognized most of them from the game, either players or spectators in the bleachers. The players were fairly evenly dispersed among men and women not in team garb—friends and intimates of one kind or another, she gathered. Seemed like everyone had a companion of some kind. Carrie sat at one corner of the row of tables nearest Gina, facing Joe with her back to the bar. A blonde Gina had noticed in the bleachers a few rows down from her sat on Carrie's left. The Rivers's coach, Harper Rivers, sat on the blonde's far side.

Gina watched and nursed her beer, trying to figure out if Carrie was with the blonde or if they were just friends. When Harper Rivers absently slid her fingers beneath the blonde's hair and stroked the nape of her neck, Gina figured they were the couple. Carrie seemed to be by herself, although she appeared to be talking and laughing with everyone else at the table. She was popular, and Gina could see why—talented, smart, gorgeous—what wasn't to like? For a newcomer, Carrie looked at home with everyone too—more at home than Gina felt, having lived in the area all her life.

Joe ambled over and ordered refills for half the table. "You planning on joining us or being your usual antisocial self the rest of the night?"

"Looks pretty crowded over there," Gina said.

He scoffed. "There's always room for another chair."

"Is the brunette next to you your hot date?"

Joe laughed. "Not hardly. Her husband is the big guy on her other side. I'm picking up my date when she gets off work at eleven."

"Another PA?"

"OR nurse. Mattie Evans."

"I remember her," Gina said. "She was a few years behind me. Played goalie for Corinth."

"Yep," Joe said carefully, the way he always did when soccer came up.

Gina let it go, easier than it used to be. Just as carefully she said, "Who's the blonde sitting next to your pitcher?"

Joe looked over his shoulder as if he needed to remind himself of who was at the table. He quirked an eyebrow at Gina. "That would be Presley Worth. She's the big boss of the hospital now."

"Carrie's boss?"

"Well, Carrie's and everybody else's, I guess. Her company bought the place, and she's in charge now."

"Yeah, I heard that. Dad negotiated contracts with her."

"With her and Abby Remy, the ER chief. My boss. Since the takeover the ER has some kind of independent deal going on with the hospital." He shrugged. "I don't pay too much attention as long as I'm getting training and a paycheck."

"So the CEO is the friend of your boss who needs the favor." Gina shook her head. Just like Joe to try fixing everyone's problems. She wouldn't have minded if he hadn't volunteered her for the same duty.

"They're more than friends. I guess you could say they're kind of related, since Presley's with Harper Rivers, and Abby is with Flannery. It's a pretty tight unit."

Gina smiled wryly. "They don't call the place the Rivers for nothing, I guess."

"Hey, they've kept the hospital going for a hundred years and are still looking after the place. And that's what matters to all of us."

"I totally agree with you. And I'm happy to do my share." She finished off her beer. "If somebody would just let me."

He signaled the bartender to get her another beer. Pushing the glass toward her, he said, "Here. I know two's your limit, so at least come and drink this with us. Let the job go for the night. You'll be out busting stone before you know it."

"Yeah," she muttered, grabbing the beer. "I hope so."

She couldn't *not* sit with them, not unless she wanted to appear outright unfriendly, so she followed him. She wasn't even sure where her resistance to joining the group was coming from. Her social skills were kind of rusty, and most of the time when Joe invited her out, it was to some kind of party where by the end of the night most people had a little too much to drink and conversation had turned to more intimate pastimes. She wasn't big on casual conversation with strangers, and she was not a one-night-stand kind of person. Not that she'd pick up a girl anywhere near where her brother could see her anyhow. It just wasn't her scene. But she wasn't so rusty she couldn't make polite conversation.

As she approached the table, Joe dragged a chair over from an adjacent table and wedged it in at the corner next to Carrie. Gina chose to think that was an accident. He couldn't possibly know the only person at the table she really wanted to talk to was Carrie.

❖

Carrie turned to her right when someone sat down beside her. For a second, she was so surprised she didn't say anything. She hadn't seen Gina come in, and she was the last person she expected to see. Gina had materialized out of nowhere, and that seemed to be happening a lot.

She'd never met the woman before that morning, and now every time she turned around, there she was. She wouldn't have thought anything of it if it hadn't been for her odd and alarming reaction. She could feel her pulse pounding in her throat, and the room was suddenly way too warm. And thank goodness the tavern was just barely light enough to see people's expressions, because her face was heated and probably flaming. None of those reactions were under her control, and all of them were completely unusual for her. And she was staring, wasn't she. She could tell by the little smirk on Gina's face. At least she hoped that was the cause and Gina wasn't actually reading the rest of what she was feeling. If she started telegraphing random, irrational lust, she'd need to take a long vacation somewhere far away.

Gina was doing some staring of her own, as if waiting for Carrie to make the first move.

"Hi," Carrie said, and wasn't that a great opening line.

"Hi," Gina said back in her husky, oh-so-casual way.

Maybe it was the slightly foggy atmosphere clouding her brain, but Gina's voice sounded distinctly smoky, even a little bit seductive. And there she went again, having the most alarming thoughts with absolutely no provocation.

"I've never seen you in here before," Carrie said, with yet another brilliant remark. Wow. What next? *We can't keep meeting like this*?

"What's so funny?" Gina asked, grinning faintly.

"I'm trying not to utter any more bad pickup lines."

"Are you picking someone up?"

"No!" Carrie blew a wisp of hair from her eyes. "Of course not."

Gina considered teasing her a little more, but she didn't want to push too far. She wanted to talk with her, not chase her away. "My brother keeps bugging me to come, but I haven't had a good reason. Until now."

Carrie cursed her total lack of cool. Now the heat reached all the way to her hairline. Hello, beet-face. She'd hated her red hair and pale, slightly freckled complexion as a child, but as she'd gotten older, she'd begun to realize red hair was a distinguishing characteristic a lot of people—okay, a lot of women—seemed to like. Right this moment, she was back to wishing her skin was any other color than pale white because there was no way to hide a blush. And when had she ever been blushing and speechless in the presence of a sexy woman?

Since that morning, apparently.

Until now, Gina had said.

"I'm going to take that remark as a non sequitur," Carrie said.

Gina laughed. "Let's just say I'm happy my brother finally talked me into going to one of his games."

"Oh? You're not usually a softball fan?"

"No, just the opposite. I love softball."

"Do you play?" Carrie asked.

"No," Gina said, her expression, even in the dim light, darkening for an instant. "No, I don't."

The conversations and laughter swirling around the table floated on the edge of Carrie's awareness as she leaned closer. Gina's eyes held all her attention. "Just a fan, then."

"Actually, I coach a team."

Carrie straightened. "You're kidding. Who? What league?"

Gina grinned. "We're local. A's Construction. Although most people in our league call us the Hammers."

Carrie's eyes narrowed. Oh, this could so not be a coincidence. She'd never seen Gina at a game before—or anywhere else, and who with a pulse could miss her? "Now you're kidding me, right?"

"Honest truth." Gina sipped her half-warm beer. "We're not all carpenters, of course—some are pipefitt—"

"I'm not talking about the name, and you know it. You coach the Hammers?"

"Yep."

"And you just decided on a whim to come to the game tonight because Joe's been bugging you about it?"

Gina's smile widened, and Lord, it was a beautiful smile, full and wide and perfectly balanced by her tapered jaw, high cheekbones, and deep-set eyes. And she was staring again. Carrie bristled, irritated with herself for letting a handsome face muddle her brain. "Well?"

"Joe has been bugging me to come out for one," Gina said, "but, okay, I might have had an interest in seeing how your team looked."

"You mean you were scouting us."

"Tell me you've never done the same thing."

Carrie smothered a grin. "I might have taken in a couple of Houlihan's games. But I haven't seen any of yours."

"Well, we're playing day after tomorrow. Why don't you come on by and see what you think." The words were out before Gina even had a chance to consider them. Inwardly, she wondered what the hell she was doing—inviting the competition to come and check out her team wasn't exactly a smart coaching strategy. Added to that, inviting Carrie, or any other woman, to a game would be exactly the first time, ever, she'd done that. All the same, she held her breath, waiting for the answer.

Carrie heard what sounded like a dare, and her natural competitive instincts kicked in. "You're on."

"Game starts at six thirty. We play out on Belmont Plateau."

"I know where. I'll make it if I can," Carrie said, pulling back just a little, giving herself room to back out. "So what did you learn tonight?"

"Joe hasn't been exaggerating. You've got a good team. And a very hot pitcher."

Carrie pulled her lower lip between her teeth, refusing to flirt back, if that's what Gina was doing. She couldn't quite get her mind around why she would be, and decided after a few seconds to take the statement at face value. "Thank you. I hope you won't be too disappointed this weekend."

"Why would I be?" Gina said, her voice dropping just a little.

"You know, when you lose."

Gina grinned. "Feeling pretty confident."

"Well, we've got a great team."

"Maybe you should come scout us out before you get your hopes up."

"Don't need to," Carrie said, enjoying the banter. "I'll bet you dinner we take three out of five."

"You're on," Gina said. "Winner gets to pick the place."

"Done." Carrie finished her first beer and poured another half glass. She lifted the pitcher toward Gina. "Fill your glass?"

Gina shook her head. "No, I'm driving and I'm done."

Carrie sipped her beer. "So why don't you play?"

"Can't," Gina said, her voice flat and hard. "My running days are over."

"Sorry," Carrie said, remembering that brief instant when she'd noticed the stiffness in Gina's gait. "Knee injuries are hell. Old ACL?"

Gina gave her a long look. "Car accident."

Carrie's chest tightened. "Oh, that's hard. I'm really sorry."

"Long time ago," Gina said with finality. Subject closed.

Carrie got the message. "You know everyone here? I didn't think to introduce you. Apologies."

Gina finished the last dregs of her beer and pushed the empty glass toward the center of the table. "No problem. I mostly came to talk to you."

Carrie drew a sharp breath. Really, were they back to the permits again? "Sorry. No business after hours."

"What makes you think I'm talking about work?"

"Aren't you?"

"If I wanted to push someone on that, I'd push your boss."

Carrie shifted, blocking Presley a little more from Gina's view. Like that would actually help. "I told you I'm in charge of the project."

Gina sensed the wall come down. She recognized the tone from when Angie stonewalled an unreasonable vendor or overbearing client. Nobody got to be second in command, no matter what name they called themselves, without being very good at their job. "I didn't come over to the table to talk about the job with anyone. Although I'm surprised you have a rule against it. You look like you'd be one to work twenty-four seven."

Carrie shook her head. "Nope. I'm highly efficient, so I don't have to work around the clock." She chuckled. "Even though my boss does, and keeping up with her is a challenge I take very seriously."

"So no business after hours is a personal rule?"

"You might say that." Carrie relaxed. "I'll introduce you to Presley if you promise to abide by it."

Gina laughed. "Do I look like a rule breaker?"

"Frankly, yes," Carrie said sweetly.

"I'll behave."

Carrie nudged Presley, who was discussing the latest superhero movie with their left fielder, Angelo Gutierrez. From what Carrie could gather, the debate was whether Wonder Woman could beat Thor in a one-on-one. Presley made the point that Wonder Woman not only had more tools at her disposal, they were far more powerful than just a hammer. Angelo countered that when a man had a hammer, all the world was a nail.

Laughing, Presley turned to Carrie. "Remind me not to debate movie heroes with anyone who works in the OR—they're way too literal."

"Noted," Carrie said. "Presley, this is Gina Antonelli. Joe's sister."

Presley stretched a hand in front of Carrie to Gina. "Hi. Presley Worth. Good to meet you."

"Same here," Gina said.

"I met Tom Antonelli. Your father?"

"Yes." Gina wondered if Presley had that no business after hours rule and suspected she didn't, but she'd already promised Carrie she wouldn't go there. Nothing was going to happen until the morning anyhow. She could wait a few hours before pushing again. "I'm looking forward to working with all of you."

Presley glanced at Carrie and nodded. "We'll see that that happens as soon as possible."

"Appreciate it." When Carrie visibly relaxed next to her, Gina was glad.

"So, Pres," Carrie said casually, "speaking of construction. Gina coaches the Hammers softball team."

Presley's brows rose. "Really? Well, we're all in for an interesting weekend."

Gina grinned. "That's one way of putting it."

"We do have an advantage," Presley said, draping an arm around Carrie's shoulders. "You've probably noticed."

"I might have," Gina said.

"She's our ace," Presley declared.

"Little pressure, Pres?" Carrie said.

"Like that ever bothered you." Presley turned her head as Harper whispered something to her from her other side, and she nodded. "I think we're headed out in a minute. Nice meeting you, Gina. We'll talk again soon, I'm sure."

"Same here. And we will." Gina glanced at Carrie as Presley and Harper called good-byes. "You're going to have some pretty disappointed fans this weekend."

Carrie rolled her eyes. "You know that part about winner choosing the restaurant?"

"Yeah." Gina caught the glint in Carrie's eyes, and her blood raced a little faster.

"I ought to warn you to get your wallet ready."

"Don't worry about that. I'd never take you for a cheap date."

"It's a bet," Carrie said carefully. "Not a date."

CHAPTER NINE

That's it for me too," Flann said to the others at the table as Harper and Presley stood to leave. She put a twenty by the empty pitcher in the center and pushed back her chair. "Next round's on me. See you all Friday night."

"Give me a call if you need anything." Harper didn't need to say she was talking about Blake. Flann understood the rest of the thought— she and Harper had been reading each other's minds since they were toddlers, being about as close as they could be without being actual twins. When she needed help, even when she didn't know it, Harper was always there.

"I will." She'd stayed just long enough to celebrate the win, but her mind had only been half there. She wouldn't have even gone to the game if Abby hadn't insisted and if she hadn't been comfortable Blake was doing okay. The surgery had gone as she'd expected, clean and quick. All the same, he was hers in a way that other patients weren't, and a part of her wanted to be sitting at home with Abby, just being there for her and for him. But if she hadn't played, Blake might have been worried that *she* was worried, and she and Abby had already talked things over. The best way for Blake to feel that what he'd done was exactly what he needed to do, and nothing out of the ordinary, was for them to behave as if the surgery was just that—one more step in his journey, no greater and no smaller than any other he had taken or would take in the future. And that with every step, they'd be there if he needed them, but their life would go on like every other family's. His transition was part of their life, not the focal point of his life or theirs.

All the same, she was happy to climb into her truck and drive the quick five minutes home. They were still in the old schoolhouse Abby had rented when she and Blake first came to town. They wouldn't be there for much longer now, thankfully. She and Abby'd decided to move to their new place, a four-bedroom farmhouse on ten acres just at the edge of town, and live with renovations rather than wait any longer to find a contractor with an opening. As soon as Blake was feeling better, they'd make the move. Of course, that might get derailed by the wedding plans.

Flann parked the truck in the narrow drive next to the white picket fence bordering the one-and-a-half-story white clapboard building. Thus far she'd escaped most of the wedding planning. Oh, she wanted to be married—she'd been the first to bring it up—not that she didn't feel married now, but she wanted her family to be united in the eyes of her family and friends and the world. She wanted that for herself and Abby and Blake. The details she'd leave to Abby and just do what she was told and be where she needed to be. Perfect. Of course, Abby might have other ideas. In which case, she'd have to adjust hers.

Smiling, Flann eased open the unlocked screen door and stole into the darkened living room. The only illumination came from the dim ceiling light in the kitchen at the far end of the main room. Their bedroom was off to the right, but Abby was curled up on the couch under an afghan.

Stepping lightly, Flann ghosted across the room to the stairs and tiptoed up to the loft to peek in on Blake. She stopped at the top, narrowed her eyes, and took in the small space in a swift glance. Okay. That was unexpected. She backed down quietly.

Abby sat upright on the sofa and ran both hands through her hair. Flann settled beside her.

"Why is Margie in Blake's bed?" Flann whispered.

"Hi, honey." Abby snuggled against her, one arm circling her waist. "She's not *in* his bed, she's *on* his bed. She came by after the game to give him a play-by-play, and when they'd finished celebrating the ass-kicking—Margie's term, by the way—they put on a movie. I think it took about ten minutes for them both to fall asleep. I called your mother, so she knows where Margie is."

"Okay," Flann said slowly. "So is that a good idea, do you think?"

Abby kissed Flann. "I think you and I should go to bed and leave them alone."

"Yeah, but, you know…my sister, our son."

"There's no blood between them, and let's not jump the gun. They've spent plenty of time in his room or hers before."

"Yeah," Flann muttered. "And they're sixteen and you know what that means."

Abby ran her fingers through Flann's hair and kissed her. "Thirtysomethings get horny too."

Flann's mind went predictably blank. Instinct took over. "Right. Bedroom."

They closed the door and she wished for the thousandth time they were already in their new place, where Blake had a normal bedroom with a door of his own. Two doors between them were better than one, and holy hell, her sister was up there too. Blake wanted the same thing, although now that she thought of it, if her sister was going to end up behind the closed door, maybe…

"You think we need to have a talk with them?" Flann asked, leaning back against the door.

"You know," Abby said, "I really love you."

Flann pulled off her jersey and the tank underneath it and tossed them onto the overstuffed chair by the window. "I know. What have I done?"

Abby wore a T-shirt and loose cotton pants, and nothing else as far as Flann could see. Watching her approach with the moonlight at her back, her breasts moving gently beneath the thin cotton, made her mouth go dry and her insides boil. Reading her expression, Abby smiled and threaded her arms around Flann's neck.

"A lot of things, all of them good," Abby said and kissed her again, pressing full-length against her.

Flann groaned softly. She'd had a long day, and contrary to what she'd let on, a stressful one. All of that dropped away as the only reality became the taste and smell and sensation of Abby surrounding her. She pressed her face to Abby's neck, scenting the shower gel she used—some combination of purple flowering things and soft breezes. "You always smell so good. And you feel better than anything I've ever known."

Abby reached between them and tugged on the waistband of Flann's tight baseball pants. "You tired?"

Flann laughed, clasping Abby's hips. "Not hardly. I could probably use a shower, though."

"I don't mind a little sweat." Abby leaned back as Flann pushed her pants down. "You know, you don't have to have the birds and the bees talk with him, but the fact you're thinking about it just makes me love you even more."

"I wasn't thinking about the baby-making so much, although one day I guess that will come up too," Flann said, kicking free of the rest of her clothes. "I was thinking more about the emotional end of things. Because it's complicated—they're really tight, everybody knows that, but when you get physical, it changes things."

"It does, but they're at that age where they're going to want to explore." Abby laughed a little. "Not that we ever actually outgrow that, but sometimes we learn a little restraint."

"Yeah?" Flann caught her around the waist, tugged her close, and propelled her over to the bed. When they tumbled down, she slid on top of her. "I haven't noticed a lot of that around here."

Abby moaned and slid her leg around the back of Flann's, drawing closer, heat to heat. "Maybe we should talk about the birds and the bees a little bit later."

"We'll do that. Later." Flann kissed her throat where the elegant curves dipped beneath her collarbone, slid a hand over her breast, and closed around the soft fullness of her. Abby arched beneath her, the press of her flesh an invitation, the strength of her fingers digging into Flann's ass a demand.

Now there were only the two of them, their hunger, their need, their wonder. Flann leaned on her elbows and bracketed Abby's shoulders, enclosing her beneath her. Fitting her hips tight between Abby's thighs, she rocked between her legs, watching the arousal build on her face.

"I love you," Abby murmured, closing her eyes as her body clamored for more, for everything. For an endless moment, she balanced on the brink of shattering. When Flann slid inside her, stroked the places that made her heart race and her body shudder, she caught her lip between her teeth, swallowed a cry. When the pleasure grew too big, too powerful to contain, she buried her face in Flann's neck, muffling her cries.

Flann gentled her caresses, stroking slow and deep. "Again," she whispered.

Abby laughed. "That was perfect. You'll have to wait for round two."

"It'll be hard, but I'll try." Flann chuckled, content. "You are so sexy I can't stand it."

Abby gripped Flann's hair, kissed her hard, and pushed until Flann rolled over. Abby leaned over her. "You'll just have to stand it for a few more minutes." She drew a finger down the center of Flann's body, smiled as Flann stiffened and groaned softly. "Or…maybe we'll just wait."

"I'll do anything you want, just name it."

Laughing, Abby stroked lower, found the spot that always pushed Flann to the edge, and circled slowly. "Anything? I'll have to give that some thought."

Flann gasped. "God, that feels good."

Abby's chest tightened, the incredible wonder of knowing she could please her stopping the breath in her chest. She knew every nuance of Flann's body now, and the knowing only heightened the desire. "I'm about to make it feel a lot better."

"God, yes. You are," Flann choked out as the world went blindingly white.

Abby wrapped Flann in her arms and pulled her head against her shoulder. She loved the moment when Flann lay unshielded, vulnerable except for her protection. Another place, another time, Flann would have been a warrior and she her shield. Abby kissed her. "I love you. I need you more than you know."

Flann tightened her arm around Abby's waist. "You and Blake, you're everything to me."

Abby pressed her cheek against Flann's hair and closed her eyes. "We know."

❖

As Presley and Harper prepared to leave the tavern, the rest of the group began to break up. Carrie said to Gina, "I'm headed out too. Early morning."

"Me too," Gina said. "I'll walk out with you."

As they rose together, Presley lifted a questioning eyebrow in Carrie's direction. Carrie gave a subtle shake of her head. Gina was just being friendly.

The parking lot was still half-full when they stepped outside. Gina paused just beyond the door, pointing left. "I'm over there."

"I'm that way." Carrie indicated the opposite direction. "I've got your card. When I have an update—"

"Wait. Stop." Gina held up her hand. "No business after hours, right?"

"You *were* listening." Carrie smiled. "Is that a hardship for you?"

"It's not usually an issue." Gina shrugged. "I like my work, day or night."

"So do I, and if the situation demands, I'm in—day or night." Carrie searched in her duffel as they talked and found her keys. "But after hours if something can wait until the next day, I let it."

"Sounds reasonable." Gina slid a hand into her back pocket. "There's one thing I forgot to ask, though."

The tavern door opened behind Carrie, and along with the noise, a cluster of people surged out. Someone bumped her from behind and she rocked forward. Gina's hand came to her hip, steadying her.

"Sorry," Carrie murmured. Another inch and she'd have been in Gina's arms. She quickly stepped back. What had Gina said? Oh, right. She wanted to ask her something. Damn it, there went her heart racing again. What did she think, Gina was going to ask her for a date? She'd already made that impossibility clear. Besides, dinner was in their future, one way or another—not a date, just dinner. Casually she said, walking toward the lot, "What did you forget?"

"If there's no business after hours, what is there?"

Well, she'd let herself in for that, hadn't she. What could she answer that wouldn't be a lot more revealing than she wanted to be with Gina? "That is nothing you need to know."

Laughing, Gina said, "Well, now I'm curious. And you might not know this about me, but when I'm curious, I always get an answer."

"Why am I not surprised," Carrie said, grinning in spite of herself. She took a step back, watching Gina watch her. She never realized how much she liked being watched by a woman. And oh boy, was it time to go home. "Good night, Gina."

Gina nodded her head, her gaze still on Carrie. "Good night, Ms. Longmire."

With a snort and a roll of her eyes, Carrie pivoted and headed across the lot to where she'd parked. Her car was so small if she hadn't known where it was, she wouldn't even be able to see it, dwarfed as it was by the pickup trucks and SUVs. The bunch that had exited just after them still lingered in the center of the gravel lot, and as she circled around them she caught snatches of postgame analysis.

A man stepped in front of her and she jerked to a halt. She recognized him instantly. The Houlihan's pitcher. Moving sideways, she said, "Excuse me."

He moved with her. "Hey, it's the ringer."

She carefully shifted her keys until she had the largest in her fist. "Close game tonight. Could go the other way next time."

"Pitched triple-A somewhere, didn't you," he said, slurring his words. "On some girlie team. That's why you think you're so hot."

"No, sorry. Never did." Carrie took another step to the side. "If you'll excuse me."

"You've got a pretty nice slider. I bet everything else slides pretty nice too."

Okay, so enough. The lot wasn't all that well lit, but they weren't alone. She didn't want a scene, but she wasn't going to be bullied, either. Carrie looked him in the eye. "Listen, the game is over. Next time we play, you're welcome to try to outpitch me."

"How about a little batting practice next time." He shoved his hands in the pockets of his sweatpants, making his intentions obvious.

Oh, please. High school again? Time to head back inside and wait this bunch out. "No thanks."

He shot out a hand as if to grab her arm and she jerked away. "Okay, listen—"

"Hey, Carrie!" Gina jogged up beside her. "I forgot to ask you for that paperwork. Probably because I hate it, but I really ought to get it tonight."

The pitcher frowned, blearily looking from Gina to Carrie. Finally he focused, more or less, on Gina. "We're having a conversation here, buddy."

Gina's smile was thin. "Oh, sorry, business. You don't mind, do you?" She slipped her hand under Carrie's elbow, moved her to the side, put her body between Carrie's and his. "You told me you had the stuff in your car?"

"Yeah," Carrie said. "I'm just back here."

"Great, thanks."

The guy muttered something under his breath, but he didn't try to stop them.

"Thanks," Carrie said once out of earshot.

"You okay?"

"Yeah, he's just a drunk asshole."

"He's also three times your size." The dark, angry undertones in Gina's voice belied her calm exterior. Her hand still clasped Carrie's arm, firm and warm. "Did he threaten you? Because if he did—"

"He didn't—just made a few lame come-ons, but I'm glad you came over." Carrie pointed to her car. "That's me. I'm good."

"You want me to follow you home?"

Carrie unlocked the Mini Cooper, slid behind the wheel, and looked out at Gina. "No, I'm fine. And it's not very far."

Gina checked the parking lot. The Houlihan's guys were gone. She propped an arm on the low roof and leaned in. "You got your cell phone handy?"

Carrie laughed. "I always do." She lifted it from the console where she'd just put it. "I even have your number in here already."

Gina studied her. "Why don't you make sure it's on speed dial."

"Believe me," Carrie said, "I'll find you if I need you."

"I'll remember that." Gina stepped back. "Good night again."

Carrie backed out and idled until Gina crossed the lot to a red pickup truck and climbed in, just in case the a-hole made another appearance. She followed Gina out to the road and turned in the opposite direction. She watched Gina's taillights until they disappeared, then put the window down and took a deep breath. Well then, that was more excitement than she'd had in a very long time, and the idiot from Houlihan's had nothing to do with it. She absently rubbed the spot on her arm where Gina's hand had rested, and swore she could still feel her fingers. The woman was hot all right, inside and out.

CHAPTER TEN

When Carrie got home, she pulled around behind the house and parked under the lean-to attached to the barn. Probably a vain attempt to keep the car clean, but at least it wouldn't be a target for flyovers. Some things about country living she didn't love, and a perpetually mud-spattered vehicle was one. As she climbed the back porch and let herself in to the kitchen, the temperature dropped ten degrees to a tolerable seventy or so. Had to be eighty outside still, and the upstairs bedroom was probably hotter. No AC was another thing not to love, although she was coming to enjoy sleeping nude with the windows open and a fan blowing the sultry air across her as she lay in bed. Decadent in a wholly refreshing way.

She wasn't quite ready to cool down in the shower and stretch out in the big double bed upstairs, though. Instead of being tired, which she should've been after a beer and having gotten up practically in the middle of the night the day before, she was wired and wide-awake. She thought about a cup of tea, but then the caffeine might be a problem if she ever wanted to sleep, and decaffeinated tea just never tasted anything like the real thing. But hot chocolate—now, that was always a good idea. She showered quickly, pulled on a pair of white boxers with candy canes all over them, the girlie version of the boy style, along with the thinnest tank top she could find, and headed barefoot down to the kitchen. Everything in there worked, but nothing was quite as it should be—not enough counter space, a fridge with a freezer that was way too small, and a four-burner stove that looked like it was new when Teddy Roosevelt was president. She wasn't exactly sure when that was, but more than a hundred years ago would be about right.

All the same, the kitchen with its window above the big square country sink looking out into the barnyard, the white screen door that led to a wide porch, and the scarred pine table, just big enough for four chairs around it that she'd bet had been in that room for almost as long as the stove, spoke of history and home in a way that worked for her. Who knew things like this would resonate after growing up in Berkeley, with a coffee shop on the corner, concerts in the park, and a house full of her parents' activist friends and students at odd hours of the day and night. She'd always had to share her space and vie for their attention. She'd known they loved her, but sometimes she'd wished life hadn't been quite so busy.

Maybe that's why the quiet and the solitude suited her more than she'd expected. If she got lonely now and then, she only had to call Presley or Abby or Mari, and she'd have a friend to share a movie and wine or ice cream with. As she'd told her annoyingly nudging little sister, the dating would come when she found someone who offered her something else—friendship, sure, but she wanted more. Sparks and fireworks and, most of all, to feel she was the one and only. Fairy-tale romance, her sister teased, but then, that's what dreams were for. And she was in no big hurry. The biggest thing on her horizon was getting a kitchen she could actually cook in and a bathroom with a shower big enough to wash her hair without cracking her elbow on the wall. Small miracles first.

Leaving the inside door open to catch what there was of a breeze, she heated milk on the stove in a small dented copper bottom pot, poured it into a mug with honest-to-God Belgian chocolate she spooned out of a tin, and stirred the hot mixture until the top was frothy and velvety dark. After licking the spoon, she left it in the sink, popped the screen door open with her hip, and wandered out to sit on the top step with her mug and the moon. The starlit sky was cloudless, and the half-moon, so perfectly formed it looked as if someone had sliced it with a knife, hovered just above the rolling hills beyond the fields surrounding her house. Harper had told her the place had been built for the generations of farm managers and their families who'd overseen the Rivers family land for a century and a half until the last fifty years, when her grandfather decided to lease the land to local farmers to plow and plant.

Across the grassy dooryard, as Ida Rivers called the patch of land behind the house, the barn was shadowed by a stand of tall oaks whose branches dipped down to nearly touch the tin roof. The story-high double doors were wide open now, with all of the animals having been moved elsewhere when Harper left to move in with Presley. The stalls and hayloft inside were invisible in the dark, but she fancied the weathered building seemed lonely, as if waiting for life to return. Maybe she'd have some animals of her own. Not that she knew the first thing about taking care of farm animals, but they couldn't be much different than dogs, right? After all, Presley had a pet chicken—correct that, rooster, the male of the species—plus a barn full of kittens. Presley loved that silly bird with its bad leg and its even badder attitude. Carrie'd always had a dog as a kid, and if she hadn't lived in city apartments for the last five or six years, she would have had one by now. A place like this was made for animals. She definitely had room for kittens, maybe a puppy. She'd have to see what Presley thought about it. She could definitely use barnyard advice for anything more exotic. Like chickens.

For now, her only company was the crickets—almost as noisy as city traffic at night—a frog croaking loudly and insistently hoping to get lucky, and the distant chorus of coyotes. At first she'd tried to convince herself they were just dogs, but they definitely weren't. Their yips and yaps and howls were eerie and haunting at first, but now as relaxing as any other night sound. She'd yet to see one and would probably be a little unnerved the first time, but she seemed to be rapidly losing her city sensibilities and replacing them with something slower and quieter and, in a strange way, deeper.

Contentment finally replaced the wire in her blood and she arched her back. Her right shoulder was a little sore, but her arm felt fine. She knew what overuse felt like, and she sure as heck knew she was more prone to it now than she ever had been when she was playing nine months out of the year. Just because she wasn't pitching that much any longer meant she had to take it easy, but she threw as often as she could during the week. Her strength was still good and her flexibility almost what it was when she'd been in college.

She'd been happy with her pitching tonight. The asshat in the parking lot had been right. Her slider had definitely been working. Sore loser, that guy. Her temper spiked just thinking about what a jerk he'd been. She'd been more angry than scared, but she wasn't naïve enough to think he hadn't been dangerous. Alcohol and bruised egos were a bad combination, especially when he'd been beaten by a girl.

Ha. Not just any girl, either. She chuckled. A hot pitcher, Gina had said.

Carrie smiled. The woman knew how to charm and had the confidence to pull it off. Most of the time. Nothing about Gina was halfway, and as irritating as that was on occasion, Carrie had to admit she liked a woman who was definite.

Gina had surprised her back there in the parking lot—coming to her rescue, which was pretty darn welcome, and managing to defuse things without getting into a standoff with the asshat. Which might have happened if Gina hadn't arrived. Carrie's temper had been starting to fray—she wasn't raised to take bull from anyone, even when they did happen to be a little bit bigger. Okay, a lot bigger. But all things considered, always better not to fight. So Gina showing up was…nice.

Somehow, she was going to end up having dinner with Gina. Win or lose—of course, she wouldn't be losing—and she needed to give some thought to the restaurant. She wasn't even going to feel bad if it was a pricey one. Not a bit. Gina looked like she would be able to handle the price tag, and she'd been the one to set the terms of the bet. She wouldn't otherwise take advantage of her. Hell, she wouldn't mind having McDonald's with her.

She caught herself and examined that idea. First of all, she didn't even like McDonald's, and what made her think she'd be spending any time with Gina? Other than this payoff. Her mind had been wandering down strange highways all day. She'd just chalk that up to starting her day in a different time zone.

Carrie rose, dusted off her backside, and swallowed the last of her hot chocolate. By the time they got to the tournament and one of them had won the bet, she might not have the slightest interest in having dinner with Gina Antonelli. All the same, the idea of having dinner with Gina made her think about things she hadn't thought about in a long time. Things like dresses and whether she needed a haircut or highlights, or exactly what shoes would go with what. Girlie thoughts. Girlie thoughts inspired by a woman.

❖

Gina took her time driving through town. The sidewalks were empty and the only cars clustered in the parking lots of Clark's pizza place, Stewart's dairy shop, and the Cumberland Farms, which was pretty much open twenty-four seven. She wasn't going anywhere in particular, just driving, restless and edgy. She'd almost circled around after leaving the tavern to try to pick up Carrie's car headed home and stopped herself at the last second. Carrie wouldn't appreciate her following her around, and she couldn't blame her.

Still, an itch between her shoulder blades had her stomach churning. The Houlihan's pitcher might've been just a drunk asshole, but he'd been a step away from putting his hands on Carrie. When she'd started across the parking lot, she'd been certain that was what he was going to do. He was looming over her, clearly blocking her way, and Carrie hadn't looked like she was going to back down or even call for help. Stubborn, and no surprise there. Seeing him threatening her had tossed Gina back to another parking lot in another time, another life. She still remembered every minute of that night although she'd mostly trained herself not to relive it. Tonight she had, the angry words in the parking lot, the crude insults, the thinly veiled threats as sharp and cutting as they'd been when she was seventeen. She remembered the car ride with Emmy scared and furious by turns, the headlights slashing the darkness behind them, closing in on them. And the last fractured seconds of the sickening roll of the car and the screaming metal.

Gina jerked the truck to the side of the road and slammed into park. Sweat rolled down between her shoulder blades. Nausea churned in her chest. Gripping the steering wheel, she closed her eyes and took a couple of slow deep breaths. Over. Done with. Gone. All of it. The plans, the dreams, the hopes and promises.

She hadn't relived that night in a very long time, not while she was awake at least. The guy in the parking lot, that was it. He'd just triggered something. The terror and the sick fear had nothing to do with Carrie. Nothing at all.

❖

"Holy smokes," Margie said in a hoarse whisper. "What time is it?"

"Nighttime," Blake mumbled. "Go back to sleep."

"I can't go back to sleep here," Margie said, bolting upright in bed. The loft was dark and the whole house was quiet. What happened to the movie they were watching? She didn't remember turning it off. She fished her phone out of her jeans. One twenty. Cripes! "I'm at your house in the middle the night."

"So? Don't jiggle the bed."

Margie went still as granite. "Whoa. Right. Sorry. Does it hurt?"

"Sore," Blake muttered. "I think if I take a pain pill, it'll be fine."

"Okay. I'll get them. Where are they?"

Blake sighed and sat up. "I think on the nightstand on your side. My mom brought everything up when we got home, but I wasn't really paying attention."

"I'm gonna turn the light on over here," Margie said, reaching for the little bedside table lamp. "Cover your eyes."

"I'm awake," Blake said, sounding just a little grouchy. "Go ahead."

"Nobody called me from home, so I guess they know I'm here." Margie flicked on the light with a shade made of multicolored glass pieces held together by thin black lines, probably not really lead anymore, in a pattern with dragonflies around the edges. It wasn't girlie, but it was pretty.

"My mom probably," Blake muttered.

"Yeah. Sounds right." Margie eased out of the bed, trying to be careful not to jostle Blake too much, and checked the labels on two pill bottles she found next to a capped bottle of water. One was an antibiotic, the other a pain medicine—she recognized it from ones she'd taken when she'd broken her arm a couple years ago. The instructions said to take one to two every four hours. They'd been up in the loft for at least six and Blake hadn't taken any, so the timing was cool. "You want one or two?"

"I think maybe just one." Blake wore a T-shirt over the compression vest and loose shorts in bed. "They kinda make me fuzzy."

She shook out a pill and handed it to him along with the bottle of spring water. "It probably won't matter if you get to go back to sleep."

"Well, I can take one now and then one later if I need it, right?"

"Yeah, you can." She pointed to the egg-shaped plastic collection containers resting on top of the covers. The tubes disappeared under Blake's shirt and connected to the drains under his skin. She'd seen them on YouTube. "You know, I think they need to be emptied."

Blake lifted one up and held it in the air. Pale pink fluid nearly filled it. "You're right. They're almost full. If they're not empty, they don't suck right."

He sounded just a little bit nervous.

Margie considered the options. "Well, either we do it, or I can wake up Flann or your mom."

"I know how to do it." Blake sat up a little straighter. "I think I might need a little help, though."

"Well, yeah." Margie tilted her head toward the small bathroom in the back corner of the loft. "In there?"

"I guess." Blake swung his legs over the side of the bed.

"Wait."

Margie skirted the end of the bed and slipped her arm around his waist as he stood. "You good?"

"Yeah," Blake said after a second. "Thanks for, you know... staying."

Margie squeezed, careful not to lean against his chest. "Well, yeah."

CHAPTER ELEVEN

When Carrie's alarm beeped at 6:45 a.m., she turned it off, avoiding the big fat snooze bar that was four times the size of the off button. She never hit snooze, which she considered a subtle form of self-delusion. If she wanted an extra half hour's sleep, she'd set the alarm for the correct time and then get up and go about her business. Efficiency was her secret obsession, although she preferred the term "organized" over "obsessive-compulsive." True, everything about her morning routine was timed down to the minute, but she couldn't really help the fact she had a precise internal clock ticking away in the back of her head. She'd obviously inherited all the time sensitivity that had passed the other members of her family by. She'd taken to getting herself up and ready for school by third grade after realizing her well-meaning parents had no sense of being on time. Not that she let time rule her life—she wasn't a slave to the clock. She just liked to be organized.

Take her work life, for example. Presley would already be at work, but that was Presley's obsession, not hers. She chose to show up at seven thirty every morning, a good hour ahead of almost everyone else in administration. She garnered both admiration and a few thinly veiled accusatory looks suggesting she was making other people look bad, but hey, she was Presley's wingman, and that required flying as high as her. Besides, she liked the challenge of meeting her talented boss on equal ground. Within reason, of course. Starting work in the dark was not reasonable.

Humming to herself, she jumped in the shower for a quick refresher, and ninety seconds later, wrapped in a towel, headed downstairs to push

Brew on the coffeepot she'd set up the night before. She didn't trust the automatic timers, having been disappointed a couple of times that cost her a good five minutes she couldn't afford. She preferred not to leave anything to chance. Halfway down the stairs, a loud crash shook the house and stopped her in her tracks.

Tree falling? She pictured the area around the house. No, none that were close enough to hit the house if they suddenly toppled over. The maples by the barn were a possibility, but surely she wouldn't feel the vibrations all this way away. Something crashing down in the kitchen? No cats or dogs or critters larger than a field mouse to knock things off the counters. A cabinet coming loose from the wall? Hopefully that wasn't the case, because she didn't have time to deal with the mess.

All was quiet now and she continued down the stairs in search of whatever had fallen. The kitchen was just as she'd left it the night before, all the chairs arranged around the table, the coffeepot waiting for her to push Brew, which was the first thing she did as she scanned the room, and all the cabinets were still firmly attached above the counters. She glanced out the back window and, from what she could see, the barn and surrounding copse of trees looked unharmed. She stepped out onto the back porch to get a better look at the yard, and froze.

Gina stood in the middle of the yard, tool belt slung across her lean jeans-clad hips, her dusty work boots planted shoulder-width apart, her head tilted back, eyes squinting ever so slightly in the early morning sun. She didn't have the hard hat today, and her hair was tousled as if she'd hastily run her hands through it. Her gray T-shirt with the faded number 20 on the chest had a rip over her right shoulder. Carrie's gaze kept returning to that small patch of skin as if it were a beacon leading her somewhere she ought to be going.

Gina raised a brow. "What are you doing here?"

Grabbing the edge of the towel she'd hastily secured in a loose roll over her chest, Carrie parroted, "What are *you* doing here?"

Gina laughed. "I'm working."

"Not here you're not. You're supposed to be…" Carrie waved a hand. *At the hospital*, except she couldn't be there because of those damnable permits that haunted her like a bad memory. "Someplace else."

Obviously enjoying herself, and irritating Carrie even more, Gina grinned and slid her hands into her back pockets, her hips tilting forward ever so slightly. The move was unspeakably sexy. "According to my work order, I'm supposed to be here renovating"—she drew a crumpled piece of paper from her pocket—"kitchen and bathroom, checking both porches for structural integrity, and adding a carport."

"Where did you get that?"

"From my father. He's the boss."

"Yes, I know that, I mean, that makes sense, but where did you get it from?" Extremely exasperated at yet another fractured conversation with the only woman she'd ever met who could leave her tongue-tied, and acutely aware she was standing half-naked in her bare feet at 7:06 in the morning and time was slipping away, Carrie snapped, "Before that. Who hired you?"

"I guess that would be whoever owns this house. As far as I know, your boss." Gina cocked her head. "Have you noticed any leaks? That roof looks like it could use an overhaul."

"Well, no one said anything to me!" Carrie stared up at the underside of the porch roof. "Really, you think it will leak?"

"I was thinking the main roof, but I'll check them all." Gina shrugged. "As to the scheduling, I guess you'll have to take that up with your boss. Where do you want me to start?"

Carrie glared. "How about by getting into your truck and leaving?"

"Not and lose half a day of work. Did I wake you?"

Carrie finally focused on the giant very ugly green dumpster beside the porch. "No. I was getting ready for work and I heard the crash."

Gina grimaced. "Look, I really am sorry about the confusion. I'm usually careful not to disturb the owners on residential jobs, but we do start early. I'll wait in the truck until you're…done."

"Oh, this is crazy," Carrie said, mollified by Gina's apologetic tone. She wasn't usually such a grump. Gina just seemed to bring out her inner cranky-pants. "Wait right here just a minute."

"You sure?" Gina asked, suddenly all helpful and making Carrie feel even worse for snapping at her. "I'm supposed to be meeting someone here at nine to go over the work, so I could just come back. I only wanted to get the equipment delivered to save time."

Carrie lost the last of her mad. Gina was just being time conscious, after all. She sighed. "I have a feeling that nine o'clock might be with me, since I live here. Let me clear this up."

"Sure. No problem."

Holding her towel even more securely, Carrie turned with as much dignity as she could muster, considering she wasn't wearing anything except terry cloth, and hurried back into the house. Once out of view of the screen door she sprinted for the stairs, tossed her towel into the bathroom, and yanked sweats and a T from her dresser. As soon as she was decent, she found her phone and checked messages. Sure enough, voice mail from Presley at 6:58, just when she would have been in the shower.

Hi, Carrie. I bet you're in the shower right now. Sorry, I got a message just a couple minutes ago that the contractor wants to start work this morning at your place. I know it's late notice. It looks like there's not much going on after the eight o'clock division head meeting, so maybe you can swing back and talk to them about what you want done after that. Really sorry about the mix-up, but I didn't want to say no. You know what they're like. She laughed. *We need to hold on to them while we have them! See you in a few.*

Carrie let out a long sigh and trod back outside. Gina regarded her expectantly. "Well, this is turning into a comedy of errors. I just got the message that you were on your way. Of course, I didn't actually *get* the message or I wouldn't have greeted you in my"—she blew out a breath and laughed, the ridiculousness of everything finally hitting her—"towel."

"I can't say I mind." Gina's smile turned slow and admiring as her gaze traveled down Carrie's now thoroughly covered form. "Kinda liked the look, but I do recognize it wasn't the best timing. So like I said, I'll wait in the truck until you get ready."

"I'll be dressed and out of here in eighteen minutes."

"That soon, huh?"

Carrie grinned at the wry note in Gina's voice. "How about I get you a cup of coffee. The pot just finished brewing."

"I'd be your slave forever," Gina said.

"That might be taking it a little too far," Carrie said primly.

"Oh, I don't know. Depends on how good the coffee is."

"Trust me, it's excellent. I'll just be a minute."

Gina put a boot up against the bottom step and leaned on her bent leg. "I'll await your pleasure."

Carrie rolled her eyes and disappeared inside. Gina settled onto the top step and stretched her legs down to the bottom stair. She'd backed the truck with the dumpster on her trailer into the drive and hadn't pulled in far enough to see the little car nestled in the turnaround in the back. She would've recognized it and made her presence known before creating a racket. Still, she was happy with the way things turned out. A glimpse of Carrie Longmire in a bath towel at seven in the morning was about the best way to start the day she could imagine. Add the fire in her eyes to the expanse of smooth creamy skin that promised to be softer than it looked, and she couldn't ask for anything more. The woman was an intoxicating combination of sharp edges and silky-smooth curves, hot tempered and surprisingly amusing. Carrie combined the power and beauty of a summer thunderstorm at its fiercest and most sultry, when the air was so hot your skin tingled with every brush of a breeze and lightning streaked across the sky with a jolt that made your heart race.

Bemused by her fanciful thoughts, Gina tilted her head back against the porch post and closed her eyes as the sun drifted across her face. The morning smelled of hay and wildflowers, quiet and peaceful, something she rarely felt. She lazily opened her eyes at the tread of footfalls coming closer and looked up. Deep green eyes, the exact color of the fields she'd driven through half an hour before, met her gaze.

"I thought you might have fallen asleep," Carrie said gently.

"No, just daydreaming." Gina shook her head, surprised at having drifted away and even more surprised at admitting it.

"Nice dreams?"

"Yeah," Gina said.

Carrie handed her a mug of coffee. "You sound surprised."

"I am. I'm not much on dreaming."

"Why is that?" Carrie sipped her coffee. 7:18. She could spare two more minutes and wished she had more. Gina's expression when she'd come upon her unawares had been softer, gentler than she'd seen before. When she'd opened her eyes, sadness had moved through them. For a tiny fraction of a time, that glimpse of vulnerability had reached inside and squeezed her heart.

"Don't believe in them."

The flat dismissal in Gina's voice should have warned her off, but the memory of the sadness drove her on. "Even the good ones?"

"Most of all those."

Carrie nodded. Some things couldn't be rushed. "So what were you daydreaming about, then?"

"I was thinking about thunderstorms," Gina said.

"You like them?"

"I do. Very much." Gina smiled, and this time her gaze as it traveled down Carrie's body was anything but sad. Carrie was glad she'd taken the time to pull on clothes, because Gina had a way of making her feel naked just by looking at her.

"I didn't realize how beautiful they were until I'd lived through a few here," Carrie said, choosing to ignore the appraisal in Gina's glance. She wasn't going to wither under a woman's heated gaze like a blossom in the noonday sun, after all. "I like to sit out on the porch and watch them coming. It's something Harper taught Presley and me to do when we all lived together. I thought she was crazy until I experienced the anticipation of watching the clouds roll in while the lightning streaked closer and closer and the thunder crashed right on top of us. I swear, the air feels so alive it dances on your skin."

"You made it sound even prettier than I was remembering," Gina said.

"We'll have to do it sometime," Carrie said and mentally slapped a hand over her mouth. "I mean…"

Gina went on as if she hadn't noticed Carrie madly backpedaling. "If I'm here sometime when you're here and a storm is coming, we'll watch the show."

Carrie nodded abruptly. "I should let you get to work. And I've got to leave in about three minutes."

"Sure. I'll just finish the coffee."

Carrie made do with the minimum of makeup and was back downstairs in two minutes. Grabbing the pot of coffee, she walked outside. "You want a refill?"

"Sure." Gina rose and held out her cup. "I can't believe how quickly you got ready. You look great."

"Hmm." Carrie poured coffee and feigned nonchalance. If she hadn't blushed while dressed in a towel and nothing else, she wasn't going to now over a little throwaway compliment. Of course, telling herself that didn't stop the heat from rising in her face. She was just grateful for whatever had possessed her to grab a dress from her closet instead of the shirt and pants she'd been planning to wear. She liked the way Gina looked at her. "Thanks."

"Well," Gina said, leaning with her back against the post, the mug cradled in her hand. "You were right. Excellent coffee. I'll see you in a couple of hours?"

"I should be here by nine ten."

"Right." Gina grinned. "I'll just finish with the dumpster and unload some equipment."

"If I'm delayed, I'll call."

"Well, you've got my number."

"I do," Carrie said breezily as she shouldered her purse and headed across the yard to her car. Gina's laughter followed her, as electric as a storm on the wind.

Abby climbed the stairs to the loft and stopped just below the landing. "You two want some breakfast?"

Margie tiptoed across the floor and started down the stairs. Trying for cool, she said, "Morning."

Abby followed her down and into the galley kitchen tucked under the loft. She smiled at Margie as if it wasn't weird at all for Margie to be coming down from Blake's bedroom first thing in the morning. Cripes!

"Hey," Margie said, playing along. Nothing unusual here. Nope.

"Is Blake awake?"

"Sort of," Margie said. "He's not exactly a morning person."

Abby laughed. "Trust me, I know that. The smell of breakfast usually drags him up, though."

Margie hopped up on one of the tall stools at the counter that divided the galley kitchen from the rest of the living space. Since Abby wasn't freaking out, she guessed she didn't need to, either. "I think he's still knocked out from yesterday."

"How about you? Can I fix you something to eat?"

"You don't have to do that," Margie said, hoping her stomach didn't growl. "I should probably get going."

"I called your mom last night," Abby said. "I didn't want her to worry."

"Thanks, I thought you probably did," Margie said. "Sorry, I kind of crashed."

"No problem. How about toast and bacon. Scrambled eggs?"

"Um, yeah, that would be great. I'm actually kind of starving."

Abby pulled fixings from the refrigerator. "Thought you might be."

"Hey, me too?" Blake called from up above them.

Abby looked up at the ceiling below Blake's space. "You need some help up there before breakfast?"

"No, we already got everything taken care of. Just need five minutes." Footsteps, and then the sound of the bathroom door closing.

Abby slid fresh-cut bread into the four-slot toaster. "I think it probably helped Blake relax to have you here last night. I appreciate it."

Margie let out a mental sigh of relief. Things really were cool. "He's good. Not even hurting too much."

"I'm glad. How are you doing?" Abby asked casually.

"Me?" Margie hesitated, searching for the real question behind the pretend one. "You mean how do I feel about Blake's surgery now?"

Abby laughed softly. "Yes. And I suppose I should've just asked that, shouldn't I."

Margie grinned. "I think I'm a lot like Flann. Not so subtle, so it's probably just best to ask what you want to know."

"You're right. She's not subtle, coming or going. One of the things I love about her." Abby laughed again. "So? How are you now that he's taken this step?"

"I'm good." Margie considered what Abby might be worried about. "We're not having sex."

Abby carefully set down the plate of toast. "Not totally my business. I'm on the fence about it, actually."

"Us having it or you asking?"

"The asking part, mostly." Abby sighed. "I just want both of you to be okay—whatever you decide to do."

"I guess we can't know for sure until we do." Margie reached for the pile of toast Abby put on the table. "Maybe someday, but we're not there yet. We're good now."

"Okay. Yes. Right." Abby blew a strand of hair from her eyes and shook her head. "Well, you made that easy."

Margie laughed. "It's not really complicated. We spent a lot of time, you know, talking about transitioning and reading and stuff. So if, whenever, it won't be a surprise."

"Just so you know," Abby said, "you *both* know, if there's anything you ever want to talk about, Flann and I are here."

"Yeah," Margie said, "I got that."

A door closed above them and Abby hurriedly put plates on the counter. "Great!"

Blake came downstairs and paused by the counter, looking curiously from Abby to Margie. "What's going on?"

Margie forked up a piece of bacon. "Your mom and I are talking about sex."

"Really, Mom?" Blake carefully slid onto a stool as Abby put a glass of juice in front of him. "Do you think you could not totally embarrass me, please?"

Abby glanced at Margie. "It's okay, we're done. Margie cleared everything up."

Margie brushed his knee with hers. "I told her we're good. For now."

Blake smiled and leaned against her shoulder. "Well, yeah."

CHAPTER TWELVE

Carrie dropped her purse into the bottom drawer of her desk at the same time as she powered up her computer with the other hand. She was already scanning her in-box as she settled into the chair behind her desk. Thirty seconds later, Presley's door opened and she poked her head out.

"Morning."

"Sorry I'm late," Carrie said absently, making lists in her head as she read. "Need anything?"

"Nope. And you're not late," Presley said. "You're still fifty minutes early."

Carrie rolled her eyes. "Maybe for someone in the other departments, but not this one."

Presley smiled. "You got my message about the construction?"

"Yes."

"Sorry. I didn't get the message from the service until first thing this morning, or I would've given you a heads-up sooner. Are you okay to meet the contractor this morning?"

"Already did, all sorted out." Carrie deleted a half dozen meeting reminders she didn't need. The critical ones were already on her calendar. "I'll swing by after the division head meeting if there's nothing else going on."

"Oh, sorry." Presley came all the way out and closed the door behind her. "He showed up this morning?"

"She," Carrie said, giving Presley her full attention. Nothing had really jumped out from her in-box, beyond the usual mini-fires that would need extinguishing sometime before noon. Nothing she couldn't handle easily. "Gina Antonelli."

"The Gina from last night."

"The very same."

Presley rearranged some file folders on the corner of Carrie's desk and settled her hip on the edge as if she planned to stay for a while.

"So," Presley said, drawing out the word. "Gina."

"Uh-huh," Carrie said, feigning innocence and ignorance, neither of which she was very good at, especially where Presley was concerned. She was a few years younger than Presley, but they'd become fast friends almost as soon as they'd met, and their working relationship had never changed that. Presley could read her even before she knew her own mind, to her never-ending annoyance. Her only recourse when she wanted to avoid discussing something personal before she was ready was to play dense. Once in a while that actually worked, although like her sisters, Presley rarely gave up when she was on the scent of something interesting.

"We were lucky to get someone out there so quickly," Presley said casually.

"I know. I'm excited about getting the renovations done." Carrie frowned. She *had* lucked out, and none of her renovation projects were really critical. "Are you sure we shouldn't be sending them over to Flann and Abby's new house instead of my place...well, Harper's place, really. At least I can live in it."

Presley shook her head. "First, it's officially your place now. And Flann and Abby can wait a little while. Abby said they weren't going to move until after Blake's recovered. And now there's the wedding to plan. Just too much going on."

"Then I guess I got lucky. I'll take it."

Presley folded her arms across her chest and gave Carrie a long look. "It looks like you might be getting lucky in other ways too."

"No idea what you're talking about." Carrie swiveled back to her monitor. "Don't you have emails to read?"

Presley laughed and didn't budge. "Gina?"

"Please," Carrie said. "Not going there."

"Why not? She's easy to look at."

"And am I so shallow that that's all that matters?" Carrie said archly.

"Of course not." Presley grinned, obviously enjoying herself.

"But it's not a bad place to start. And you already know she's good with her hands."

Carrie colored. "You did not just say that. Really."

"Well. Come on. She looked pretty interested last night."

"Oh, really. And how can you tell that?"

"How about she didn't have a single word to say to anyone else at the table, including her brother. She sat down and never took her eyes off you."

If Presley had noticed Gina's attentions, Carrie couldn't have been imagining the connection she'd sensed between them. Heat and a flurry of nerves whirled inside her. No use pretending she didn't like the teasing and the sexy looks Gina had directed at her. Presley would see right through the pretense, and she'd only be fooling herself. Not her approach to a challenge or an unexpected development that threw her life a little off-kilter. "I'm not saying I wouldn't be interested. I'm just saying at the moment, there's nothing on the agenda."

"Well, Carrie," Presley said with exaggerated patience, "maybe you need to *put* something on the agenda. It's not like you to wait for someone else to make the first move."

"Oh, and on what do you base that judgment?"

"On the fact that I've seen you at a party when there was someone who interested you."

Carrie rolled her eyes. "Really? You're bringing up that sorority reunion again? I knew I never should've dragged you along."

"Well, you did. And…let me see…the dark-haired Solana, wasn't it? With the bedroom eyes and the…well, everything, actually. Wasn't she the one you zeroed in on the minute you saw her?"

"Yes, okay. But we only got as far as necking."

Presley laughed again. "Necking? Maybe that's why your agenda is so thin."

Carrie pushed her chair back and pretended to glare. "Just because you are now an old married lady getting regular sex does not mean you're an expert on everyone else's love life and can start giving advice to everyone you know."

"True enough," Presley said with a nod. "About the happily married, and the regular sex. As to the advice, I would say if you're free and she's free, and there's a little bit of a spark, I would fan the flames. And enjoy myself if I were you."

"Thank you very much. I will take it under advisement."

"And you'll be sure to tell me if anything comes of your deliberations." Presley glanced at her watch. "Well, now that we have that settled, I'd better work for the next ten minutes."

"We have twelve," Carrie said.

Presley stood and shook her head. "How you do that, exactly?"

"No idea. I just always know."

"Handy habit. Maybe you should pay attention to the rest of your intuition. Could be interesting."

"Thank you and go read your email."

"Going."

Presley disappeared back into her office, and Carrie refocused on her computer. Intuition sounded a whole lot like risky business to her. She wasn't above taking a chance and trying something new, or someone new. She never risked too much without being sure, and she'd never been sure enough of anyone or her own feelings to risk everything.

Gina was a different story. Gina already occupied more of her thoughts than anyone ever had in such a short time. Right at this moment, when she should be reviewing the items for the upcoming meeting, she was thinking about Gina.

Still, she smiled to herself. Sixty-seven minutes from now. She might not have an agenda, but she did have an appointment.

❖

"I'm due in to the ER at ten," Abby said. "You two need anything before I go?"

Margie carried her plate and Blake's to the sink and rinsed them. "I'm scheduled to work with Mari this afternoon, one to five, so I'll be leaving soon."

"You need a ride anywhere?" Abby asked.

"If you could drop me off at Lee's Crossing corner, I can walk the rest of the way home."

Abby smiled. "I think I've got plenty of time to take you all the way out to the homestead." She glanced at Blake, questioningly. "You okay with being here alone?"

"Sure." He shrugged dismissively. "I'm fine. There's nothing to do until the drains come out, and I can handle them okay." He tugged at the compression vest under his loose T. "Flann said maybe I can get the drains out today. Then I can take a shower, right?"

"How much did they drain last time?"

"I've emptied them twice. They were both pretty full each time."

Abby pressed her lips together. "Well, Flann's the boss, but usually it needs to be less than an ounce every eight hours before they can come out, and you might not be there yet. I think you might need them at least until tonight."

"Yeah," Blake sighed. "That's what I figured, but boy, they're a real pain."

"How about the incisions—are they bothering you much?"

Blake shook his head. "Nope. Other than the drains and the stupid vest, I feel fine."

"Good. But just because you feel good, don't overdo it."

"I know, I know. No lifting, stretching, or tugging with my arms."

"And still no driving," Abby added.

"Right," Blake mumbled.

Abby smothered a smile. "I'm going to shower and get ready to go." She looked at Margie. "Half an hour, okay?"

"Sure."

Abby disappeared into the bedroom and closed the door behind her.

Blake leaned close. "Did my mom really ask you if we were having sex?"

"Not in so many words." Margie settled back up on the stool. "You okay here? You want to go lie down?"

Blake winced. "I'm already sick of bed. I don't see why I can't sit in the ER just as easily. I could do intake or something."

"Yeah. Until that got boring and you wanted to do something else." She shook her head. "You know the biggest complication is fluid collection, and that comes from doing too much too soon."

Blake grimaced. "I know, I know." He heaved a sigh. "So what did my mom say?"

Margie glanced toward the closed bedroom door. "She kind of hinted at it in a roundabout way, you know, the way parents do when they're not sure what to say."

"That's not really like her. Usually she gets right to it."

Margie rolled her eyes. "Yeah, but this is sex."

"Yeah. I know. Everybody gets weird around sex, but she's a doctor!"

"Uh-huh. And you're her kid, and Mom trumps Doc."

Blake grinned. "Sometimes. So what did you say?"

"That we weren't."

"That's cool, then," Blake said after a pause.

Margie heard the uncertainty in his voice. "We don't usually get weird about sex. So what's up?"

Blake fidgeted with his juice glass, turning it on the countertop. "Well, you know, we talked about a lot of stuff about sex in general, but we haven't talked about me…and you. Specifically."

"We haven't?" Margie frowned. "I thought we kind of both agreed we were good the way things are now, and if anything changed, that would be cool too."

Blake nodded vigorously. "Right, we did, and I agree. Totally."

"Then?"

Blake blew out a long breath. "Wow. This is harder than I thought. No wonder parents talk in big circles and lame metaphors."

"Well, we've never needed to do that before." Margie laughed. "And really, you suck at metaphors. So whatever's on your mind, you should just come out with it. I don't think anything is going to surprise me all that much."

Blake relaxed. "How come you can make the hard things so easy to talk about?"

"Seriously?" Margie shrugged. "I think because, as long as I can remember, Harper and Flann and Carson—even my mom and dad—have always talked about everything that's happening in front of me. If it was important, or just part of everyday life, they didn't try to cover up the hard parts. At dinner when my dad would get home from the hospital or when Harper and Flann started treating patients, they'd talk sometimes about sad things or scary things. And you could tell that helped them feel better. When Bill went to war, Carson would talk about being afraid of him not coming home." She thought for a minute. "You know what it is? Nobody pretended to be strong or brave all the time, and that made it easier when it was my turn to talk about hard stuff. So your hard stuff is not scary to me."

Blake stared at her. "I knew that, right away. I got really lucky you were the first person I met here."

"Thank you. And same here." Margie grinned. "So back to the sex—what are you afraid of telling me?"

Blake shot her a look. "That's subtle."

Margie laughed. "You already know I don't do subtle. What's bothering you?"

"Besides the fact that my mother is inquiring about my sex life?"

"Oh, come on. What makes you think you're any different? Every one of my sisters, plus my parents, has checked in with me. More than once." Margie laughed. "Do I want to talk about anything. Do I know whoever I decide to date is okay with them. No hurry, of course. And sex is natural and normal—and big ditto on the no hurry where that's concerned."

"I know. But it is different for me," Blake said quietly. "Me dating somebody comes with a whole extra set of issues."

"Okay, maybe."

"Maybe?"

"I think dating and sex is different for everybody, and everybody has issues," Margie said. "None of us feel the same about our bodies or, you know, necessarily feel confident hooking up with somebody else. Even if you're cisgender het, you can have issues, and what if you're not? I don't have to tell you about the whole coming-out thing."

"Yeah, but at least for cis people, gay or straight, their parts match what's on the inside," Blake said with the first hint of bitterness she'd ever heard from him.

"Oh. Yeah. Okay." Margie leaned on her elbow and studied him. "That's true. It doesn't mean I'm any more comfortable with my body than other people, even someone trans like you, but I get where being trans does add a factor."

Blake laughed. "A factor? Wow, I'll say."

"Does it bother you a lot?" Margie stopped. "Boy, that was a stupid question. I guess it must. I'm sorry."

"No, that's okay. It bothers me a lot less than it ever used to. Being able to live all the time as who I am makes a big difference, but I worry, you know, that other people aren't going to be able to relate."

"In bed, you mean."

"Yeah."

"Is this a general or a specific thing?"

Blake grinned a little. "I mostly want to know what you think. Since I'm not, you know, with anybody that way."

Margie tried to imagine how she'd feel if she hadn't known Blake was trans all along and then found out when they were ready to date. "Since I've always known you were trans, I also know pretty much about your body, so it doesn't seem like such a big thing. I know *you*, and that's what matters. I guess if I were someone else who didn't know you were trans, that would be different."

"Yeah, I know."

Margie sighed. "You're right. This isn't so easy to explain. So—specifically, if we were going to, you know, hook up. What do you want to know?"

Blake pushed his glass and met her gaze. "How does me being trans work for you? Have you thought about it?"

Margie blushed, and that was embarrassing. She was much cooler than that! Laughing at herself, she said, "Well, sure. I mean, sixteen and all."

Blake's heart lightened with a sensation he realized was hope. "Yeah, and?"

"Let's be scientific for a second."

"Oh, sure." Blake grinned. "You're stalling, Rivers."

"No, I'm not!" Margie smirked. "Okay, maybe a little." She leaned closer and lowered her voice. "I think getting to touch you…and you touching me…would be awesome. And as long as it feels good, both ways, your body is your body. That it's you is what matters."

Blake let out a breath. "That's good. That's…real good."

Margie poked his arm. "As far as I'm concerned, your body is just part of you, and if…whenever…that's going to be what matters. That it's you."

Abby emerged, car keys in hand. "You ready, Margie?"

"Uh-huh."

"Blake, you okay?" Abby asked. "You two look awfully serious."

"Oh," Margie put in, "we were just talking about having sex."

Blake groaned. "Margie, jeez."

Abby looked from one to the other. "What's the verdict?"

Laughing, Margie pointed to Blake. "She's your mom."

"Not fair—it's two against one." Blake sighed. "We've decided it will be awesome...if, whenever."

"Oh," Abby said casually. "That sounds just right, then."

"That's what I said." Margie kissed Blake's cheek. "I'll call you later. Don't go anywhere."

Blake rolled his eyes. "Yeah. Like I can."

He watched his mom and his best friend head out the door, feeling really, really lucky to be him.

CHAPTER THIRTEEN

When Carrie and Presley arrived in the Harold Rivers conference room, named after one of the Rivers forebears and past hospital presidents, the room was nearly filled with the heads of all the major departments—medicine, surgery, pediatrics, cardiology, psychiatry, intensive care, and all the other subspecialties. The meeting was only the second division head meeting Presley had held since taking over the reins of the hospital earlier that year, and the department chairs and co-chairs had turned out in force. Sussing out the new power in town, most likely.

Edward Rivers, the medical staff president and Presley's father-in-law, stood by the big coffee urn on the table at the rear of the room with Harper, the chief of medicine and next in line after her father to head the medical staff. Flann came in wearing scrubs a minute before the meeting was about to start and joined her sister and father. Abby followed a few seconds later, although she wasn't technically part of the hospital staff in the same way everyone else was. Part of the restructuring Presley had orchestrated to ease the hospital's overwhelming financial burden had separated the emergency services department into its own domain. Abby's status was more akin to Edward Rivers's, but she settled in among the other heads of departments with a cup of coffee and a casual greeting.

Carrie passed on more coffee—for some reason her nerves were jangling—and sat on Presley's left. She opened her iPad, scanned the agenda, which she knew Presley would have committed to memory as she never worked from notes, and prepared to jot down key points of discussion, disagreement, or, hopefully, consensus.

"Let's get started," Presley said, handing out slim blue folders containing the agenda and printouts of flowcharts and financials. Carrie had initially recommended Presley use PowerPoint, but Presley felt this was more personal and, for some of the staff, more what they were used to. She didn't need to impress anyone or prove she was in charge. What she needed was to convince the skeptics among them she was one of them, with the same goals for the well-being of the hospital and its staff as them, and win their support. SunView Health Consortium might have bailed out the hospital, but as Carrie knew only too well, they were far from safe shores.

Presley began her presentation and Carrie settled into the zone. She had long ago realized she was good at her job because she wasn't an expert just at time management, which came naturally, but something else that also came naturally. She could mentally multitask, listening to what was happening around her, homing in on the important parts, while another part of her brain worked out other issues.

The other issue today was different and uncharacteristically bothersome. As she followed Presley working through the agenda, noting and annotating as department heads jousted for funding, space, prime clinic hours, and all the other issues that division heads were expected to secure for their people, she was thinking about her next meeting. Her meeting with Gina Antonelli.

Gina shouldn't even be on her radar, but there she was. Grinning with that little hint of arrogant self-confidence, taunting her with dares, and catching her by surprise with the ghosts of sadness in her expressive eyes when she thought no one was looking. Now that Carrie had seen those haunted passages written on Gina's face, she wanted to know more, wanted to know why, and, inexplicably, wanted to make them go away.

The urge to search out, to know the reasons behind Gina's contradictions, raised questions she couldn't answer, and couldn't ignore. Listen to her intuition, Presley had said. Risky advice in this case. The trouble was, she didn't entirely trust her intuition where Gina was concerned. Usually she was confident in her decision-making and relied on intuition mixed with a healthy dose of reason. She set goals, she met them, and she satisfied her competitive needs on the ball field, where intuition often ruled her actions more than in any other arena. But interpersonally, she was careful, a little more cautious. She had goals there too. She wanted some of the things her parents had—an equal partnership, a genuine liking for one another, a lifetime of challenging and supporting one another. Her mother was the go-getter, the activist, the one who saw a problem and charged out to the front lines to meet it. Her father, the philosophy professor, examined all sides and pointed out the rationales of even those he disagreed with. If she could think of one word to describe him, it would be "fair."

Growing up, if she'd been punished, she always knew whatever the verdict, whatever the price, it would be fair. That was one of the main reasons she liked working for Presley so much. Presley was a ruthless businesswoman, and she played to win, but never underhandedly. She never cut corners, she never undercut her competition in any way other than offering better quality at a better price. She was fair and she was honest. Carrie wanted all that in a relationship. Openness, honesty, fairness as the foundation. And at the heart? She wanted what she couldn't define with reason or logic. She wanted to matter to a woman the way no one else did. She wanted a woman who stole her heart and claimed her passion.

So she enjoyed casual relationships—had had quite a few pleasant friendships with women. Shared experiences, shared pleasures, and, now and again, mutually pleasant sex. She was pretty sure she was more cautious about sex than most of the women she'd dated, which might account for why she didn't have a serious girlfriend. Sex mattered. She enjoyed it, sure, and she was by no means a prude. She didn't think one had to have a lifelong commitment to share physical intimacies, but there had to be something more than casual liking. A spark, and if she admitted deep down, for her, passion. She wanted to really *want* someone, to hunger, and to be hungered for. And yeah, she was waiting for it.

"I think that covers everything," Presley said, closing her slim blue folder. "Doctors? Anything else?"

Carrie mentally jerked to attention. Holy crackers. She'd missed the last five minutes or so of conversation! How had that happened? She felt her face warming and lowered her head, hoping no one would notice. She glanced at her iPad and let out a long sigh. She'd actually noted the time and made a notation just a couple minutes ago. She must've been listening, and she couldn't remember what had prompted her notation, but she was thankful her subconscious mind was still in the game. All around her, people were rising, breaking into small groups, and talking about patients or the latest sports scores.

Flann and Harper paused at the end of the table by Carrie and Presley.

Harper murmured to Flann, "How's Blake doing?"

"He's fine," Flann said. "Handling his own drains. Not too uncomfortable."

"That's great news."

"Yep," Flann said. "So Margie spent the night with him."

Harper cocked her head. "Define spent the night."

Flann grinned. "Slept on his bed with him."

"Okay." Harper rubbed her chin. "I didn't pick up on that moving in that direction, I guess."

"I'm not sure exactly what there is to pick up on or if they know where they're headed yet," Flann said. "I'll let you know."

"Do we need to have the talk again with Margie?"

"I think if we do she's going to hurt us."

Harper grinned. "Yeah, I think you're right." She clapped Flann on the shoulder. "I'm going to stop by and see him later this afternoon. Let me know if there's any change before then."

"Will do," Flann said, as she turned away to talk to another surgeon.

Harper leaned in to Presley. "Nice job, boss."

"You only have to call me that at home, darling," Presley said, too quietly for anyone except Carrie to hear.

Carrie smothered a smile.

"That went well," Harper said. "Somehow you managed to make both medicine and surgery happy. Not an easy task."

"You're right," Presley said. "You and Flann are both tough negotiators."

Harper grinned. "We've had a lot of practice competing with one another."

"I know. It shows."

"See you for lunch?" Harper said.

Presley gathered up her papers. "Check with me about noon. I might have to reschedule a conference call."

Harper briefly touched her cheek. "Will do. I love you."

Presley smiled and murmured, "I love you too."

As Carrie and Presley walked out together, Presley asked, "Everything all right?"

"Yes," Carrie said. "Why?"

"No reason."

"Did I miss something in there?" Carrie worried she'd dropped the ball and not noticed.

Presley laughed. "Oh, not at all. It's just you're the queen of focus, after all, so any little hint of distraction stands out."

"You noticed." Carrie sighed. "I'm sorry. I don't know what's wrong with me. My mind seems to be wandering."

"You have nothing to apologize for. I'm convinced you use more of your brain than the average human being. You can afford to let some of it rest now and then."

Carrie didn't agree, but she didn't argue with the boss when the boss was cutting her a break. "I'll have those notes ready for you by noon."

"Nothing transpired we didn't anticipate," Presley said. "End of day is fine."

"All right, thanks," Carrie said, intending to get them done by noon regardless.

Presley paused by Carrie's desk. "Are you leaving to meet with Gina now?"

"Yes, if that's all right with you." Carrie tucked her iPad into her purse and checked her watch to confirm she was right about the time. 9:08.

"Of course. Let me know how it goes."

"Sure," Carrie said briskly. "I'm sure nothing very exciting is going to happen."

She thought about that as she walked to her car, wondering why her pulse raced with what felt a whole lot like anticipation.

❖

Carrie wanted to hurry, but she kept to the speed limit just to prove to herself she wasn't rushing to see Gina, and turned off the two-lane onto the narrow dirt road that ran between two cornfields and up to her new home, only nine minutes late for their appointment. From the road, her place looked like many of the other unassuming farmhouses dotted throughout the countryside, a two-story white clapboard house with a brick chimney rising above a slate roof, the wide front door flanked by tall windows and fronted by a small porch. She couldn't see the back porch that ran the full width of the house, but all the farmhouses she'd been in had had one just like it. Farm families lived in the kitchen and out on the porch much more than in the formal rooms near the front. Her kitchen was easily her favorite room already, and she couldn't wait to give it the subtle updates it needed.

She slowed as she neared the house, skirting two pickup trucks and the ugly green dumpster that took up most of her driveway. Gina's truck, at least she assumed it was hers since that was the only one she'd seen that morning, was parked in the back where she usually left her Mini. She pulled in behind Gina's truck and headed for the house. Two men were erecting a wooden chute from one of the second-story windows down into the dumpster. She assumed that was how they planned to get rid of whatever they were knocking down inside the house. They stopped to watch her as she climbed the steps to the porch, and she smiled in their direction.

"Gina around?"

The older of the two, who looked to be in his midthirties, wearing a red T-shirt and blue jeans with his work boots, tilted his head toward the upper open window. "Upstairs."

"Thanks."

The temperature inside was headed toward uncomfortably warm already as the sun came in through the windows and bathed the rooms on the east side of the house. Fine flecks of dust floated in the air, making it feel warmer than it probably was. She left her bag on the sofa in the living room and headed upstairs. "Gina?"

"In here," Gina called back.

Carrie turned into the first room at the top of the stairs, an eight-foot square with one small window that had probably been a bedroom but was too small for one, in her opinion. She'd thought about using it for a walk-in closet, considering that all the other closets were way too small to be useful.

Gina stood with her hands on her hips by the window, looking down on the men at the dumpster. The sun on her face gilded the strong line of her profile, and Carrie thought she'd never seen a more striking woman.

Gina looked over her shoulder and smiled. "Hi."

"Hi." Carrie swallowed. "Sorry I'm late."

"Not by much."

"Going on eleven minutes."

"Stop. That's scary."

Carrie laughed. "Really?"

"No. It's fascinating, really."

"Oh." There went her vocabulary out the window again. Carrie ordered her brain to function. "So—it looks like you're under way."

"Just prepping. Where are you planning on staying until we're done?" Gina asked.

Abruptly, Carrie's brain cleared. "Sorry? I'm not planning on staying anywhere except here."

Somehow Gina managed to look surprised even as her eyebrows drew down into a frown. "That's gonna be a little difficult if you want your bathroom renovated. You know, in terms of taking showers and whatnot."

"Oh. Well, how long is it going to take for you to finish the bathroom?" She could camp with Mari for a night or two.

Gina lifted a shoulder. "Hard to tell. Figure at least ten days from when we get to it."

Ten days? Carrie knew her mouth was open. That couldn't be very attractive, and she pressed her lips together in a thin line. "Ten days? Why?"

"Well, once the demo's done, we have to do the framing, order the materials, get your new fixtures—get the place painted, the floor finished, everything in and plumbed." Gina spread her hands. "At least ten days. And to be safe? Three weeks."

"And what am I supposed to do for the, you know, facilities during that period of time?"

Gina gave her a look. "Stay somewhere else?"

"Why is it we always seem to have circular conversations?"

Gina laughed. "Maybe because we have different mental pictures of things."

"Well, my picture is very clear, and it doesn't consist of me moving out since I just moved in. Can you start somewhere else besides the bathroom?"

"Sure," Gina said, "but if we do, it's probably going to take longer to get everything done, and when we get to it, you won't save much time. I'd rather start with the places where we know we're going to have to do a full overhaul—framing, drywall, floors—"

"Yes, yes, I know, fixtures, plumbing, I got that."

"You're quick."

"Don't flatter me."

Gina grinned. "Wasn't."

"All right, why don't we try to come up with a game plan that works for us both."

"Very reasonable. That's why we're having this meeting, after all."

"Correct. Good."

Gina had a great smile.

Carrie's skin prickled. "Are you laughing at me?"

"Nope."

"Not even a little?"

Gina waggled a hand. "Maybe a little. I haven't seen you flummoxed before. It's kind of—"

"Please do not say cute."

"Ah…okay."

Carrie laughed. "And I'm not flummoxed. I'm reassessing. Readjusting expectations."

Gina studied her. "You can do that that fast?"

"Sure. I'm…flexible."

"Handy," Gina murmured.

"So can we discuss what we need to do here?" Carrie felt more on stable ground now. At least they were on the same side for a change. She just wished every single encounter with Gina didn't leave her a little bit off-kilter. She'd never had trouble sorting out project details, devising a timetable, and constructing compromises and work-arounds with anyone. She was good at all of that. And every one of those organizational skills disappeared the minute she looked at Gina. What she needed was to move this discussion onto her home field. Like the kitchen. "How about we do this over something cool to drink and a little bit of shade. It's already so hot inside. You're going to die working up here."

"We'll be okay. We'll bring in fans. Besides, we're used to it."

Carrie shook her head. "It must be awfully uncomfortable this time of year."

"Nah," Gina said. "This is nothing. Now, January, that gets ugly."

Carrie shivered. "Tell me about it. California girl, remember?"

"Oh yeah, I forgot. Wimp."

Carrie arched a brow. "I'm going to make you regret that the first time I'm on the mound."

"I won't be batting, remember," Gina said.

"Then I'll think of some other way to make you suffer."

Gina laughed. "Can't wait."

Smiling, Carrie spun on her heel and headed downstairs, listening for the sound of Gina's footsteps behind her. She knew she was there—she could feel the air moving between them, heavy and hot and somehow filled with expectation. Like a long summer night when the hours stretched forever and the only way to make love was slow and lazy.

"Lemonade?" Carrie busied herself at the fridge while resolutely putting thoughts of warm nights and warmer bodies from her mind.

"That sounds great. Did you make it yourself?"

Carrie glanced over her shoulder. "Of course. Me and Minute Maid."

"Somehow, I couldn't see you squeezing lemons."

"I'll have you know, I make a very mean sun tea. And that requires slicing lemons, among other secret ingredients."

"Can't wait to taste it."

"Then I'll have to make some." Carrie concentrated on putting ice into glasses. Really. Now she was making her tea. Life didn't get any stranger than that.

Gina pulled out a chair at the table and unfolded a sheet of drawing paper she'd pulled from a back pocket. Carrie poured lemonade and carried the glasses to the table. She took the chair on Gina's right and handed her the lemonade.

"Thanks. Okay," Gina said, quickly sketching the borders of the kitchen and outlining the counters and appliances. "This is what we have to start."

Carrie tilted her head to study the sketch. The proportions all looked right, as if they'd been outlined on graph paper rather than freehand. "You're really good at that."

"Plenty of practice," Gina said absently. "So tell me what you see that doesn't work and what you want to change."

Leaning closer, Carrie pointed to various spots on the drawing, explaining where she needed more room for cooking or serving or just simple things like unloading groceries.

"Okay." Gina paused to clear her head, distracted by the hint of violets that could only be Carrie's scent mixing with the tang of lemons. Their bare forearms touched as they each pointed out places on the drawing, and Gina was drawn in by the softness of Carrie's skin and the light perspiration on her own, her thoughts suddenly tangled with the image of their bodies mingling. "Um…"

"Sorry?" Carrie said, sounding as hazy as Gina felt. "I think I lost the plot."

"No," Gina murmured, "I'm not explaining very well." She moved her chair a few inches away, breaking the unintentional contact, giving herself a little room to breathe. "We've already got good space to work with in here, plenty of room, it's just a question of altering the dynamics of the flow, of how the workspace is used." She quickly mapped several alternative layouts. "See what I mean? With this one, you'll have a good view out the window as you prep, but it means moving the table and chairs in this direction, cutting down on the breeze through the back door when you're at the table. If you want to keep the table where it is, we can switch things around"—she pointed—"here and here. Still good triangulation between the major kitchen working points but makes the table more the centerpiece."

"Definitely that way," Carrie said. "I can do with compromising a little on the workflow to keep the view out the back door and maximize the breeze. I like the way the air feels around here."

"I know what you mean. So do I," Gina said.

"So if you start down here," Carrie said, "I'll have the upstairs pretty much to myself while this stage is ongoing, right?"

"True, but the bathroom is still going to have to be torn up pretty quickly. We can leave working fixtures for you, but it won't be pretty."

"I don't need pretty. I just need hot water."

"I took a walk through the first floor while I was waiting," Gina said slowly, sketching again. "What do you think about this—there's that long, narrow room underneath the staircase that's not really useful for much of anything. We could put a second bathroom in there."

"A full bath?"

"Stall shower, but one big enough to accommodate. If we did that first, you'd have the use of that while we're working upstairs. It means more of a project, and the expense—"

"Do it, absolutely. I'll have to clear it with Harper, but I want it." Carrie smiled. "That's a great idea."

Gina put her pencil down and shifted in her chair, sipping her lemonade. "You sound surprised."

"Not at all. I just didn't expect you to be so...interested, I guess. You know, this must be a pretty small job to you."

"Every job is important to me," Gina said. "It's what I do."

"Well then, I'm glad you're doing this one."

To her surprise, Gina nodded. "Yeah, so am I."

Carrie sighed. She hated to do it, just when they were getting along, but pretending they weren't avoiding the elephant in the room was getting tiring. And she was terrible at pretending. "What happens when you start the hospital project? I guess this gets put on hold?"

"If I say yes, will you stall on getting the permits on that one?"

Carrie considered dumping lemonade on her head.

Gina laughed. "Quick, tell me what you were thinking just then."

"How you'd look with lemons in your hair." Carrie laughed when Gina chuckled. "You know that was an insulting remark, right?"

"You're right. I'm sorry. No excuse, ma'am."

Carrie'd heard Joe say the same thing when he'd apologized to Harper for dropping a fly ball in center field. "Are you ex-military too, like Joe? He mentioned his sister was—"

Gina rose abruptly. "Not this sister. I'm the one who didn't make the cut."

"Oh," Carrie said softly. "I'm sorry if—"

"You didn't. I did. No excuses there, either." Gina rolled up the papers and shoved them in her back pocket. "We've got enough to get started. I ought to get to work."

"Yes. Me too." Carrie watched her stride outside, shoulders stiff. Every time they crossed paths she was left with more questions, and the same disquieting urge to extinguish the pain Gina worked so hard to hide.

CHAPTER FOURTEEN

The roads were empty at midday, and Carrie made it back to her desk before eleven. Forsaking lunch, she set about typing up the summary of that morning's meeting. She emailed it to Presley at 11:31. Five minutes later, Presley appeared in the doorway.

"Everything okay at the house?" Presley asked.

"More or less." Carrie pushed her chair back and swiveled to face Presley. "I guess I hadn't really thought the entire thing through. Like what it would actually be like living there during the renovations."

"You mean other than being annoying and disruptive?"

"That and not having a working bathroom for longer than a couple of days."

"Huh." Presley nodded, forehead furrowed in her typical problem-solving expression. "I guess you can't talk them into doing it piecemeal rather than tearing it out right away?"

Carrie huffed. "I don't think talking Gina into anything is a realistic possibility. And it *does* make sense to get the big projects out of the way all at once."

"You can always move back in with us until it's done. We already miss you."

"I know you mean it, and I appreciate the offer, really." Carrie lifted a shoulder. "It's strange, because it's been great living with the two of you, but it just doesn't seem right somehow now. And to tell you the truth, I'm kind of liking my solitude."

"Believe me, I get that. I adore Harper, but I'm not sorry our schedules don't always line up." Presley smiled. "But if you need emergency accommodations, you have an open invitation."

"Thanks. I do need to get together with you to talk about some of Gina's recommendations. And we have to talk about expense."

"Well, we might be able to kill two birds with one stone. Mari called an emergency wedding planning meeting for tonight. Wine and nibbles at my place after work. Harper will probably be home at some point, and you can let us know what Gina had to say."

"Okay, that will work."

"Good. I'm going to grab lunch with Harper."

"Don't forget your one o'clock with the planning board."

"I've got it." Presley emerged a minute later. "Want to join us? I know you haven't eaten yet."

"Oh. No thanks. I'm going to tackle this permit situation again, even if it will mean I'm going to lose my contractor before we even get started."

"I'm sure they'll come up with someone to handle them both. Business, after all."

"I'm sure you're right," Carrie said, just as sure Gina would bolt at the first opportunity to get back to the real job at the hospital. Not that she could really blame her.

"I'll be back in forty-five minutes," Presley said on her way past. "Text me if you want me to bring you anything."

"Thanks."

Carrie pulled up the number for the county licensing office. She had her priorities in order, and the hospital project came first. She ignored the swift surge of disappointment when she considered she wouldn't have Gina showing up every day to work at her house, and dialed the number. Like Presley said, it was just business.

❖

Gina pulled into the company lot at ten minutes to four. Joe's Mustang was parked next to her dad's truck by the side of the trailer, and when she walked inside, she found the two of them kicked back with a couple of beers.

"You're just in time." Joe pointed to the cooler by the desk. "I stopped by that new microbrewery on the other side of town. It's pretty good."

"Thanks." Gina fished out a bottle of beer, checked the label, and smiled. Groundhog Day. The image of the fat gopher sitting up with an ear of corn in one paw and a brown bottle in the other made her smile. She popped the top and took a long swallow. Some of the dust of the day disappeared along with the beginnings of an ache between her shoulder blades. She hadn't done any serious demo that didn't involve a crane and a wrecking ball in a long time. Today she'd been swinging a sledgehammer, ripping down drywall with a crowbar, and tossing debris out a window into the chute. All the same, she felt good. Nothing like looking at the bones of a room after spending a day stripping it down to feel she'd accomplished something. Honest work. Honest sweat. Honest aches and pains. "You're right, the beer's good."

"So," Joe said with exaggerated casualness, "how's the new job going?"

Gina fixed him with a stare. "You mean the project you dragged me into to impress your boss?"

"Hey, I'm not doing this for personal gain." Joe affected the innocent look that always got him out of trouble when they were kids. "*Antonelli Construction* is going to impress my boss because we're helping out her best friend, who just happens to run the whole hospital."

"Not we," Gina pointed out. "Me. And as to running the hospital, actually I think Carrie does that."

Joe pounced. "Carrie. Would that be our pitcher, the hot redhead you couldn't take your eyes off last night?"

"Hey!" Gina said, sounding a warning before she had a chance to think. "Careful."

"What?" Joe still had that innocent look that didn't fool her for a second. "Only stating the truth, right? She's our pitcher and she's damn well ho—"

Tom Antonelli cleared his throat. "That's enough, Joseph. We don't talk about ladies that way in our family."

"Yes, sir." Joe stared down at his shoes.

He'd been joking, trying to get a rise out of her, but they didn't argue with their father. You never won. Gina kept a blush off her face by sheer force of will and, with an even greater surge of willpower, managed not to come down on her brother for treating Carrie like a sex object, even in jest. The back of her neck was hot and she itched to declare discussing Carrie off-limits. If she did that, she'd never hear the end of Joe's pestering as to why she should be so protective of a client when he was just playing with her. Since she couldn't answer the question in her own mind, she punted and said to her father, "Carrie Longmire is the executive admin for the CEO over at the Rivers and seems to be the go-to person if you want something done."

Her father said, "Then that's the person we need to know. How's it going there?"

"Nothing out of the ordinary. We might be adding a little bit more to the work order, especially since she doesn't want to be without a bathroom and doesn't want to move out."

Joe laughed. "She's going to change her mind soon enough when you barbarians start showing up at seven in the morning."

"I don't think she really knows what she's in for," Gina said slowly. "Besides, I'm probably not gonna be there very long. As soon as the ER project gets under way—"

"Vince can handle that until you finish over there," Tom said.

Vince? Vince could handle the auto parts store construction well enough, but the hospital was a couple million dollar project with a crew four times what Vince was used to running. Gina put her bottle down slowly, waiting for the rush of heat to leave her brain so she could come up with something that wasn't going to force her father into an ultimatum before she could argue the point. Once an order came down, it never changed.

"Vince isn't really up to speed on the project, Dad," she said quietly, watching Joe ease back in his chair as if physically drawing out of the line of fire. Oh, now he had nothing to say about any of it. No help there, so she soldiered on, hoping to avoid a minefield. "Besides, he doesn't know this crew—"

"Then he needs to learn," Tom said with a note of finality in his voice. "You're going to be sitting in my chair one of these days, Gina, and he's going to need to be able to do everything that you do now."

"You're right, although," Gina said, keeping her gaze fixed on her father's, knowing that the only way to negotiate with him was to never give an inch, "that's a good long time in the future, and—"

As if he hadn't heard her, Tom said, "As soon as you've finished up where you are now, we'll move you back over to the hospital. We'll make sure that Vince reviews everything with you ahead of time. You can handle oversight at a distance. That'll be good for you."

"Sir," Gina said sharply, "this other thing isn't that important right no—"

"That job is just what your brother said it is—a goodwill gesture to the right people at the right time. Besides, it's honest work."

Honest work. True. Gina knew when she'd lost the battle. She couldn't even honestly say she didn't want to do Carrie's renovations. She'd enjoyed sitting down with her in the warm, sunlit kitchen to discuss designs a lot more than she'd enjoyed the last date she'd had. She couldn't even remember the details of that. She sighed. "Yes, sir."

Tom put his half-finished beer on his tabletop. "Since I've got you both here, there's something we need to discuss."

Out of the corner of her eye, Gina saw Joe tense and straighten up, all the levity leaving his face. The beer curdled in her stomach, and she set her bottle on the floor between her boots. She was surprised when Joe said nothing, handing the conversational baton to her. "What's going on, Dad?"

"Probably nothing, and it's nothing that I want to leave this room until I say differently."

Gina swallowed, her throat so dry it felt like cut glass.

Her father sighed, sounding exasperated and, oddly for him, uncomfortable. "The two of you don't have to look so serious. I just need to take a few days away from work. Gina, you'll be in charge of the business. Joe, keep your eye out on the family. Nothing the two of you haven't done before."

"Where are you going?" Gina said.

"Florida. I've got a business thing down there."

Gina did something she'd never done before. She challenged him. "Dad, that's a bullshit story, and it won't fly with anybody."

His expression hardened. "Is that the way you talk around your father?"

"Calling bullshit when it's bullshit is just honest talk. Something *you* taught us." Gina shook her head. "As long as I've known you, you haven't gone anywhere for more than a day. You don't even take Mom on vacation."

"Your mother's idea of a vacation is having help with the grocery shopping." He smiled briefly. "All right, I have to have some tests, and it's easier if they do them all at once while I stay in the hospital." He must have known they wouldn't accept that as an answer. He grimaced. "Something to do with an irregular heartbeat."

Gina's stomach dropped. Joe jerked as if he'd been zapped with a live wire.

"How long have you known about this?" Joe asked, finally finding his voice.

"Not that long. A couple months."

"A couple months? Jesus, Dad—"

Tom thundered, "*Joseph.*"

"Sorry. Sorry. But come on, why have you been putting this off?"

"I've been busy."

"Does Mom know?" Gina asked.

For the first time, his stern composure wavered. "Not yet. I want to know what we're dealing with before saying anything. There's no point—"

"You have to tell her," Gina said. "It's the right thing to do. It's the fair thing to do."

"Your mother's and my relationship is none of your concern," he said sharply.

Gina set her jaw. "That's not true. We're family. We all look out for each other. You taught us that too."

He let out a long breath. "I wish that the lot of you weren't quite so much like me, especially you."

"Thanks."

"When?" Joe said. "And where?"

"I'm going into the city," Tom said. "I figure then everybody won't know my business."

"I'd like to know the name of the doctor," Joe said. "I just want to make sure you're seeing the best person."

"Fair enough." Tom resumed drinking his beer. "Sometime in the next few weeks. I'll let you know exactly when." He looked from Joe to Gina. "And in the meantime, the both of you will keep doing your jobs exactly as you're doing now, understood?"

"Yes, sir," Joe and Gina said simultaneously.

Gina picked up her beer but didn't drink it while they all pretended nothing had happened. She'd had a lot of practice doing that in the last eight years, and it never got any easier. The only way she'd ever found to block out fear and pain and disappointment was to act as if she had everything she wanted and needed, and she was so damn tired of the lie.

CHAPTER FIFTEEN

Carrie arrived at Presley and Harper's farm at ten to six, and as she drove down the driveway, she'd already begun to think of it as *their* house, not hers any longer, even though she'd only been gone a short time. Her mother had asked her if she was lonely, the first night they'd talked on the phone after her move, and she was surprised to realize she wasn't. She was rapidly coming to like her own little corner of the countryside, something that prompted her parents to express wonder over and her sister to proclaim she'd lost her mind. Of course, she'd like it a lot more when she had a bigger bathroom. Just thinking about the house and the changes she wanted to make immediately made her think of Gina. She'd been debating calling her since she left the hospital, and the indecision alone had made her hold off.

She glanced at her phone in the console as she drove past the rambling three-story farmhouse and parked in front of the barn. She did have a good excuse—it wasn't as if she was calling her just to hear her voice or aimlessly chat, after all.

"Oh, what the hell," she muttered, and brought up Gina's number. When she was switched through to voice mail, a pang of disappointment almost had her hanging up. Now, that was silly. "Hi, Gina. It's Carrie. Carrie Longmire. I have an update for you—nothing urgent. It can wait until tomorrow. Have a good night."

She disconnected and closed her eyes. *How about being a little more obvious, Carrie? If it could wait, why bother calling in the first place?*

Since she couldn't undo the call, she resolutely decided to forget it. As she walked to the house, a series of squawks and the fluttering of wings signaled the arrival of a brightly plumed maroon and midnight blue bird who hopped toward her adroitly on one leg, head cocked as he stopped a few feet away to study her.

"Hi, Rooster," Carrie said, holding out her empty hands. "Sorry, buddy. No grapes at the moment. Isn't it about time you started rounding up your girls and getting them to bed?"

Rooster merely squawked, expressing his disdain that she had arrived with nothing to offer him. A gaggle of pullets straggled around the side of the barn, seeming to have grown much bigger than they had been only a few days before. She smiled at the young chickens, Rooster's new flock. Deciding that she was no longer of interest, Rooster strutted away in his entirely arrogant if slightly lopsided fashion across the yard with the chickens following along. Smiling, Carrie headed for the back porch. She could definitely do chickens. She could do without the five a.m. crowing, however, and decided that one rooster in the extended family was plenty. Presley and Harper, carrying glasses of wine, walked out from the kitchen at the same time as she climbed the stairs.

"Hey," Presley said. "Help yourself on the counter inside."

"Thanks," Carrie said. "Hi, Harp."

"Hey, Carrie. How's it going?"

"It's all good." She realized after she'd given the stock answer that things did feel good, maybe even exciting in a way she hadn't noticed in a long time. Must be the new digs, a new adventure. She poured herself some wine and joined them on the porch, settling onto the top step and sipping the merlot as she watched Rooster and the chickens busily peck and scratch.

"Presley says the contractor's shown up out at the little farm." Harper stretched a hand out, and Presley twined her fingers through Harper's.

Their unconscious movements, automatic and perfectly in sync, were yet another reason Carrie had decided it was time to move out. They were a couple in a way she hadn't noticed so much before. She didn't know if the wedding was what had made the difference, or, more likely, the promises they had made that had nothing to do with the ceremony itself.

"She arrived with a dumpster bright and early this morning." She probably winced because Harper laughed and Presley smiled. Feigning indignation, she said, "Really? Does everyone around here have to get up before daybreak? Is it some kind of rule?"

"You know what they say—" Harper began.

"Don't even think about mentioning worms before I've had anything to eat," Carrie said. "In fact, don't mention them at any time."

"I can see I'm going to have to take you fishing."

Presley laughed. "Oh, darling. The day that happens, I'm going to be very worried the apocalypse will be next."

Harper grinned.

"Anyhow," Carrie said, deciding she wasn't going to rise to the bait, "that's what I wanted to talk to you about. I know you said you were planning on renovating the place even if you'd stayed, but it's turning into a much bigger project." She shrugged, smiled a little sheepishly. "I'm afraid I've got some ideas that might be a little more than you planned for."

Harper glanced at Presley. "So before we get to that, we've been talking."

"You've changed your mind. You're going to sell the place?" Carrie swallowed her disappointment. "No, wait. Margie wants it. Of course it should be hers. After all, it's been in the family—"

Harper shook her head. "No, that's not it. Margie isn't ready to think about where she wants to live, but if she plans to stay local, my father will likely deed part of the homestead land to her and build. Otherwise she'll buy somewhere like we did. But we do want to sell."

"Oh. Well, then I guess I should start looking—"

"What we were thinking," Presley said, "is a lease-to-buy plan with you, unless you've got some long-range plans I don't know about?"

"You mean, like looking for another job?" Carrie said it lightly, but Presley wasn't smiling. Carrie put her glass down and looked from Harper to Presley. "Wow, don't you know me better than that?"

"Living here is a lot different than Phoenix," Presley said.

"No kidding. For one thing, I understand it snows here. I can't wait."

Harper smiled at the sarcasm in her voice.

"I was just thinking last night when I got home from work and I sat on the back porch," Carrie said, "that I liked the way the air smelled. I can't ever remember thinking that before about any place I've lived. I was also considering getting some animals—a dog or cat, or a chicken. Or two."

Presley laughed softly. "Oh. I think you've got the country bug."

"Yeah, I totally love this place. You happen to be pretty important too." Carrie huffed. "I can't believe you don't know how much you mean to me. Considering all of that, *and* since I happen to be kick-ass at my job and I'm only going to be getting better, why would I want to be anywhere else?"

"If you get any better at your job," Presley said, "I'm going to start worrying about mine." She let out a long breath. "It's just that we've never talked about this before and a lot has changed since we arrived. I don't know what I would do without you at the hospital, but especially here." She touched her chest over her heart.

"So, the answer is," Carrie said around the rush of feeling that filled her throat, "I'm not going anywhere, and yes, I want the house!"

"I'll set something up with an attorney," Presley said.

"Let me know what I need to do," Carrie said. "In the meantime, about the renovations—I want to add a bathroom downstairs. Gina came up with this amazing plan to tuck one under the stairs."

"Like I said," Harper put in, "I was planning to renovate regardless, but we can look at all the numbers when we sit down with the attorney."

"All right. I'd like to tell Gina to go ahead, if that works for you two."

Presley eyed her with a speculative expression. "Absolutely."

"Well, that takes one problem off my plate, then." Carrie paused as two cars pulled in beside hers across the yard. Abby and Mari climbed out of one and Carson Rivers from the other. The three approached the back porch and everyone called greetings.

Carson was unmistakably a Rivers sister with Harper's quiet humor and Flann's ceaseless energy and drive.

"Where's the munchkin?" Harper asked, referring to her nephew Davey, Carson's son.

"I left him with Mama." Carson lifted her arms and twirled in a circle. "Free as a bird for a couple of hours."

Presley said, "There's wine and salad and Lila's cold chicken inside. More wine in the rack."

"I'm only having one glass." Carson headed for the kitchen. "But I'm going to enjoy every drop."

"I'll bring out the chicken," Abby offered and followed her in.

When Mari sat down, Carrie shoulder bumped her. "Hi, cuz. How are things?"

"Good. Busy."

"And outside of work?"

Mari smiled shyly. "Glenn and I are looking for a place to rent."

"Oh hey, that's fabulous." Carrie inwardly chided herself for the brief flare of envy. She couldn't be happier for Mari and Glenn, who were clearly mad for one another. And since when did it bother her when her friends were happy? "I better be the first one to hear when you decide."

"Promise," Mari said.

Abby came out with a tray of chicken piled high on a platter along with plates and napkins. "We have nourishment. On to the battle."

Harper rose and snatched a chicken leg from the heap. "Well, I'm outta here."

Presley grabbed her by the back pocket and pulled her to a halt. "Really? You think you're getting out of helping?"

"Hey. I'm available for manual labor, chauffeuring, and moral support. But menus, flowers, and music? I respectfully pass."

Presley laughed. "Just remember what you volunteered for."

Harper leaned down and kissed her on her way inside. "Always."

Mari pulled her tablet from her bag, swiped several times, and then said, "Alrighty. Item number one. Dates, preferred and backup."

Forty-five minutes later, they had outlined all the basic areas of attack, apportioned tasks, and set a calendar for getting back together with updates.

Abby shook her head. "I don't know how I would've managed any of this without all of you."

"That's the whole point—you're not supposed to." Mari slid her tablet away, looking happy with the initial plan.

Conversation shifted as they all caught up, and at 8:42, Carrie said, "I should get home. Gina and the rest will probably be showing up at first light again tomorrow."

Carson began picking up empty glasses. "Who's Gina?"

"The contractor who's doing the renovations. Gina Antonelli."

Carson paused, empty wineglasses dangling between her fingers. "I know that name. She's local, right?"

"I don't know," Carrie said, realizing she knew little about Gina personally. Gina somehow managed never to talk about herself. "I think so, though—she coaches a local ball team and seems to know everyone around here."

Mari interjected, "Her brother Joe is a PA student interning with us in the ER, and he mentioned family nearby."

"Okay," Carson said. "I know them. Gina was the one in the accident."

Carrie carefully set her glass down, torn between wanting to know more and uncomfortable that they were talking about Gina when she wasn't around.

"What accident?" Mari asked.

"It was a while ago, but you know how it is around here," Carson said. "When anything out of the ordinary happens, everyone either knows the person or knows someone who does. Gina's sister was in my class." She shook her head. "And the tragedies are never forgotten."

"A tragedy?" Carrie asked quietly, her stomach knotting.

"Yeah, Gina and another girl in her class were in a car accident right at the end of their senior year. The girl was killed, and Gina was pretty badly injured, as I remember."

"Oh. Oh God." Carrie shuddered. The haunted look in Gina's eyes made sense now, as did her veiled references to an old injury that she obviously didn't want to talk about. Her heart hurt just thinking about it.

Mari asked, "Who was driving?"

"Um, the friend. Emily Wilcox, that was her name," Carson said. "Gina was a passenger. I remember there was a lot of speculation about what exactly had happened. No one really talked about all the details, but I know they were going pretty fast. It wasn't a drug or alcohol situation. Just careless driving." She shook her head. "Teenagers. They think they're going to live forever."

Mari gathered up the plates. "Don't I know it. We see too many of them in the ER."

The conversation shifted again, and Carrie stood to help clean up, unable to think of anything except Gina.

❖

Abby walked beside Carrie to the cars. "You okay? You're quiet tonight."

"What?" Carrie said. "Oh. Yes. Fine. Just a lot going on."

"I know." Abby sighed. "I keep waiting for things to slow down, but they never do."

"How's Blake? I was thinking of stopping by to see him. Do you think he'll still be awake?"

"He's back to keeping teen hours," Abby said with fond exasperation. "He'll be up late tonight and up late in the morning, at least until he feels well enough and Flann gives him the green light to go back to his shifts in the ER. He'll be glad to see you."

"Do you mind the interruption?" Carrie said.

"Not at all." Abby smiled. "Flann is late doing a gallbladder, so I'm planning on curling up in bed with a book after I stop at Stewart's and get the ice cream I promised Blake."

"I'm just going to say hello, so if I don't see you, I'll catch up with you soon," Carrie said.

"'Night," Abby called.

Carrie waved good-bye, got into the car, and put the top down. She'd always been an air-conditioning addict until this summer, when she decided she liked the way the breezes played across her skin, even if they were warm. Every now and then, a cool one snuck in like a gift, and the wait was worth mussing her hair and sweating a little. Besides, she had a better view with the top down. The sky was bright, the stars brighter, and the clouds silvered along the edges as the moon danced in and out behind them. Town was quiet as she drove through and parked in front of Abby and Flann's. A light burned in the first floor, and as always, just the screen door separated the inside from the night.

"Hello?" she called as she climbed the stairs, not wanting to surprise Blake if he was dozing.

"Hey," Blake called, "come on in."

Blake and Margie were sprawled on the couch, each with a book propped open in their lap. Blake wore a baggy T and loose sweatpants. Margie had on shorts and a tank top. Both were barefoot, a bag of chips between them.

Carrie laughed. "Hey, sorry to barge in. I just wanted to see how you were doing."

"Pretty good," Blake said, looking more like himself than he had the last time she'd seen him. His color was back, and his eyes were bright and happy.

"That's terrific. Your mom's getting ice cream, but you need anything else?"

"Just to get these drains out." He made a face and pointed to the two plastic bulbs protruding from below his shirt. "Flann said maybe before I go to bed. I'm waiting up for her no matter how late she is."

"That's good news, then."

"I'll say."

Margie said, "You want something to drink or anything? We've got chips and soda, and I'm pretty sure Flann has beer."

"No, thanks. I had my one glass of wine for the night already."

"Oh yeah," Margie said. "Wedding planning, right?"

"Yep."

"How'd it go?" Blake asked.

"Great. We're getting to be old hands at this."

"Maybe you should start a sideline," Margie said. "The Wedding Doctors or something."

Carrie laughed. "No way. It's fun doing it for your friends, but I don't think I'd want to do it for strangers. Too much pressure."

"Oh yeah, like your regular job is so easy."

"Nah," Carrie said, "piece of cake."

"So when are we going to get our new MRI suite?" Blake said.

Carrie grimaced. "Not you too."

"Mom was telling Flann about the delays. It's good we're getting more patients through the ER, but it can get pretty crowded at peak hours."

"I know. I know. And I'm working on it. Soon."

"Awesome."

Obviously Blake was on the mend. Carrie tilted her head toward the door. "I'll let you two get back to your exciting entertainment. I just wanted to see how you were doing."

"Thanks," Blake said, suddenly seeming shy. "That was nice of you."

"Just get well quick. Hey, you two going to be able to come to the games this weekend?"

"Absolutely," Margie and Blake said together, then looked at each other and laughed.

"Good. Then I'll see you in a few." Carrie waved and let herself out. She turned the car around and headed back out of town, thinking they were cute together. She wondered briefly if they were just friends, and then thought just friends was a good thing. Sometimes friendships lasted a whole lot longer than anything else. She had good friends and they meant everything, but now and then, she thought about more. And she seemed to be doing that more often lately.

Just as she pulled in behind her house, her cell phone rang. She grabbed it and answered as she headed toward the porch. "Hello?"

"Is this too late to be calling?"

Carrie thumped her bag down on the top step and sat beside it. "No. Gina?"

"I got your message."

Carrie blushed. Thankfully, Gina couldn't see her. "Oh. Sorry. I should've waited until tomorrow."

"I thought it must be important, since you did say no business after hours."

Carrie smiled at the teasing hint in Gina's voice. "And you never forget anything. Apparently."

"Not anything you have to say," Gina said.

Just teasing, doesn't mean a thing. Carrie's thoughts tumbled around like loose change in a washing machine, jangling inside her head and making too much noise for her to keep control of the conversation. Why did that happen every time she was in Gina Antonelli's vicinity?

"Carrie?"

She even liked the way Gina said her name. "I'm here. Sorry. Anyhow. I thought you'd want to know we're making some progress."

"Does that mean we're ready to start digging?"

Carrie sighed. "Not exactly, but I finally connected with the person we need on this at the county, and he assured me he's going to be making calls and pushing things through as fast as possible."

"Uh-huh." Gina sounded underenthused. "I don't have a lot of faith in people who push paper."

"Hey. I push a lot of paper myself."

"I bet you don't. I bet you just dispatch problems with a wave of your hand, the magician behind the curtain."

Carrie laughed. "I wish."

"What time is it?" Gina said.

"Right now?"

"Yes."

"Nine forty-seven."

Gina was silent for a moment. "Yep. Scary. And like I said—magician."

"You don't strike me as the type to be frightened by women."

"Maybe I'm just afraid of superefficient, smart, and..."

"And what?" Carrie asked, holding her breath.

"Competent women."

She let the breath out.

Gina laughed. "I should also add very attractive."

"Attractive is a little better than competent," Carrie muttered.

"You'll be at the game tomorrow night?" Gina said, abruptly changing the subject.

Disappointed at the sudden distance, Carrie said lightly, "Absolutely. I need to scout out your weaknesses before the tournament."

"What makes you think we have any?" Gina said.

"Oh. I'll find them."

"Maybe I *should* be worried, then."

Carrie took a long breath. "I don't think so."

"Then I'll look forward to seeing you in the morning."

"Oh. Yes." There she went again, losing her powers of speech. "Right. Tomorrow, then."

"Good night, Carrie," Gina said gently.

"'Night," Carrie murmured as the line went silent. She sat on the steps with her phone cradled in her palms and watched the stars revolve overhead. She told herself the warmth in her chest and the tingle of excitement were all due to the painfully beautiful summer's night.

CHAPTER SIXTEEN

Carrie opened her eyes at 5:35 a.m. and wondered what was wrong with her. She should not be awake. She should have been asleep for another seventy-five minutes. She'd gotten up at this unnatural hour intentionally when necessary, true, but this was not planned. She depended on her internal clock to wake her at the time she decided upon when falling asleep, and this morning for some reason, her clock had betrayed her.

Funny, she didn't feel tired. If anything, her body hummed with anticipation, as if she was facing a day filled with special plans and not another day at the office. Not that she resented going to work, because she didn't. Usually she woke in work mode, and by the time she was finishing her first cup of coffee, she was already sorting through the problems she'd have to deal with. That was her job. She took care of the problems so Presley wouldn't have to. She smiled to herself, thinking about Gina's assumption that she was the receptionist. She was that too. She was the voice and very often the face that staff, drug reps, patients, families, and bankers heard or saw before they ever met Presley. That was part of her job as well, and an important one. Managing people was every bit as important as managing infrastructure, even more so. Companies ran on people, not budgets and agendas. She and Pres were a good match.

But she was still awake way too early. Since she wouldn't be able to go back to sleep, she headed downstairs barefoot to start coffee and enjoy the quietude. Presley had gifted her with half a dozen of Lila's blueberry corn muffins before she'd left the night before, and she'd fallen asleep thinking about having one of them for breakfast. She put some in the toaster oven to warm, took butter out, and added cream to her coffee. At a few minutes after six, she carried the coffee and muffin outside and sat down to enjoy them both. She'd barely made a dent in either one when the quiet sound of an engine heralded an approaching vehicle. Gina's truck slowly, almost stealthily, pulled into the yard, and the anticipation bubbling through Carrie's veins ratcheted up a notch or twenty.

Great—now what?

She had two choices. She could stay where she was in her boxers and tank top and pretend she wasn't the least bit embarrassed, or she could run inside and find something more suitable, comb her hair, put on some makeup, maybe a dress and a sexy pair of sandals. And wouldn't that be obvious. Nope, she was staying where she was, in her pajamas, no makeup, and not even an old pair of flip-flops, let alone sexy sandals. At least she'd splashed water on her face.

Gina parked by the barn where she had the day before and sat with the engine running, as if that would somehow buy her time. She'd seen Carrie the instant she'd pulled around the house. She shouldn't even be here so early, and she didn't want to compound the offense by barging in on Carrie's private time. Then again, she couldn't stay in her truck for another forty-five minutes.

Gina climbed out of her truck and quietly closed the door. She'd been awake since before five, restless for no good reason she could put a finger on. She'd had trouble falling asleep thinking about what her father'd sprung on her and Joe about his health issue, wondering if her mother knew yet, fighting the fear that things were more serious than he'd let on. Hell, things *had* to be more serious if he agreed to tests that might take a couple days in the hospital. When she'd worked herself up to the point where she was thinking about everything in her life she couldn't change or fix, she was on the verge of being awake the entire night. Ordinarily when that happened, every few nights or so, she'd go over the next day's job, replay a ball game, or turn on the light and read a book until she was tired enough to stop thinking. But last night she didn't do any of those things.

She'd thought about the night in the tavern sitting with Carrie after the game and the phone call the night before, and how talking to her brought out something she'd almost forgotten—the ability to joke and play a little bit with a woman she liked. Heat crawled down her spine, reminding her not to BS herself. She liked Carrie, sure, she was smart and funny and quick and sharp. She was also very, very attractive. That hadn't helped her get to sleep, either.

And now here she was at 6:20, her hands in her pockets, feeling a little awkward.

"Sorry." Gina stopped at the bottom of the porch steps and shrugged. "I'm early and disturbing you. I'll just wait—"

"I'm up early too," Carrie said, "and I've got fresh coffee and the world's best blueberry corn muffins. Anything sound good?"

"Better than good." Gina grinned. Things didn't only sound good, they looked mind-blowing. Carrie wore a white tank top, and although Gina was careful not to drop her gaze, she was pretty positive there wasn't anything underneath. If that wasn't enough to short-circuit her already steaming brain, Carrie's long, tanned legs extended from pale blue boxers covered in— "Are those fishies on your boxers?"

Carrie looked down and turned an adorable shade of strawberry. "Oh my God. Yes. Christmas gift from my sister, who has really weird taste in clothes."

"I dunno, I think they're pretty nice." Gina rocked slowly on her heels, content to stay just where she was as long as the view never changed.

Carrie snorted and waved a hand at herself. "Obviously, I wasn't expecting company."

"I think you look great," Gina said.

"Well, thank you for not looking all that closely." Carrie stood. "Come on in—get your coffee and something to eat."

"If you're sure?"

"Totally, come on. I'm ready for a refill and, for some weird reason, I put three muffins in to warm this morning." Carrie smiled. "I must have known you were coming."

"Huh. And I ended up here a good forty minutes early. You think it's something in the muffins?"

"I hope not—because I still intend to eat them." Laughing, Carrie popped a muffin on a plate and handed it to Gina.

"I ought to warn you, construction workers are a little bit like cats." Gina spread a slab of butter on the muffin and poured a cup of coffee. "If you feed us, we'll keep hanging around."

"As long as you don't leave dead mice on my back porch, I'm

not going to complain." Carrie leaned back against the counter and gave Gina a slow smile that shot straight to her midsection, leaving her as breathless as a punch. Carrie's smile grew, as if she knew she was twisting Gina up, tight as a bowstring.

"It's really nice outside," Carrie said. "Let's go back."

"Okay, but my guys will be showing up at seven." Gina probably wasn't being very subtle, but she didn't want the guys seeing Carrie dressed like this. For some reason, she wanted to keep the image of her, relaxed and casually beautiful, all to herself. And thinking about the way they'd be looking at her, just natural, but still, the picture made the back of her neck itch. Not that she would blame them. But Carrie wasn't just any girl. She was…Carrie.

"We'll hear them coming, right?" Carrie said.

"Yep." Gina sat down and put her back against the post, and Carrie settled opposite her, mirroring her position. Their knees nearly touched as they balanced muffins and coffee in their laps. Right at that moment, Gina couldn't think of another place she'd rather be.

"So, how long have you been doing construction?" Carrie asked.

Gina tensed. No reason to be nervous—just a casual question. "Since I got out of high school. Almost seven years now."

Carrie did some quick math. Gina was just about her age. "Family business, right?"

"Right." Gina took a long swallow of coffee, fighting the discomfort of talking about herself, something she rarely did with anyone, even family these days.

"Did you always know you'd be joining your father?" Carrie broke her muffin apart and picked up a piece.

"No," Gina said, her throat tightening. She swallowed. "That came later. So, how about you? Are you following in the family footsteps somehow?"

Carrie laughed. "No way. My parents are slightly aghast I'm in the corporate world."

Gina breathed a little easier. On safer ground now. "Seems like a big accomplishment to me to be where you are."

"Thanks," Carrie said, coloring faintly. "I think they're happy for me. They just wonder where they went wrong." Carrie laughed, no sting in her words. "My father is a college professor—he teaches philosophy. My mom is…basically an instigator. She calls it being a political activist, but mostly she gets people together in support of one cause or another and makes a lot of noise in the right places."

"Wow. That sounds kind of wild."

Carrie rolled her eyes. "Oh, trust me, it can be. We had some pretty interesting discussions and meetings around my house growing up."

"Sounds like the opposite of mine," Gina said.

"How so?"

"Well, there's four of us kids, my two sisters and Joe. My father is an ex-Marine, so we were kind of raised like recruits. Sometimes there wasn't a lot of discussion."

"I think the middle ground is probably the best," Carrie said pensively, licking crumbs off her fingertip. "Kids need things to be clear and rules are helpful, but they also need to be able to think for themselves and question authority—" She laughed. "God, I can't believe I said that. It's a T-shirt slogan."

"I know what you mean, though." Gina had a hard time concentrating while watching Carrie lick her fingertips. The tip of her tongue danced over the pale pink flesh, flicking away crumbs, sliding across the seam of her lips, playful and sensuous and downright mesmerizing. She swallowed hard. Maybe having coffee and muffins with Carrie was a bad idea. One thing about construction work was it demanded concentration, and she needed to have a clear head. Otherwise she'd be dealing with hammered thumbs or worse. But for the next few minutes at least, she was going to enjoy the warm sensation curling in her belly. The sensation she hadn't experienced in a very long time.

Gina blinked, realizing Carrie was watching her with a curious smile. "Sorry."

Carrie smiled. "Why?"

"I have a feeling I was staring."

"I don't mind." Carrie took her time breaking off another piece of muffin. "You have beautiful eyes. When you're concentrating, they get darker."

"Ah…thanks," Gina murmured. Good thing Carrie didn't mind, since she couldn't seem to stop herself from looking at her.

"Don't tell me you've never heard that before."

"I can't say that I have."

"Then I'm glad I'm the first." Carrie would have asked her how that could possibly be, would have teased her a little, flirted a little, except for the quicksilver flash of pain that passed over her face. Okay—past relationships were a touchy subject. Of course, that made her all the more curious. And before she went too much farther down the road she seemed to be pulled down without any intention on her part, she really needed to know if there was a *present* relationship.

One part of her wished she didn't know about Gina's accident. That might be something else Gina didn't want her to know. She didn't probe, afraid to put that pain back in her eyes, even if she did want to know everything about her—especially what Gina thought about when she looked at her with that intense, slow gaze, and what brought the flashes of the devil into her eyes when she teased, or the faraway look she got when she sat on the porch looking out over the fields.

"The guys will be here soon." Gina stood abruptly and brushed the crumbs from her lap. "Thanks for breakfast."

"Anytime." Carrie rose too, leaving her cup and plate on the porch. She was running behind, should have been in the shower five minutes ago, and she still didn't want the day to start—or this moment to end. "Consider the coffee a standing offer. I can't vouch for the muffins, though."

"I suppose I could do the food part." Gina smiled. "What's your pleasure?"

"That's a dangerous line," Carrie said, relieved to see the clouds lifting from Gina's eyes. "It could be complicated."

"Oh, I don't know," Gina said slowly. "I can always get a couple different things, if you're not sure what you like."

"I'm pretty sure I know what that is." Carrie waited for the comeback, but none came. Only Gina's gaze moving languorously over her face, dropping to her mouth, heavy and thick and sweet as honey slowly coating her tongue. Gina suddenly seemed to be standing closer—had Gina moved? Had she? The air was so oddly still. The morning had been filled with the ever-present distant rumble of tractors, the twittering of birds building nests under the eaves of the house, the rush of water in the creek that ran a hundred yards away. All that disappeared, leaving only the drumbeat of her heart echoing in the silence.

Carrie obeyed the demand of something she barely recognized— the subtle, undeniable, irresistible bending of a flower toward the sun, the ebb and flow of waves against the shore, the slip of twilight into night. Inexorable, as natural as breathing. She lifted on her toes and leaned into her. Gina didn't move away.

When Carrie kissed her, her mind was absolutely clear, bright and sharp against the sweet softness of Gina's mouth. Gina's lips were warm and, after a heartbeat, gently questing, answering Carrie's careful explorations with her own. Carrie rested her fingertips lightly on Gina's bare arm. Gina's muscles rippled beneath her touch, and heat flooded Carrie's depths. She gasped, her lips parted slightly against Gina's. Through half-closed lids, she found Gina's smoky gaze and drifted in the hazy heat.

Gina chuckled low in her throat and Carrie's pulse jumped, slow-rolling storm clouds building inside. Gina tilted her head ever so slightly, her lips moving over Carrie's until they fit perfectly, breath to breath. No other parts of their bodies touched, but Gina's heart beat through Carrie's fingertips, a distant thunder, steady and strong and hinting of sweet danger. Carrie could have kissed her forever, standing in that one spot in the perfect silence, would have slid her fingers over smooth slick skin, searching for the places that made Gina gasp, if the rumble of a truck coming down the drive hadn't fractured the stillness like a scream splintering crystal. She backed away, feeling Gina's captivating gaze follow her.

"Well," Carrie said, breathless and unable to hide it, "that wasn't exactly what I was going to ask for."

A battered black Dodge Ram pickup pulled in behind Gina's and two guys in sleeveless tees and canvas work pants tumbled out, cardboard coffee cups in their hands, some conversation Carrie couldn't catch bouncing back and forth between them.

"Come to think of it," Carrie said, "I didn't ask at all, did I."

Gina sucked in a breath, looked toward the men in the yard. "I better get to work."

"Me too." Carrie waited for Gina to say something else—what, she had no idea. *Let's do that again, let's not do that again. Why the hell did you do that?* She couldn't answer that question, so she was glad Gina didn't ask. She was vaguely aware of the two guys approaching and wondered how she and Gina looked to the two of them—her standing there with not very much on and Gina just inches away. Hopefully not as exposed as she felt. She backed up toward her screen door and the safety beyond.

"Don't forget the game tonight," Gina said, watching her go. Frankie and Manny were right behind her, and as much as she didn't want Carrie to disappear, she didn't want the guys looking at her.

"I won't." Carrie slipped inside. The screen banged shut, and Carrie's silhouette was framed in the door.

Gina started breathing again, but her legs were still rooted in place. The rest of her was a tangle of nerves and questions and confusion. She should have said something. *You didn't need to ask. Permission granted. God, you can really kiss.*

Her lips were numb. Her head was buzzing. She fell back on habit and jammed her hands into her pockets. Carrie looked out at her, a little worried crease between her eyes.

"Thanks for the coffee," Gina called.

"You're welcome."

The shadows shifted, sunlight slanted across the porch, and Carrie was gone. Gina let out a sharp, pained breath. Her chest hurt, the emptiness she'd gotten used to burning like a flame reborn from embers.

"Everything okay, boss?" Manny stood at the foot of the stairs frowning up at her.

"Yeah. Great." Gina jumped down to join them, glad her legs held her up. She wondered if Manny could tell she was lying—no one ever seemed to be able to except Joe, who always knew when she was faking normal. The day stretched out before her like a prison sentence, timeless and empty. Only the evening and the promise of seeing Carrie again held any hint of reprieve.

CHAPTER SEVENTEEN

Carrie walked upstairs into her bedroom, closed the door, and methodically stripped off her clothes. Voices drifted up through her open window, floating on the same breeze that washed across her heated skin. She could pick out Gina's mellifluous alto offset by the deep rumble of a bass note and a lilting tenor accompaniment, but her perceptions were too stultified to make sense of the words. Her body was the strangest combination of numb and electrified—as if when she stepped off the porch and into her own kitchen she had somehow passed through a charged barrier or an invisible magnetic field that simultaneously stimulated every nerve ending while turning her mind and the tips of her fingers and toes into a state of frozen animation. Not altogether unpleasant, especially the tingling that accompanied every uneven breath. When she reached out to turn on the shower, she wondered for an instant whose hand that was. Taking a step back, she shook her head.

Okay, time to do a reality check.

She closed her eyes and took a deep breath. After a minute she could finally hear herself think, having never realized before she actually *could*. Thankfully, she was still her. All her limbs were still attached to the appropriate places. She hadn't suddenly been teleported into an alternate reality. Even if she wasn't behaving like herself, she was in fact still the woman she'd always been. Even as she comforted herself with her rational thoughts, she wondered if she really knew the woman she'd always been. She'd never thought of herself as lacking in confidence, and she always went after the things that she cared about. Her goals, her pleasures, the things that satisfied her—she didn't wait for them to come to her, she sought them out, she made them happen. The one area where she was always careful not to rush, though, was women. She knew what she wanted with women and had nurtured the picture for a long time. She didn't mind waiting until she was certain she'd found it. Gina did not fit the picture at all—she was distant and secretive and broody. She was sexy and seductive, but for all of her confidence, she hadn't made the first move. Or any move.

"Really? That's what's got you turned around?" Carrie murmured, hoping the sound of her own voice would restore her sense of balance. "You were really waiting for someone else to take the first step? Wow. That doesn't fit with the picture, either."

Time to readjust her picture of her own wants and desires, that was for sure. She stepped into the lukewarm water and adjusted the taps until it was as cool as she could stand without shivering. Time to get honest with herself. She'd kissed Gina Antonelli, and that was definitely off script. But oh, what a kiss. She'd kissed enough women to know what a good kiss was, and this one was off the charts. Gina had the softest, warmest, most demanding mouth she'd ever encountered. Her lips still smoldered from the hot glide of Gina's mouth and the taunting, teasing, knowing press of her tongue. Carrie swallowed a groan and ran her hands down her sides, lingering on the dip just above her hip bones where Gina's hands had lightly rested, simply making contact for a fleeting minute or two. And as light as that contact had been, she could still feel the imprint of Gina's hands on her flesh, never mind she'd been fully clothed at the time.

And thank goodness both of them had been fully covered and standing out on the porch in the full light of day, or she really might have ended up in uncharted waters. If those two guys hadn't shown up, she could very clearly see herself dragging Gina up the stairs and into the bedroom. Just thinking about another kiss and the possibility of Gina's hand skimming under her clothes and over her bare skin stirred a pulse beating pleasantly between her thighs. At least, the insistent thrum of desire would be pleasant if she was the least bit inclined to do anything about it, which she wasn't. Satisfying her own needs was enjoyable under most circumstances, but this time she had a feeling she'd be left wanting. Sometimes less than everything was worse than nothing at all.

Sometimes, settling was the same as losing, and one thing she never intended to do was lose before she'd even begun to play.

Carrie closed her eyes and tilted her head back as water streamed over her face, down her breasts, and along the swell of her thighs. With the memory of Gina's mouth on hers, she let herself imagine Gina's fingertips exploring and teasing and pleasing her. When the torture reached a painful pitch, she groaned and opened her eyes. There was only so much she could take. Even as she stood under the icy needles, heat raced beneath her skin. She bet steam was rising from her body, and God, she wanted one more taste of Gina.

She cut off the water with a frustrated twist of the knob, stepped out of the shower, and grabbed a towel. On autopilot, she dried off and blow-dried her hair for a few perfunctory minutes until her patience withered and died. At least the tangles looked intentional, rather then simply neglected. She'd planned on wearing tailored pants and a semicasual shirt, but opted instead for a straight tan skirt that ended a bit above her knees and a sleeveless silk shirt in a light shade of tangerine. She slipped into low-heeled sandals, headed downstairs for her bag, and stepped out onto the back porch feeling a lot more in control. Not being in her pajamas any longer was a plus. Gina turned at the sound of the screen door banging shut and stopped in her tracks, a hammer dangling from her right hand. Even from twenty feet away, Carrie could see Gina's stunned gaze travel down her body and back up to her face. She smiled, pleased she'd decided on the change of clothes. She almost imagined she could hear Gina swallow.

"Need me for anything before I go?" Carrie called.

Gina's heart kick-started back into motion, and she managed to get her legs to follow suit. She strode across the yard and stopped at the foot of the steps. The view up into Carrie's face was better than a summer sunrise—bright and brilliant and breathtaking. "Another speed record. I would've sworn it would take you a good two hours to look as good as you do right now."

"Thanks. Trade secret," Carrie said. "So maybe I'll see you at the game tonight."

"Right. Okay."

Carrie slipped past her and before she could get too far away, Gina called, "Hey, Carrie."

Carrie looked back over her shoulder, raising a brow in question.

Running on instinct, Gina said, "How about I pick you up after work, we grab something quick to eat and head over to the field together."

"Well, that depends."

"What are your terms?" Gina said.

"No pizza, no fast food."

"Okay, that's a challenge. But I accept."

Laughing, Carrie shook her head. "That's okay. Pizza is always good."

"Five o'clock at the hospital?"

Carrie nodded. "Unless there's an emergency, that will work."

"You have my number. If anything changes, let me know."

"I will. You have a good day." Carrie strode over to her zippy little car, started the engine, and zoomed away without looking back.

Gina shoved her hands in her pockets and turned to watch her until she disappeared around a bend in the driveway.

Manny came around the corner. "Hey, boss? We good to go?"

"Yeah," Gina said slowly, despite having no idea where she was headed, only knowing she wanted to go. "We're good."

❖

At a little after three p.m., Gina unbuckled her tool belt, slung it into the truck, and signaled to Manny and Frankie to finish up. "Let's call it, guys."

Another day of demo upstairs and they'd be able to start framing. Decent progress. She'd have to let Carrie know they'd be pulling the bathroom apart soon. As soon as she thought about Carrie, which she'd avoided doing with superhuman willpower all day, the kiss came roaring back into her consciousness and into every cell in her body. Her heart raced and her stomach did a full revolution with her standing still. She wiped sweat from her forehead with the back of her arm. If she was being honest, she liked the feeling.

"What do you think, boss," Manny said, mopping his neck with a red bandanna he'd pulled from his back pocket. "Are they going to pull us out of here when the job over at the hospital gets started?"

"Can't say for sure," Gina said, although she'd be willing to bet money the three of them plus a few more would be stuck here for the next few weeks. She didn't see her father changing his mind. She couldn't remember him changing his mind in recent history, for that matter.

Manny scowled. "Yeah, well, I don't mind doing this kind of thing, and it's pleasant working out here." He scanned the yard. "Pretty." He grinned. "And the owner's not bad to look at, either."

Gina gritted her teeth and let it go. Manny was harmless, and what he thought about Carrie was none of her business anyhow. Still, a twist of irritation and a whole lot of possessiveness hit her in the midsection and gnawed at her. "A job like this is a change from the big stuff, I'll give you that." She shrugged. "Once in a while it's nice to do some custom work."

"Can't argue," Manny said. "Well, I gotta get home. I promised the wife I'd watch the kids so she could have a girls' night." He shook his head. "I still can't figure out exactly what they do, but if she doesn't get to go, she's mighty unhappy."

Gina smiled. Manny was the kind of guy who looked rough and unfinished on the outside, but a day didn't go by he didn't mention his wife and children with pride. At the end of the day he was all about family. Gina understood that. She'd expected the same for herself, once upon a time. She could name the day when she'd stopped seeing that picture, but she couldn't recall when she'd finally accepted it.

"You'd better take off, then," Gina said, climbing into her truck. "I'll see you both in the morning."

She had a couple of hours to kill before she picked up Carrie and plenty of time to head home to take a shower. Time enough to take care of the thorn that kept stabbing at her insides all day. She made it to the Rivers in fifteen minutes, and as she'd figured, Joe's Mustang was still in the ER lot. Whenever she needed to find him, that was always the first place she looked. She rarely called him because if he was busy, she didn't want to interrupt him.

The patient part of the ER lot was mostly empty, a good sign. She parked next to Joe's muscle car and walked inside, pausing by reception to make sure no big crisis was under way. A baby cried somewhere in the depths of the ER, a phone rang at the central station, and muffled voices carried down the corridor. Nothing unusual. She waited by the desk until someone appeared.

"Hi, Gina." Pam, the nurse she'd met the last time she'd come looking for Joe, smiled at her. Today she wore skinny jeans, a white polo shirt, and teal running shoes. A stethoscope was looped around her neck, and an ID badge hung on a multicolored lanyard between her breasts. "What can I do for you?"

"I was looking for Joe. Is he busy?"

"I think he's almost finished. You want me to check?"

"No, that's okay. I'll just wait."

"I was about to take a break. Buy you a cup of coffee?"

Gina hesitated. She couldn't just hang around in the hall, and she didn't have a good reason to say no. "Ah…sure. That would be great."

Pam smiled. "Great. I'll tell Joe to text me when he's done."

"I appreciate it. Thanks."

Pam returned a minute later. "He's putting a cast on a six-year-old. Another monkey bar arm casualty."

Gina shook her head as they walked down the hall toward the cafeteria. "That was me when I was a kid. I loved the monkey bars. Broke my collarbone. My big sister broke her arm."

Pam laughed. "What about Joe?"

"Oh, he never got hurt. He always fell on his head."

"Well, I'm glad to see that all of you recovered." Smiling, Pam briefly ran her fingers down Gina's arm.

"Yeah, we did," Gina said, although she wasn't too sure, thinking about all the broken parts of her, inside and out. Maybe nothing would show up on an X-ray, but something somewhere deep inside felt wrong. Most of the time, she ignored the simmering discontent, just as she did the nagging discomfort in her ruined knee. These days, she was having a harder time convincing herself everything was fine.

The silence stretched and Pam studied her. "So, Joe happened to mention you're single."

Gina shook her head with a wry grin. "That's my brother. Mr. Subtle. Sorry if he embarrassed you."

"He didn't. I think working where we do," Pam said, pouring coffee from the big urn in the cafeteria, "you lose subtle really fast. What's the point of waiting when you might never get the chance to do what you want? There's kind of a live-now attitude for most of us, anyhow."

Gina poured her own coffee. "I can't take issue with that. And Joe is right as far as he knows."

They sat at a small table by the door and Pam added creamers to her coffee, studying Gina as she stirred them in. "As far as he knows. Okay, let me translate that. There's someone and you haven't mentioned her to him, or you'd like there to be someone."

"No, to the first. As to the rest, I'm a really bad bet for relationships."

Pam nodded. "How about an evening of something we both like—a movie, dinner, or whatever else comes up."

"I appreciate the invitation."

"But you're not ready."

Gina smiled thinly. Not ready was an understatement. Being ready meant changing everything. She mostly wasn't ready to think about what she wanted, and what she couldn't bear to have or lose again. "Something like that."

"Good enough. If things change, let me know. I think we might have a good time."

"Thanks," Gina said.

Pam's cell phone buzzed and she checked it. "Joe texted—he's done."

"I should head back," Gina said.

"Me too."

As they walked out to the hall together, Carrie came around the corner, a distant look on her face. She almost passed them by before she blinked and focused on Gina, her brows drawing down. "Gina?"

"Hey," Gina said, struck nearly mute as she always seemed to be when she first caught sight of Carrie. She looked even better than she had that morning. A stray lock of red-gold hair curled just in front of her ear and Gina had to fight not to reach out and brush it back with a finger.

Carrie smiled uncertainly in the silence, glanced at Pam and back to Gina. "Well, it was nice to see you again."

"Right." Gina looked after Carrie as she hurried past, sure she'd missed something and not clear what. Sighing, she muttered, "Perfect."

Pam laughed lightly as they started walking again. "Would that be the somebody you're not sure about exactly?"

"No," Gina said quickly. "She's actually a client. I'm…well, it doesn't matter. No problem."

"Uh-huh," Pam said brightly. When they reached the ER, she gave a little wave. "Thanks for the coffee, and remember what I said."

"Right. I will. Thanks again." Gina walked over to the workstation where Joe stood entering data into a tablet.

"Be right with you," he mumbled.

"Take your time." Gina replayed the brief encounter with Carrie and thought of all the things she should have said. Too late now. Cripes, what bad timing. Not that it mattered what Carrie thought about her and Pam. Not that there was anything to think.

"I see you and Pam connected," Joe said, sliding his tablet into a slot at the counter with his name on it. "Nice going."

"There's no connection. We had coffee." Gina scowled at him.

"First step," Joe needled.

"Just let it go."

He must have heard the warning in her voice. His expression sobered. "So what's up. Problem?"

Gina shook her head. "Sorry to bug you, it's just...Have you got a couple of minutes?"

"Sure. I'm waiting on some tests to come back, and things are quiet right now. You want a cup of coffee?"

Gina thought of Carrie and the cafeteria. "No, I'm good."

"Let's walk outside, then," Joe said.

They ended up leaning against her truck, a position almost as familiar to her as sitting in her own living room.

"So?" Joe said.

"It's about Dad. What do you think is really going on? Do we need to worry?"

Joe rubbed his face. "I wish to hell I knew. He won't tell me anything, and I can't exactly pry into his medical history. It's just not right."

"Yeah, but he's our father."

"Yeah, he is. And he's got a right to his privacy just like anybody else."

Gina dropped her head back against the cab of the truck, folded her arms across her chest, and closed her eyes. "I just have this really bad feeling. I'm being paranoid, right?"

"I don't know. Maybe. I hope so. Right now I don't think there's much we can do except wait and make it really clear to him he's got to tell us what's going on."

She cracked an eye and gave him a look. "And how well do you think that's going to work?"

He sighed. "I guess we're gonna have to talk to Mom."

"Man, if we do that before he tells her, he's gonna order us out to the garage for the rest of our lives."

Joe laughed. When they were kids and in trouble, their punishment was they had to move into the garage for however long he deemed appropriate for their crime. Sleeping on old sleeping bags with the mice wasn't so bad, but they weren't allowed to eat with the family, which basically meant foraging in the kitchen for things to eat after meals were over. It wasn't really much of a punishment, except the part where they missed dinner. "I hope that's as bad as we can expect."

"I know," Gina finally said. "I think we're going to have to wait. Hopefully he'll talk to Mom and the rest of us, and it won't turn out to be anything serious."

"Yeah. Waiting sucks." Joe sighed. "So what's really up with you and Pam?"

"Not a thing," Gina snapped. "We were having coffee, okay?"

Joe's brows shot up. "Whoa. Okay. Just wondering."

Gina pushed away from the truck. "Nothing to wonder about."

"You'll be at the game tonight?" Joe said, obviously making an effort to change the subject and make peace.

"Where else?"

"I'll be done at four. You want to get some pizza before you head over to the field? I don't have anything on tonight, so I'm going to go to the game."

Damn it, she could feel herself blushing. "Uh, no thanks." She huffed out a breath. "I sorta have plans to…you know, meet somebody for dinner."

Joe's eyes widened. "You're kidding me."

Gina clenched her jaw. "Can we not talk about this?"

"Hell no. We are so going to talk about it. What does *sorta have plans for dinner* mean?"

"Just what I said."

"With who?"

"Carrie Longmire."

Joe whistled. "Wow. Really."

"Yes," Gina said through her teeth, "really."

He grinned. "Okay, I'm impressed."

"There's nothing to be impressed about. We're just going to have something to eat before the game, okay? So let it go."

He held his hands up as if surrendering. "Okay. Absolutely. Just a little friendly sorta date." He started laughing and she punched him in the arm. He muttered an epithet their mother would scold him for and just laughed harder.

"I gotta go." Gina turned around and stalked to her truck, her brother's laughter following her. She needed to shower and figure out exactly what she was going to do for a casual dinner that had somehow become a date.

CHAPTER EIGHTEEN

At four forty-five, Carrie texted Presley. *Leaving at five. All quiet. Text if you need me.*

She'd skipped lunch to get caught up and had spent the afternoon hoping no emergencies would arise. The planets must've been aligned. Other than a few routine problems, easily handled, nothing had come up that she'd had to put through to Presley. The only potential disturbance on the horizon was her dinner with Gina, branded as a disturbance only because she had no idea what to expect or exactly what to make of it. The invitation had come out of nowhere and her acceptance had been just as spontaneous, not that she would've said no under any circumstances.

The idea of a casual meetup with Gina was…nice. Very nice. Exciting even. Carrie laughed to herself. Okay, so she was a little bit nervous and a lot intrigued. Not that all that much could happen in an hour, after all, and that's about all they'd have time for before Gina had to get to the field for the pregame warm-ups. A quick sandwich somewhere and on to the game. They could easily fill an hour talking softball if nothing else. Considering how little Gina talked about herself, that was all they might have to fall back on.

Of course, there was *one* other little matter she had to clear up, and considering the kiss she wasn't thinking about—*at all*—she'd have to get to it sooner rather than later. The matter being the status of Gina and the ER nurse she was with earlier. Carrie recognized the brunette from seeing her around the hospital and at some of the staff events, but she didn't know her other than to say hello. She was attractive, very, and it sure looked as if she and Gina were sharing a personal moment.

Her timing was usually a lot better than this—she didn't go around kissing women who had other involvements. Not that she went around kissing women out of the blue. Oh no. She only did that with Gina. She was usually a whole lot clearer too—she asked specifically about other relationships and got specific answers before venturing past the conversation stage. Obviously, she'd missed a few steps with Gina. Totally unlike her.

"Not smart, Longmire," Carrie muttered.

Presley's door opened and she stuck her head out. "What aren't you telling me?"

"Sorry?" Carrie flushed. "Could you hear me?"

"Only metaphorically. So? What's up?"

"Oh. Nothing."

"Uh-uh. Exhibit A." Presley held up one finger. "It's not quite five o'clock and you never leave before six." She held up a second finger. "Exhibit B. You never tell me when you're leaving because you know I don't care what hours you keep. Therefore, your leaving must have some significance." She came all the way out and closed her office door, holding up a third finger. "Exhibit C. You look guilty."

Carrie bristled. "I do not."

Presley grinned. "You do a little bit. More like you're keeping a secret, actually. Ergo, what aren't you telling me?"

"Absolutely nothing. I swear. I'm going to scout out the Hammers tonight. Just a little pre-tournament preparation."

"Okay. I'll buy that. The game is at what? Seven?"

"Six forty-five," Carrie said cautiously, sensing a trap.

Presley nodded. "And it's about ten minutes from the hospital. And you're leaving early."

"You know," Carrie said, "it's very annoying when someone knows your schedule as well as you know mine. Especially when that someone is your boss."

"What about when that someone is your best friend-slash-boss?"

"Even worse."

"You don't have to tell me if you don't want to." Presley looked contrite. "And I'm sorry if I'm being nosy."

"Oh, stop—you're not being nosy—at least not any more than I'd be given the same circumstances." Carrie pushed a hand through her hair. "Besides, it's hard to criticize when you're totally right on all counts. I'm acting like I've been body-snatched. I feel like it too."

Presley laughed. "Well, tell me quick, before the pod swallows you up."

"You're going to be disappointed. I'm just having dinner with Gina."

Presley pressed her lips together and nodded sagely. "That would explain the behavior. And I'm not going to even ask you for the details… beforehand. Only for a full report after."

Carrie gave up on getting any more work done, closed her programs, and logged out of her computer. She rose and grabbed her bag. "See, what you really should be asking me about is the kiss."

"There was a kiss?" Presley's arm shot out and grabbed her before she could step away. "You're not going anywhere."

"Yes, I am," Carrie protested. "I need to be downstairs in six minutes."

"Then talk fast."

"Actually, I can tell you everything in under thirty seconds." Carrie looked over her shoulder just to be certain no one lurked in the hall beyond the reception area. She lowered her voice as extra protection. "I was overcome by a moment of insanity, possibly inspired by a blueberry corn muffin and Gina's tool belt. And I kissed her this morning."

Presley narrowed her eyes. "This morning. You kissed her. When and where and for how long?"

"Perhaps it was the unnatural hour that led to my temporary irrationality," Carrie said. "I would put it at somewhere between six forty and six fifty. I can't be entirely certain, as I seem to have had some mental dysfunction at the time."

"Wow. What were you doing up before six forty-five?"

"I couldn't sleep. And Gina was early. And there was coffee and this urge…" Carrie held up her hands. "And then it happened."

"You do realize this is a significant occurrence."

Carrie vehemently disagreed, shaking her head to demonstrate. "It doesn't have to be. It was a kiss. People do that all the time and

it doesn't have any particular significance attached to it. To say good
night. Or thank you after a date. Or…or hello after having been apart
for a while. And since we haven't even had a date—"

"Exactly." Presley pounced. "That's what makes it significant.
None of the usual reasons apply. What did she do?"

"Picked up her metaphorical hammer and went back to work."

"Did she say anything?"

"I have to get back to work."

"No, you don't, you're done for the day."

Carrie smiled wryly. "No, that's what Gina said. *I have to get to
work.*"

"Oh boy." Presley laughed. "Knocked her off the rails, didn't
you?"

"That's what I would've thought, but she asked me to dinner just
a few minutes later."

"So she recovers fast," Presley said lightly.

Carrie blushed. Great—how about advertising she had sex on the
brain.

"She seems really nice," Presley said, pretending to ignore
Carrie's hormone spike. "In addition to the hotness factor. I hope you
have a great time."

"I'm sure it will be just a simple dinner," Carrie said. "No reason
to make too much of it."

"Why don't you just try to have fun and not think it to death. I
promise I won't harangue you too much, but you should probably call
me later."

Laughing, Carrie shouldered her bag. "I really shouldn't kiss and
tell."

"Oh, don't be ridiculous. Talk to you later."

Carrie took the stairs down to the lobby, not wanting to wait for
the elevator. She'd probably be early, but she didn't mind a few extra
minutes of anticipation. Like Presley said, no reason she couldn't enjoy
a simple dinner with an interesting woman.

❖

Gina leaned against the fluted two-story marble column in the
spacious hospital lobby, watching the clock set high at the junction

with the arched ceiling, its ornate gilded hands moving at a snail's pace toward five p.m. She knew from experience just how long five minutes could feel, especially when filled with helpless terror. She'd forgotten just how pleasurable those same minutes could be when her heart was thudding and her stomach churned with nervous excitement. The clock-watching helped keep her from twitching out of her skin.

Out of the corner of her eye, she watched the alcove where the elevators opened. Thirty seconds to go. She had a bet with herself that Carrie would materialize on the dot of five.

"You're early."

Gina jumped and spun around. Her heart made a bid for freedom, pounding against the back of her ribs. "Whoa."

"Scare you?"

"Nope," Gina said, recovering her cool as quickly as she could. "You're early too, by the way. Twenty-two seconds, to be exact."

Carrie laughed. "You're timing me?"

"Just a little bet with myself. Where'd you come from?"

"Oh!" Carrie pointed behind her. "I came down the staircase. The hall behind the columns turns left into the admin wing. It seems silly to walk all the way around to the elevators. I don't even know why they added one, way on the other side of the lobby."

"You see that a lot in old buildings like this," Gina said as they walked out through the main hospital doors, down the marble steps, and along the flagstone walkways between flower beds and stone benches shaded by maple trees. "The administration wing was added after the main body of the hospital—about eighty years ago, I think." She shrugged. "You always have to break through a wall somewhere with an addition, and a lot of times the easiest way to do that is to connect where it works structurally, but not necessarily for flow…" She trailed off and glanced at Carrie. "And you probably didn't need to know that, did you."

Carrie shook her head. "I love learning the history of this place. I've never worked anywhere like it before. The hospital itself is like…" She caught her lip between her teeth, sighed. "I know it sounds a little crazy, but it feels alive. Like an important member of the community."

"Hey, it doesn't sound strange to me. And besides, you're right. The history of this whole town lives in this place. Almost everyone was born here, almost everyone has someone who's died here. If the community has a heart, this is it."

"It must feel special to think about adding to it," Carrie said. "In a hundred years, someone will probably be talking about the addition you put on."

"Let's hope they're not cursing it. But yeah, it feels like a responsibility and an honor both." Gina slipped her palm under Carrie's elbow, guiding her onto a gravel walkway. "My truck's over here."

"I can follow you in my car," Carrie said. "Then you won't have to drive me back after the game."

Gina shook her head and opened the passenger side of her truck. "I don't mind. Besides, I don't think you'll want to take that pretty little car where we're going."

"Oh? Where are we going?"

Gina grinned. "Field trip."

Carrie stopped dead. "Ah, in case you haven't noticed, I'm wearing a skirt and sandals with heels. I'm not equipped to go hiking."

"Oh, I noticed the skirt. And I like the sandals, even if they seem impractical." Gina held out her hand and Carrie took it, automatically climbing up into the truck.

"Impractical? Oh my God. What a heathen."

"Guilty." Gina leaned against the door, her grin widening. "Don't worry, though. I promise you won't have to walk very far, and if the going gets too rough, I'll carry you."

Carrie threw back her head and laughed. "Oh, right. That's so not happening."

"Offer stands." Gina closed the door, sprinted around to the other side, and climbed behind the wheel. She headed down the winding road to town, turned left, and in five minutes, they were driving through the countryside.

"Are you going to tell me where we're going?" Carrie asked.

Gina shook her head. "It wouldn't be a surprise if I did that."

"I don't remember you saying that it was going to be a surprise dinner."

"It was kind of a spur-of-the moment thing."

"Dinner, or the surprise part?"

Gina glanced over at her. Carrie had rolled the window down, and the wind blew her hair into long gleaming golden red tangles. "How come you're not complaining about your hair?"

Carrie frowned. "My hair? Why? Is there something wrong with it?"

Gina reached over and caught some of the flyaway strands in her fingers, the back of her hand lightly brushing Carrie's neck. "Not a thing. It's just you're not fussing about the wind messing it up."

Carrie shifted to face her, and Gina's fingers rested against the side of her jaw for a fleeting instant. Carrie tensed, and Gina slowly pulled her hand back and settled it on the wheel.

"Do women usually complain about that when you're driving?"

"It doesn't come up very often," Gina said, her voice dropping.

"I don't mind it. I'm in love with the air around here," Carrie said. "I've never smelled air so good, and I love the way it feels on my skin. So if you don't mind a few tangles, neither do I."

Gina steadfastly stared straight ahead. The churning in her stomach had moved on to a full burn. Carrie had no idea how sensual she looked with a faint flush to her cheeks, a bright gleam in her eyes, and a mane of red hair framing her face. The sexy shirt and skirt were a nice addition, but she would have looked just as heart-stopping in a faded T and jeans. "I like your hair a lot. I especially like it when it's a little messed up."

"I'm really afraid that you're referring to bedhead. Did I have bedhead this morning?"

Gina shot her a quick look, remembering how hot she'd looked in that tank top and boxer shorts and no shoes. "You looked gorgeous this morning. Made it kinda hard to breathe, to tell you the truth."

"Well," Carrie said, instantly breathless herself. "I won't take issue with that."

If Gina kept saying things like that to her while looking at her as if she wanted to peel her clothes off, she was going to combust. Thankfully, Gina put her blinker on and turned down a narrow dirt lane that rapidly deteriorated into an overgrown tractor path. The rough excuse for a road demanded all her attention and gave Carrie a chance to corral her runaway libido.

"I'm very glad we're not walking," Carrie said. "And you were right about my car. I can't believe your truck actually fits down here."

"We're almost there. Doing all right?"

"I'm good." Carrie glanced behind her as Gina turned into a stand of pines. She could no longer see the road. The air was noticeably cooler as dappled sunlight streamed through the dense branches overhead. She heard birds and nothing else. "Where are we?"

"On the back border of my grandmother's farm."

"So you *are* from around here," Carrie said, feeling as if she'd won the lottery with that little tidbit. "Where does your grandmother live?"

"She doesn't. She passed on five years ago. I live in her house, and this is my land now."

"Oh." Carrie craned her neck and couldn't see anything that looked like pastures or a farmhouse. "Do you live here?"

"Yep. The front forty is over that rise we passed coming in, but I didn't think you'd enjoy taking the tractor path to get here, so we came the long way around."

"How much of it is there?"

"Not all that much. About a hundred acres now."

Carrie laughed. A hundred acres. "Yeah, kind of a small place."

Gina stopped the truck, leaned over, and lifted a clean patchwork quilt from the back of the cab. "Can you carry that?"

"Sure."

"Okay. Wait just a second." Gina jumped out, pulled a wicker basket from behind the seat, and circled around to open Carrie's door. "Hungry?"

Carrie clutched the blanket to her chest, reached for Gina's hand, and carefully climbed down. The ground beneath the ceiling of evergreens was layered with a fragrant carpet of pine needles, soft and yielding beneath her feet. Their tangy sweet fragrance rose to tease her with every step.

"We're having a picnic, aren't we," Carrie said softly.

"Yeah. Is that okay with you?"

Carrie nodded, still holding Gina's hand and wondering if Gina realized it. They were having a picnic, alone in a hidden spot that Gina chose, a million miles away from her everyday life. Oh, that was more than all right with her.

"I love the idea."

"Good," Gina said, relief flooding through her. "You said no pizza and no McDonald's. My choices were limited, so I thought I could wow you with location instead."

Carrie glanced sideways at her. Gina had changed out of the work clothes she'd been wearing earlier into a short-sleeved washed denim shirt, dark jeans, and running shoes. Her hair was as windblown as Carrie's felt, but not long enough to actually tangle. Instead, the dark locks looked wild and as untouched as their surroundings. A lot like Gina. "Oh, believe me, the wow factor is good."

Gina led her down a slope and stopped by the side of a pond bordered on the far side by a thicket of rushes and marshy grasses. She held her hand out for the quilt and spread it on a grassy patch by the edge of the water. Carrie sat down, kicked off her sandals, and stretched out her legs. She watched as Gina knelt and opened the picnic basket, her amazement growing as Gina removed two wineglasses, folded linen napkins, two plates, utensils, and a bottle of wine.

"I'd almost think you had this planned," Carrie said. "How did you manage this so quickly?"

Gina worked the corkscrew into the top of the red wine bottle. "The picnic basket has been in my grandmother's pantry—well, my pantry now—for as long as I can remember. Same thing with the napkins. They're in the sideboard along with a lace tablecloth that I can't imagine ever using. The wineglasses, well, everybody has wineglasses, right? Plates from the cupboard, quilt from the bedroom, and—" She reached into the picnic basket and removed two covered dishes and set them on the quilt next to the plates. "Confession time. I called my mother and said I needed food for a picnic right away."

Carrie laughed. "You didn't."

"What else was I to do? You already nixed my number one and two choices."

"I wouldn't mind sandwiches. I said no McDonald's."

"McDonald's makes sandwiches."

"Those are not sandwiches. And stop trying to distract me. What did your mother say when you said you needed food for an emergency picnic?"

Gina looked away, but not before Carrie saw the shadows clouding her eyes. "She didn't ask."

"Hey," Carrie said gently, stroking the back of her hand, "this is amazing. Thank you."

Gina refocused on her, and the tension left her face. "Well, my mother's chicken is a wonder to behold. So is her potato salad. You ready?"

"Oh, more than ready."

Gina uncovered the dishes, scooped out salad onto the plates, and added pieces of cold chicken to each. She handed the plate to Carrie, poured wine for both of them, and stretched out beside Carrie. She tipped her glass to Carrie. "Enjoy."

"I already am," Carrie said softly, her eyes never leaving Gina's. Finally, she tried the potato salad and moaned in appreciation. "Oh my God. This is fabulous."

"Yeah, there's not a whole lot of point in learning to cook when food like this is pretty easy to come by."

"Speak for yourself. Neither of my parents has much in the way of culinary expertise." Carrie sipped the wine, a nice choice of zinfandel. "But I do make a mean grilled cheese sandwich."

"I like grilled cheese."

"I'll remember that the first time I have you to dinner."

"All right." Gina leaned on an elbow, as relaxed as Carrie had ever seen her.

Whatever memory had brought out the shadows had passed.

Carrie stretched her bare toes toward the still pond. A blue heron lifted out of the reeds on the far side and wafted majestically into the sky. Frogs thrummed a deep chorus, and a pair of dragonflies flitted by in the midst of an aerial mating dance. The air sang with the promise of endless summer. "This place is amazing. Does anyone ever come here?"

"Not anymore. I used to swim here when I was a kid." Gina looked around and slowly shook her head. "It seemed so much bigger then."

"Perspective," Carrie murmured. "Things always seem different, unchangeable and forever, when we're young."

"I haven't been here since high school."

"I'm glad you brought me."

Gina captured Carrie's hand and slowly entwined their fingers. "Me too."

CHAPTER NINETEEN

A shaft of sunlight reflected off the still surface of the pond and illuminated Gina's face, painting the angle of her jaw and the arch of her cheekbone in brilliant gold. A butterfly lifted from a stand of wild tiger lilies, its multihued wings sparkling in the air. Carrie committed the mental snapshot to memory, hoping she could hold the image forever. In that still, quiet moment, she understood beauty as something that lived in the heart.

"I'm afraid to breathe," she whispered. "I might break the spell."

"You won't."

"I love that you brought me here. I'm just having a little trouble thinking right now." Carrie brushed her thumb over Gina's fingers. "This place is amazing, and you're very beautiful."

"I can't think of anything except you right now," Gina murmured, sliding closer until their shoulders and thighs touched, food forgotten, the taste of wine still on her lips. "I have to kiss you."

"Before you do," Carrie murmured, caught in the shifting depths of Gina's fierce gaze, "tell me there isn't someone with a claim on you."

Gina stilled, her fingers tightening on Carrie's. "What if I can't?"

The disappointment was piercing, larger than she expected, huger than it had any right to be. But there it was. A sharp, cold blade sweeping around her heart, severing ties that promised to bleed forever. "Then I think you probably shouldn't kiss me."

Gina had lived with one truth for so long she couldn't find another, but she gripped Carrie's hand, held her still when she would have pulled away. "What if I told you it was an old claim, a memory more than anything else?"

"Then I'd say it must've been a powerful love." Another time, Carrie would have asked who, would have asked more, but she knew, somewhere inside, what the answer must be. Today, this moment, the only answer she needed was the desire in Gina's eyes.

"There's no one today—not Pam, if that's what you were thinking." Gina knew they were balanced on the edge of possibility, on one side of the precipice a retreat into the world she'd defined for herself, convinced herself she wanted, and on the other side, a dangerous path she wasn't sure she could take. All she knew was in this moment, she hungered. "She's a friend of my brother's, and I barely know her."

"A kiss might be a very bad idea," Carrie murmured, caught between desire and confusion and unable to look away from Gina's mouth. A kiss was just a kiss, she'd said that before, hadn't she? How could she have been so wrong.

"Why?" Gina curled Carrie's hand against her chest, letting Carrie feel the flight of her heart, the rush of her breath. "Can't you tell how much I want you?"

Carrie pressed her palm flat against Gina's chest. Gina trembled, a fine shiver that raked through her like wind in flames. "You have to get to the game."

Gina laughed unsteadily. "Who are you trying to convince? Yourself or me?"

"Oh, I don't need to be convinced about the kiss." Carrie traced a finger along the edge of Gina's jaw, slid her fingers to her nape, stroked the soft skin beneath the collar of her shirt. "I've been thinking about another kiss since—"

Gina's mouth stopped her words, stopped her breath, stopped every single thought. Gina's mouth was a hot demand, insistent and possessive. Gina's kiss asked no questions, offered no answers, only claimed.

The kiss pierced Carrie's deepest reaches like a clarion call.

This is who I am. Here is what I want. Let me have you.

Carrie grasped Gina's shoulders and surged against her, crushing her breasts to Gina's chest. Gina gasped and deepened the kiss, her lips a relentless victor, taking and taking until Carrie couldn't breathe. She twisted her fist in Gina's hair and dug her fingers into the rigid muscles of Gina's shoulders, dragging Gina over and down. Then she was on her back, and Gina was above her, braced on one arm, the other hand on her hip, and Carrie had to close her eyes against the sunlight blazing in Gina's eyes.

Gina's leg slid over hers and wedged between her bare thighs, catapulting Carrie to a screaming pinnacle of need. Carrie's skirt rode up to her hips, molding around Gina's rough denim-covered thigh the way she wanted to encase Gina inside her. She arched and grasped Gina's ass, pulling her tighter, writhing against the unbearable pressure tormenting her swollen flesh. Gina made a growling sound low in her throat, her fingers tightening on Carrie's hip, and abruptly rolled on top of her, her weight a tantalizing promise of power and possession.

Carrie rubbed the thin cover of her silk panties against Gina's jeans, and the ache grew more urgent. She curled her calf over Gina's, desperate for just a little more, just a little harder, God, just *right there*.

Gina drove her leg harder, higher, obeying Carrie's demand.

"God! Wait!" Carrie broke away, throwing her head back as she struggled not to come.

Breathing hard, Gina buried her face in Carrie's neck. "I'm about to lose it."

Carrie brushed her mouth over Gina's ear. "So am I. I'm right on the edge of crazy. Do. Not. Move."

"I better." Gina shoved herself up on both arms and planted her palms on the quilt on either side of Carrie's shoulders. Carrie's face was flushed, her eyes bright, her lips swollen. Gina hungered for her, starving for all the years she'd pretended not to feel the gnawing ache in her depths. "If I touch you again, I'm going to put my hands on your skin and I'm not going to stop."

Carrie swallowed, torn between unbearable need and a deeper demand she couldn't define. "You should get off me right now. Another second, and I'm going to beg for your hands all over me."

Gina groaned and closed her eyes, forcing herself to roll over onto her back, her chest heaving, her heart threatening to explode. Carrie's hand grazed her bare arm, fingers gliding lower. She clasped them desperately. The sun burned against her closed lids. She might be dying, the pleasure was so sharp. "I can call one of the guys, have them stand in for me tonight at the game."

"And then what?"

Gina turned her head. Carrie watched her from beneath half-lowered lids, her eyes deep pools of desire, daring her to drown. "Then I can take off all your clothes and make love to you right here until…"

"Until?"

"Until you can't breathe anymore. Until I can't move anymore."

Carrie laughed, sounding a little insane to her own ears. "The first time you do that, I intend to be in a bed."

"Negotiable?"

"Maybe, but not tonight."

Gina rolled over, gently clasped Carrie's jaw, and turned her face until she could kiss her. She was careful with the kiss when she'd been reckless before, gentle where she'd been rough. "I hear you. I just want you so damn much."

"I know." Carrie smiled a little tremulously. "It's safe to say you make me crazy like nobody else. Which is a good reason to stop."

"Why?"

"I don't know. I'm just…"

"Afraid?" Gina wondered what Carrie saw in her eyes, beneath the terrible need. Could she see the terror, the remorse, the guilt?

"Maybe." Carrie pushed herself up, pulled her skirt down. "I don't usually lose my mind from a kiss." She glanced at Gina. "We should go or I'm going to make you kiss me again, and I don't think I'm going to let you stop this time."

Gina lowered her forehead to Carrie's and groaned. "I'm not sure I can walk yet."

"Good." Carrie pushed away, tucked in her shirt, and pulled on her sandals with shaking fingers. Gina scared the hell out of her. No one had ever turned her on so much, so fast, and made her want to be taken so badly. She needed time to figure out what she was doing. She needed not to make a mistake. If she hadn't already.

❖

Abby stopped halfway up the staircase to the loft and rapped on top of the wooden railing to announce herself. "Blake? Okay to come up?"

"Yeah," Blake called.

Abby climbed the rest of the way up and stopped at the foot of Blake's bed. He was propped up on two pillows in his usual attire of cut-off sweats and a loose short-sleeved T-shirt, his laptop propped up against his knees. His hair was a half an inch longer then he usually wore it and tousled, his unlined face free from pain. His face had changed in the last two years, especially since he'd started hormone therapy. Like all boys his age, his facial bones had started to grow heavier, his jaw thicker, his features losing their youthful, androgynous beauty and edging toward handsome. His body, too, had changed even before the surgery. He'd gotten taller, added muscle to his torso.

She stood just taking him in, the familiar push-pull of love and worry washing over her. She would have worried about him under any circumstances. Growing up was always difficult, fraught with challenges and changes, and as her life in the ER testified to every day, victim to danger and fickle fate. Blake wasn't that much different than any other teenager in so many ways, except one, and every day those differences grew less apparent.

"What, Mom?" Blake regarded her curiously. "Are you worrying about something again?"

Abby laughed. "You are not supposed to be able to tell what your mother is thinking."

He rolled his eyes. "Then maybe you shouldn't think so loud."

"Good advice. How are you doing?"

He shrugged. "I'm fine. I'm really bored."

"I've got a couple of surprises for you."

"Yeah?" He dumped his laptop onto the bed and sat up straighter.

"Flann stopped down to the ER this afternoon and dropped off a new vest for you."

He grimaced. "Oh, my favorite thing."

"I think you'll like this one better than the binder one. It's lightweight, zips up the front, and doesn't have much in the way of shoulder straps. Flann says it's your step-down vest."

"It's gotta be better than the corset I'm wearing." He swung his legs over the side of the bed and stood up. "Can I change into it now?"

"Sure. You want some help?" He usually said no and she expected him to again. Being independent was very important to him, and she suspected he was still a little shy about having anyone see him without a shirt on.

"Okay, thanks," he said after a pause. "I think the Steri-Strips are ready to come off too."

"We've got some new ones. I can reapply them if it looks like you need them." Abby hesitated. "Unless you want Flann to do it."

Blake grinned. "Don't worry, I know you can do it just as well."

Abby laughed. "You probably don't want to mention that to the God of surgery."

"No way," Blake said. "So do you want to do it now?"

"Sure."

He gripped the bottom of his T-shirt, and as she had done hundreds of times, probably thousands of times in their life together, she stepped forward, grasped the bottom edge, and lifted it up over his head as he raised his arms into the air.

As his head came through and she freed the material, Blake smiled. "I could probably have done that by myself."

"Habit. It's a mother thing."

"Yeah." He released the Velcro straps that ran along each side of his binder, unzipped the center portion, and carefully unwrapped it from his chest. He sighed and wriggled his shoulders. "Boy, that thing sucks. What's the new one look like?"

Carefully not looking at him yet, Abby opened the plastic bag and extracted the replacement vest, a lightweight white stretch material that was more fitted and styled like an undershirt. She held it up.

"Oh yeah, that's a lot better." Blake sat down on the side of the bed. "So, what do you think?"

Abby placed the vest along with her second package on the bed and pulled over a chair so she could sit. She tilted the shade on the bedside lamp to focus the light on his chest. Two or three flesh-colored paper strips covered the lower edge of each nipple. Their edges curled loosely and she doubted they were doing much good at this point. Scattered black and blue marks, already fading, dotted his upper chest and sides. Except for a little swelling right underneath his nipples, his chest looked like any other adolescent boy's. "Everything looks great. You're right, those Steri-Strips need to come off."

Blake gently ran his fingers over his chest. "It's kind of amazing."

"It is."

He met her gaze. "Not what you expected when I was born, huh?"

Abby took his free hand. "You know, from the time you were little and didn't always do what I expected you to do, I reminded myself you would be your own person one day. Every parent has to learn that lesson sooner or later. All I wanted for you was happiness and that you have the life you want and the love you deserve. Nothing has changed about that."

"Just so you know," Blake said, allowing her to hold his hand, a rare treat these days, "I'm really happy."

"Then we're definitely headed in the right direction." Abby leaned over and kissed his cheek. "How about I change the Steri-Strips, and we'll get you into the new vest."

"Can I ask you something?" Blake said as Abby gently peeled off the Steri-Strips.

"Sure." Abby opened another package, cleaned the incisions with a cotton swab, and reapplied the paper strips.

"It's about your favorite topic."

Abby glanced up at him. "Okay, that would be books, movies, or...?"

He grinned, looking as if he was trying to cover his discomfort. "Sex."

"Aha. All right. Shoot."

"Do you think you can love somebody without having sex with them?"

"That's an easy one." Abby sat back in the chair. "Absolutely. I love a lot of people who I've never had sex with. Harper and Presley, for example. I love both of them. Presley's been my best friend since you were a baby, and I can't imagine not having her nearby now that we're close again."

"Have you ever wanted to have sex with someone you loved, but didn't?"

"That's getting harder. A few times I thought I was in love and the other person didn't feel the same, so no sex. I can think of at least one time when I had really serious feelings for someone who was with someone else. So that was a no sex time too." Abby wanted to ask why he was asking and who he was asking about, but when he was talking wasn't the time for her to probe. It was time for her to listen and hope she had the right answers. Or at least answers that helped him find his own.

"How about sex with somebody you *didn't* love. You know, just sex."

She laughed shortly. "Okay, so now you're getting personal. Some things have to be private."

He grinned. "Theoretically, then."

"I think what you're asking me is if love and sex always go together."

Blake was analytical. He got that from her. He didn't jump to conclusions. He thought things through, and she could see him thinking about what he was really asking. Finally, he said, "I think that's right. So I guess my question is about when you ought to have sex—because sometimes it seems like your body's in the driver's seat."

"Wow. Okay." Abby took a deep breath. "First, let me say I think sexual feelings are perfectly natural under all kinds of circumstances. We have hormones and all kinds of neurochemicals that influence the way we feel physically and sexually—"

"I know that part, Mom."

"Right. So let's just assume that all sexual feelings are okay."

"Okay."

"So then the question is when, right?" Abby said.

He nodded.

"I don't need to say first of all when it's consensual, but I will just for the record."

Blake rolled his eyes. "Well, of course."

"I think the next step after mutual desire is mutual understanding." She didn't need to spell out things for him. He was too smart for that. If she tried, he'd just be insulted.

After a moment, Blake said, "You mean making sure that it means the same thing to both people."

"As much as is possible." Abby sighed. "Unfortunately, sometimes people have sex for reasons that aren't the same as what they say."

"But how are you supposed to know that?"

Abby blew out a breath. "Unfortunately, you can't always. If something feels off, if you have this sense that the other person is using sex for something other than connecting and expressing love and desire, then I would say you want to wait."

"Man, that must be why everybody says sex is complicated."

"It's a tough one, baby," Abby said.

He winced at the endearment.

"I'm sorry. I know. But really, I'm probably going to call you that until you're fifty."

"Great."

Abby smiled. "So is this helping at all?"

"I think so. I kinda came to the same conclusions."

"Good. Wanting to be physical with someone you care about is a natural thing. If you can, talk about it first." She patted his leg. "And I happen to know you're a very good communicator."

"Yeah, okay." Blake relaxed. "So what's in the other bag?"

Abby laughed. "Your other present."

"Yeah?" His voice lifted in anticipation.

She handed it to him, and he instantly dug inside and pulled out a T-shirt. He held it up, his eyes widening.

The black shirt was emblazoned with the logo of the old rock band the Doors. Abby couldn't figure out exactly why so many teenagers seemed to love music that was already old when she was young, but she'd heard enough of it on the station Margie and Blake favored to figure out what he liked.

"Oh, wow. This is great." Blake frowned. "But it's a medium."

"I know," Abby said gently. "I don't see any reason why you can't wear a T-shirt that fits you now."

He lowered the shirt, gripping it in his fists. He always wore extra-large T-shirts to hide what little breast tissue hadn't resolved with the hormone therapy. Now he wouldn't have to. "I think you're way too cool to be a mom."

Abby blinked at the stinging in her eyes. "Well, I am, and always will be yours. Come on, let's get you into the shirt. You ready?"

He rose, zipped up the new vest, and lifted his arms. Laughing, Abby pulled the shirt down over his head, the way she'd done thousands of times.

CHAPTER TWENTY

D id you learn anything tonight?" Gina asked as she pulled out of the dusty field onto the dirt road bordering the ball field.

Carrie rolled down her window and let in the twilight. The sun dropped low off to the west, taking with it some of the heat of the day and promising a brief respite. She'd sleep with the windows open tonight. "Not as much as I thought I would."

"Why is that?"

"I was a little distracted."

Gina grinned and watched the road. "Why is that?"

Carrie laughed. Gina had a knack for teasing her into revealing more than she wanted to, before she was ready. Before she even understood herself what she was feeling. That ability to pull her out of herself, out of her head, was part of Gina's considerable charm, and part of what scared her. Gina walked through her normal self-defenses as if they weren't even there, a skill that made her damn near irresistible. Carrie played for time to organize her thoughts by watching the lights reflected in the side-view mirror. A steady stream of pickups and SUVs followed them to the first intersection, some peeling off right and others falling in behind them on the way back to town. Everywhere else, the darkness closed in, leaving her and Gina in their own private world. "I was trying to watch the game and assess the management strategy at the same time."

"That's a lot to take in."

"Uh-huh. Especially when every time I looked at the coach, I remembered kissing her. And a few other things." So much for keeping the parts she didn't fully know what to make of to herself. The place where they'd picnicked had only been a few minutes away from the ball field, and her body, hell, her entire system—mind *and* body—was supercharged by the time she got out of the truck and followed Gina to the Hammers' bench. Some of Gina's team members had given Carrie a second look and then cast an inquiring glance at Gina, but Gina didn't introduce her to anyone. She was just as glad. She didn't really have the concentration to make small talk. She'd found an empty corner on one of the benches and stayed there for the whole game. Half the time she'd actually been able to pay attention. The other half she'd spent working hard to ignore the insistent pounding of arousal that rose from her depths and spread into every cell of her body. She'd managed not to confess to *that*, at least. "Like I said. Distracting."

"You might've noticed I wasn't looking in your direction." Gina glanced at her, the heat in her gaze obvious even in reflected light off the dash. "At least not when I could help myself."

"And why is that?" Carrie's pulse spiked. So maybe she hadn't been the only one suffering for the last three hours.

"Every time I caught sight of you, I thought about how good it felt with you underneath me, and then I instantly imagined how good it would feel to be insi—"

Carrie snapped up a hand. "Enough. Don't get me started again."

Gina gave an altogether arrogant and self-satisfied chuckle. "Can't see why not."

"Because you're going to be dropping me off at my car in approximately four minutes and twenty-eight seconds. And I need to concentrate to drive the rest of the way home."

Gina turned her head, gave Carrie a long look. "I could drive you all the way home."

That was an invitation she couldn't possibly misinterpret. Part of her leapt up and screamed, *Yes. Absolutely. Hurry.* Another part grabbed her by the back of her neck and shook her like a puppy about to wander into traffic. If she let Gina drive her home, she would take Gina inside and upstairs to her bedroom. And they'd still be there in the morning, she was certain of that. She wanted it, desperately, and she didn't know why. Oh, her body knew why—Gina was incredibly sexy and stirred her up to a fever pitch just by kissing her. If she let Gina go any further than that, Carrie was pretty sure she'd disintegrate in a fireball. But she needed to understand what was going on besides being more turned on than any woman had ever gotten her before, because she wasn't about just sex. She never had been. In fact, sex had never been the number one motivator in any kind of relationship. Of course, thinking back, every single relationship seemed pale and nearly transparent compared to this one.

"You're thinking awfully hard," Gina said.

"That's where you're wrong," Carrie said quietly. "I'm not thinking at all. And that worries me."

"Then I'll take you back to your car." Gina didn't sound angry or even upset. Just definite. "Because the last thing I want between us is regrets."

"And you're so certain about jumping into bed?" Carrie asked.

Gina's laugh was short and hard. "Hell no. All I know is I can't stop thinking about you, and every time I think about you, I have this ache so huge to touch you I can't breathe."

Carrie let out a long shaky breath. "Well, a line like that will get you pretty far."

"It's no line." Gina whipped into the drive to the Rivers and gunned the truck up the twisting road to the hospital. She pulled in next to Carrie's Mini and braked to a sharp stop. "But you don't know me well enough to know that."

"You don't talk much about yourself," Carrie murmured, "but your actions speak pretty loudly."

Gina stretched an arm across the seats and stroked Carrie's cheek. "I want to make love to you. Plain enough?"

"Oh," Carrie said, her breath catching. "You don't know how much I want to take you up on that."

"But?"

Carrie tilted her head and Gina's fingers feathered down her throat. She shivered and desire twisted in her depths. She didn't trust herself alone in the dark with Gina and Gina's hands on her for very long. If she gave the word, Gina would drive her home right now, and they'd be in bed before the engine cooled. A big part of her would be very satisfied come morning. She opened the door, and when Gina opened hers, she shook her head. "I really like it when you come around and hand me out like this is a carriage and I'm a princess." She laughed.

"But I'm afraid any contact right at this moment would be all kinds of dangerous."

"Are you afraid of me?" Gina murmured, dark and oh so very dangerously sexy.

"More of me, I guess." Carrie paused. "You do have secrets, and I…I think maybe they scare us both."

Gina went still, her hand cupped on Carrie's neck. After a long moment, her thumb brushed over Carrie's jaw and her hand fell away. "Some secrets should stay buried."

"Only you can decide that, but if I end up in bed with you, I'm going to find those secrets hard to ignore." Carrie slid her leg out, feeling her skirt climb up her thigh as she swiveled around and dropped to the ground. "So I'm going to say good night, before I do."

"I'm sorry."

"Don't be. That was the best picnic and, without a doubt, the best kiss I've ever had. Good night."

The truck door closed and Gina sat with the motor running, the headlights angled toward Carrie's car as she watched her make her way across the lot. She wanted her, but she couldn't deny the relief that flooded through her. She'd never been afraid of her desire before, but she'd been young and stupid when she'd first fallen in love. She wasn't a kid anymore, and she ought to know better. The places inside that Carrie wanted her to expose had died a long time ago, and Carrie deserved more than just her need. She knew how dangerous selfish need could be. When Carrie got in her car, closed the door, and started the engine, Gina backed around and swiftly headed out. She didn't look back.

❖

"Hey, Carrie, you want to ride over to the game with me and Joe?" Flann said at five forty-five on the first night of the tournament.

Carrie hesitated. She wasn't exactly feeling sociable, but she needed to get into game mode double-quick. For the next three hours, at least, she couldn't afford to think about anything except what she needed to do to help her team win. To help her team beat the Hammers. Gina's team. Gina, whom she'd seen for all of ten minutes in the last couple of days, when they passed each other in the morning at her house. Gina and her guys arrived together promptly at seven a.m. Gina, apparently, wasn't having any trouble sleeping, unlike Carrie, who not only woke up every few hours but lay awake thinking of things she didn't want to think about. She forced herself to at least close her eyes and pretend to relax until her normal wake-up time and left for work as usual at seven fifteen. By then Gina and her crew had set up their saws and air guns and ladders and whatnots. Carrie nodded to them as she went to the car and received a perfectly polite and noncommittal response from Gina along with hearty hellos from the guys. And that was that.

Gina hadn't called her.

To be fair, she hadn't called Gina, either. She wasn't entirely sure why. She'd gotten way past the point of not calling up girls she was interested in by the end of high school. She didn't want to think she was trying to force Gina into proving something. Even worse, she didn't want to think she was being a coward and avoiding her own feelings. To be honest, it was probably a little bit of both. She'd told Gina she wasn't ready to go any further than the kiss, which was true enough as far as it went. She definitely *wanted* to go further than the kiss. She hadn't been thinking about much else in the last forty-eight hours and had proven her theory that coming by herself to thoughts of Gina making her come was definitely not enough to satisfy. Orgasms were always good. Did anyone ever have a bad orgasm? But none of them left her satisfied. Somewhat less than crazy, maybe, but the persistent wanting still remained.

"Carrie?" Flann was looking at her with a curious expression.

"Oh. Sure. Now?"

"If you're ready." Flann narrowed her eyes. Like she didn't know Carrie was always ready to go two hours ahead of game time. "Joe's due to be outside in five minutes. And it's pretty much that time."

"Right. Okay. Give me two minutes."

Flann grinned. "Sure. I want to say hi to Abby anyhow."

"Don't get hung up in the ER," Carrie warned, trying for normal. The last couple days, normal had been eluding her. "That means no quick check of patient charts just to see what's going on, and no waylaying Abby in the hall to fool around."

"Hey, I never waylay her in the hall." Flann's grin widened. "Now, the on-call room, maybe—"

"That's probably information you should keep to yourself." Carrie resolutely logged out, grabbed her bag, and swore off thinking about Gina until after they'd beaten her team.

"How's your arm feel?" Flann said.

Carrie pressed her lips together grimly. "My arm feels good. I can go three games in the next two days."

"Let's just see how it goes. See you downstairs in five minutes." Flann waved and disappeared around the corner.

"Yeah," Carrie said with a sigh. That's what she'd been telling herself about everything since she drove away from Gina in the dark. Wait and see. If she only knew what she was waiting for.

❖

Gina leaned against the end of the bleachers by her bench as trucks and cars pulled in on the opposite side of the field. The Rivers team congregated on the sidelines to start their warm-ups. Flann headed out to the mound to pitch batting practice. Carrie arrived with Joe and, after sitting to pull on cleats, walked down the third-base line with Harper. Gina eased back enough so Carrie wouldn't notice her staring. Carrie looked great in her uniform, but then she looked great in everything. She'd tied back her hair and looped the tail through the back of her cap. She tossed the first warm-up pitch to Harper, her expression focused but relaxed. Her form was natural and a beautiful thing to watch. Gina smiled to herself. Who was she kidding. *Everything* about Carrie was beautiful, her pitching technique being just one of a million things she could think of. Her sense of humor, her focus, her determination, even her crazy absolute sense of time painted a fascinating picture of a complicated, captivating woman. And the sexiest woman Gina had ever seen.

"Good luck tonight," Joe said, appearing out of nowhere beside her.

Gina squelched the urge to jump and turned slowly, blanking her expression. "Shouldn't you be out on the field warming up?"

"Yeah. I'm on my way out. Thought I'd send condolences before the game."

"You wish."

"Hey, it's not personal, you know."

Gina laughed. "What are you talking about, it's always been personal. We've been trying to beat each other at just about everything since we were kids."

Joe laughed too. "True enough. The only thing we never competed for was girls."

"No need to do that," Gina said quietly. "I got there first, remember?"

Joe winced. "Sorry. Sometimes I'm an ass."

"No, you're not," Gina said softly. "You just don't live in the past."

"Maybe you should think about changing that a little bit yourself."

Gina shook her head, keeping track of Carrie. Looking at her was the only way to dull the ache in her gut she'd been walking around with for two days.

Joe turned his head, followed her gaze, and murmured, "She's probably a little out of your league."

Gina snapped her gaze to his. "What the fuck?"

Joe grinned. "Language."

Two kids, a boy and a girl, walked by holding hands. The taller one, a dark-haired boy, called hello to Joe.

"Hey, how you doing?" Joe called back.

"Great," the boy said with a big smile, and the pair walked on, swinging their clasped hands, to join a group of teens by the Rivers's bleachers.

"That's my boss's son," Joe said. "The kid I was telling you about who had the surg—"

"Let me repeat," Gina said slowly. "But *what* the fuck?"

"Just checking."

"Checking what?"

"If you still had a pulse, bonehead. Mom told me about the emergency picnic. It was with Carrie, wasn't it?"

Gina blew out a breath. Joe couldn't wind her up any more than she already was over Carrie. "Yeah."

"So are you bringing her to dinner?"

"I can't even figure out if I should call her again."

"What are you running from, Gina?" Joe said. "The only thing chasing you are ghosts."

She would've argued if she could. If he hadn't been right. "I gotta get ready for the game. You ought to do the same thing. Especially considering what a crappy outfielder you are."

"Gina…"

"Good luck tonight, Joe," Gina said softly and turned away.

❖

Carrie burned a strike into Harper's glove for her last warm-up. Harper stood, nodded. "You're ready."

Carrie felt ready. She had the edge. She wanted to win. It wasn't about beating the other team now—it was about winning the game. Winning was a pure desire, not personal, not retribution, simply the goal of the game. Sauntering back to the bench, she pulled off her glove and tucked it under her arm. She sat down and waited for the ump to call the coaches and captains. She knew exactly where Gina was without looking at her. Some radar pulled her attention every few seconds to a point on the field and there she would be. Talking to her team, clipboard in her hands, reading off the lineup. Standing to one side with the starting pitcher, undoubtedly reviewing their scouting report on the Rivers's batters. Sliding her hands into the back pockets of her skintight black baseball pants, staring out at the field. Avoiding looking in Carrie's direction.

Flann dropped down beside her. "You okay?"

"I'm good," Carrie said, reluctantly pulling her gaze away from Gina.

"You looked good warming up."

Carrie turned to Flann and caught a glimpse of Gina looking her way. She smiled. "I *am* good."

A minute later the ump signaled the coaches, captains, and co-captains to gather in front of the dugout. Carrie, co-captain with Flann, followed Harper and Flann to the field and stopped in the semicircle facing Gina and the Hammers' captains.

"Rivers is home team," the ump said.

While he went over the obligatory rules review, Carrie finally looked at Gina. She'd braced herself for the contact, and still a shiver ran between her shoulder blades. Gina's gaze, so raw and unapologetically hungry, was a thundercloud racing to engulf her, all rage and power. Carrie jerked and caught her breath. A smile flickered at the corner of Gina's mouth. Carrie glared and Gina laughed. She'd felt it too.

"Let's play ball," the ump said, and the circle broke, releasing Carrie from the spell.

CHAPTER TWENTY-ONE

At the top of the sixth inning, Carrie grabbed her glove, gearing up to head out to the mound with a score of 1–0, in favor of the Hammers. She wasn't concerned. Softball was a game, and all games included intangibles—a little bit of luck, good or bad, could swing a close game to one team or the other. The Hammers were good, with savvy, powerful hitters who could read pitches and make something happen even when a pitch was perfect. Sometimes, a batter got lucky and connected with a good pitch that for anyone else would've been a swing and a miss, but for them was a hit over the fence. She'd given up a home run in the second inning to the Hammers' first baseman, a brunette who hadn't been hitting all that well all season.

But everyone turned the corner eventually, and tonight was the brunette's night. She'd almost slammed another one out of the park her next at bat and was robbed when Joe practically climbed the fence to make the catch at the last second. And to complete the perfect storm, the Hammers were pitching well and the Rivers were hitting flat. Their big hitters, Flann, Glenn, and Rob, were grounding out or popping up. Carrie wasn't worried about them—yet. Batters went through the same kind of slump pitchers did at times, and all it would take was one of them to connect for the tide to turn. She just needed to keep the score close until their bats got hot again. They had four innings left to play and home-field advantage, so they'd be batting last. Now was not the time to panic. Now was the time to bear down and use every skill she had.

Harper walked over. "You good to keep going?"

"Damn right." Carrie surveyed the Hammers. Top of the order, their leadoff batter was already warming up, swinging his bat as if he planned to come out and blow one by everyone. She smiled. That one run stung worse than stepping on a nest of wasps, but despite their slim lead, the Hammers hadn't hammered her yet tonight. She'd held them to that single run and no further hits. Between innings, Gina had switched her lineup, bringing in a power hitter she'd been holding in reserve. Maybe she thought—mistakenly—Carrie was getting tired. Maybe she figured her hitters were due for a kill. She was wrong.

"Okay," Harper said, "if you can keep us close, we'll find a way to get you some runs of our own."

"They've got one run too many already. They're not getting any others." Carrie scanned the field for Gina, found her with her head bent toward a shorter woman, her expression even from this distance set and determined. Carrie loved looking at her. She loved the intensity that radiated from her, like a corona of heat shimmering in the air. She loved the way she stood, hands on her hips, legs slightly parted, strong, tight, wired with tension and power. She shivered, remembering the press of Gina's body above her. Oh, bad, bad idea. Now was not the time to be remembering that, especially considering that all the times she'd mentally replayed it hadn't dulled the thrill at all. She sucked in a breath and said to Harper, "Okay. Let's—"

Somewhere from the vicinity of the Rivers's bench, a phone rang. A few seconds later, another joined in. Harper grimaced and Carrie turned around to see Abby stand up in the bleachers behind them, her phone to her ear.

Flann, who'd been halfway out to the field, jogged back and pulled her phone from her backpack by the bench. Joe followed right after her and sorted through his gear, coming up with his.

Flann checked the readout and looked at Harper. "9-1-1 text. They're calling us in. Sorry."

"Go," Harper said. "I'll be over as soon as I finish here, in case you need extra hands."

Abby came down the steps and joined Flann. "Ride with me?"

"Sure," Flann said. "Got details?"

"Not much," Abby said. "MVA, multiple vehicles, multiple victims, on their way."

"Right."

"Hey," Joe said. "Can I catch a ride back too?"

Abby nodded, and in seconds, the three of them along with three other Rivers players jogged toward where the vehicles were parked.

Harper blew out a breath and glanced at Carrie. "Well, we're through the fifth, so the game's official. We're gonna have to forfeit."

"I hate to give it up, but it's just a game," Carrie said.

"And there's always a next time. Go home and rest your arm. We'll take them tomorrow."

"Damn right. Let's go call it." Carrie followed Harper over to the ump as Gina and her captain walked toward them.

"We have to forfeit," Harper said. "We just lost half our team. Emergency over at the Rivers."

The ump nodded. "Damn shame. Hope everybody's okay over there."

Gina held her hand out to Harper. "Sorry about this."

"Happens sometimes." Harper shook Gina's hand.

Gina glanced from Harper to Carrie. "So tomorrow at three."

"We'll be there," Harper said.

The others walked away, leaving Gina and Carrie staring at each other as their teams packed up on either side of the field.

"What happened?" Gina asked.

"Mass casualty alert in the ER," Carrie said. "It's always a risk when half your team are medical staff."

"That sucks all the way around," Gina said.

"Yeah, pretty much puts things in perspective." Carrie grimaced. "A few minutes ago all I could think about was what I had to do to best you. Now…that seems a lot less important."

"Yeah," Gina said. "Listen, Carrie…" She paused as Margie and Blake hurried across the field to them.

"Hey, Carrie," Margie said. "Harper's heading to the hospital to see if she can help out, and Abby was our ride. Can you take us back to Blake's?"

Carrie shook her head. "Sorry, guys. I came with Flann, so I need to find a ride myself. Come on, we can—"

"I'll take you all where you need to go." Gina glanced at the kids. "As long as you two don't mind cramming onto the bench in the back of the cab."

"Hey, no, that's great. Thanks!" Margie held out her hand. "I'm Margie Rivers."

"Gina Antonelli." Gina turned and shook Blake's hand. "Hi."

He smiled, a shy but friendly smile. "Blake Remy."

"I have to touch base with my team and help get the gear collected. Ten minutes?" Gina said.

"Same here," Carrie said. "Meet you by the bleachers."

"Got it." Gina jogged over to her bench, thanked the ump, and signed the game sheet noting their win. Her team gathered bats, gloves, and other gear without the usual post-win celebration. No one was happy about chalking up a win by forfeit, even more so considering why the opponent had to forfeit. Being one game up in a best-of-five series was usually a nice position, but there was no sweetness in this win.

When everything was sorted, Gina shouldered her backpack and crossed to the other side of the field where Carrie waited with the teenagers by the bench. The night hadn't ended the way she'd wanted it to, but she'd won an unexpected gift—a few minutes with Carrie. The anticipation of being near her, even with a crowd, lightened some of the darkness that had settled in her chest the last two days. She pretended not to notice Carrie watching her every step of the way, but she couldn't prevent the force of Carrie's gaze from lighting a fire inside her. By the time she reached Carrie, every muscle was tight and every nerve jangling. Carrie must've known, because her smile was satisfied. Maybe even a little bit victorious. Well, she was right. Gina was pretty much at her mercy, since just being around her made her head spin.

"Ready?" Carrie said brightly.

"You could say that." Gina kept her voice low so Margie and Blake, standing with some other teenagers a little ways away, wouldn't hear. "I didn't get a chance to talk to you before the game, so I'm glad—"

"It kind of felt like you were avoiding me," Carrie said quietly. "If that's the case, we're both adults, and we can—"

Gina winced. "No, no! That's not it. I wanted to call, but then I didn't know what to say and—I'm sorr—"

"Hey, no. Forget I said anything. Really. It's fine," Carrie said. "I appreciate the ride tonight."

"No problem," Gina said, taking the hint. Sorry wasn't going to cut it. She needed to say a lot more than that. She picked up Carrie's bag before Carrie could, and they went to collect Margie and Blake.

The bleachers were mostly empty, a few stragglers hanging around in the parking lot and on the field.

As they cut across uneven rows of cornstalks and pasture grass toward Gina's truck, Carrie murmured, "Oh, terrific."

The guy from Houlihan's who'd hassled Carrie outside the tavern leaned against a beat-up Ford truck, a can of beer in his hand and a sneer on his face. Gina stepped quickly around to Carrie's other side, walking between Carrie and the guy. Margie and Blake followed five or ten feet behind them, loosely holding hands and talking about some video game. As they walked past, he tossed the beer can in their direction, just far enough away from Gina he could claim he hadn't meant anything by it.

"Fucking queers," he muttered.

Carrie sucked in a breath, and Gina stiffened. She'd been here before. She knew how it ended. Not tonight, though. Not this time. She wasn't seventeen any longer.

"Hey, thanks!" Margie called, as if he'd just congratulated them on winning an award. "You have a nice night too."

He scowled, his face darkening as he tried to decipher what she'd said. By then, they were all well past him.

"Has he been bothering you?" Carrie asked.

"No," Margie said, shrugging. "He's just a jerk."

"Be careful around him just the same," Gina said.

"Don't worry, we will be," Blake said emphatically.

Blake didn't look scared or embarrassed, and Gina was glad for that. Surprised too, at both of them. They seemed so sure of who they were. If she hadn't known Blake's story, she wouldn't have guessed. He was just a boy. The girl with him, Margie, was just a girl, pretty, bright-eyed, confident. Two ordinary teens. Gina thought back to herself at that age, the secrets she'd kept from her family, from her friends. Only Emmy had known her, and Emmy hadn't wanted anyone else to know about them. These kids were so different, and she wondered why she hadn't been as brave or as honest.

"So, how's it going, Blake?" Carrie said. "You look great. Nice T-shirt."

Blake grinned. "Yeah, my mom got it for me. Kind of like, you know, a coming-out shirt."

Carrie laughed and Gina savored it. Carrie's laughter was exciting as the promises of sunrise. She unlocked the truck and everyone piled in. The ride to Blake's house in town was quick, with the kids talking behind them and Carrie sitting silently beside her. The gulf between them was cold, and Gina knew why. At least, her part in it. She'd kept Carrie at a distance even while she was giving in to her need for her. She wanted Carrie, needed the light she brought to the shadows in her heart, but she didn't want the risk. She'd hoped to take without giving. Her silence had created this gulf, and the chasm was killing her as surely as any price she might pay for being vulnerable.

"That's it," Blake said, pointing out his house.

Gina pulled over and the kids piled out of the truck. Gina hesitated before pulling away. "Take you home?"

"My car's at the hospital, if you don't mind driving me up there," Carrie said.

"I don't mind," Gina said carefully, feeling her way along a precipice, uncertain of the path but positive if she misstepped, the fall would be a long one. "But it's early and we could grab a drink, some food somewhere maybe."

Gina expected Carrie to say no, couldn't blame her. She sounded desperate, but then she was. Carrie was all that stood between her and a long night filled with regrets and recriminations.

Carrie regarded her cautiously. "I'm still too wound up from the game to eat. Your team's probably at the tavern, and I don't really feel like socializing."

"How about wine for starters? My place isn't far, and I can take you back to your car later."

"That works," Carrie said.

Five minutes later, Gina pulled into the drive beside her house and turned off the engine. Still an hour to go before sunset, but cloud banks were building off to the west, making the night unnaturally dark. "Storm coming."

"I can feel it in the air," Carrie said.

"Wait right there." Gina hopped out and hustled around to Carrie's side. She opened the door and held out her hand. "Come out back with me and watch the lightning?"

Carrie's eyes widened before she slowly smiled and took Gina's hand. "Yes."

CHAPTER TWENTY-TWO

The temperature's dropping," Gina said as Carrie followed her down a dirt drive separated from a pasture by a board fence. The lights nearest the house were barely a glimmer on the crest of a distant hill. "Are you cold?"

"No," Carrie said. "It feels good. I haven't cooled down from the game yet."

"Still up for a glass of wine?" Gina asked.

"That would be great. Thanks." Carrie climbed the steps onto a wide back porch dominated just to one side of the screen door by a wooden glider big enough for three that swung gently in the rising breeze. A single rocker accompanied it. She sat on the glider.

Gina paused by the back door. "I've got white or red."

"White."

"Hungry?"

Carrie smiled. Oh, she was hungry, all right, but not for what Gina was offering just then, and tonight was not the night to tease about it. Her skin was as raw as if she'd scraped off a few layers in a slide gone wrong, and the shadows in Gina's eyes said she felt the same. "I've still got game nerves—kills the appetite for a while anyhow."

"Funny," Gina murmured. "You never look nervous."

"I'm good at hiding it."

"Are you nervous now?" Gina's question was so quiet Carrie wondered if she even meant to speak out loud.

"No," Carrie said. "You never make me nervous—a lot of other things, but not that."

"Good." Gina rubbed the back of her neck. "I might be a little."

"You don't have to be," Carrie whispered. "You're safe with me."

Gina's smile was rueful. "Maybe I don't want to be safe."

"Let me know when you decide."

Gina nodded. "I'll be right back."

Gina disappeared inside and Carrie swung the rocker gently with one foot, taking in Gina's home. The house fit somewhere between the size of hers and the big sprawling farmhouse Harper and Presley lived in. Gina's was two neat stories, white clapboard with gingerbread trim around the eaves and porch roof, a slate roof, and a full porch front and back. The barn, off to her right and a hundred feet away, was bigger than the house, as often seemed to be the case, and looked well kept up and freshly painted. She didn't see any sign of animals, and the fenced pastures looked to be planted in corn and hay. The cornfields swept almost to the horizon on three sides of the barn, meeting the slowly billowing blue-black clouds amassing where land and sky joined. The scent of ozone and summer heat tickled her nose. Her skin moistened in the humid twilight.

The screen door creaked and Gina appeared with two glasses of wine. She held one out to Carrie and sat down beside her.

"I can so use this," Carrie said. She hadn't expected the invitation and was content to let Gina take the lead. The quiet was soothing—not even the crickets were chirping—and watching the storm slowly churn closer while safe and protected under the wide expanse of the porch roof was oddly peaceful.

"Margie and Blake," Gina said, "you know them pretty well?"

"Mmm," Carrie said, sipping the wine, surprised by the question. "Margie is Harper and Flann's youngest sister. And Blake is Abby's son. Abby and Presley are best friends from college."

"Tight group." Gina sprawled beside her, one arm stretched out along the back, her fingers almost touching Carrie's shoulder. Her leg was an inch away from Carrie's knee. The tension radiating from her rivaled the explosive promise of the thunderclouds drawing nearer.

"Pretty much family all the way around," Carrie said.

"And you too. You were living with Harper and Presley for a while, right?"

"Yes. Presley and I shared the house when we first moved here." Carrie laughed. "God, there are no secrets in this place."

"Not true," Gina said. "They're just buried deep."

"Are you speaking from experience?" Carrie asked carefully.

"Joe told me about Blake's surgery," Gina said as if Carrie hadn't spoken. "I wouldn't know if he hadn't said anything."

"Blake's transitioning is not a secret," Carrie said, "but hopefully it won't be news after a while, either."

"He seems to be pretty cool about it."

"He's a remarkable kid, and so are his mom and Flann. And Margie and his other friends are totally unfazed by it."

Gina let out a long breath. "Not everyone is, though. Like the asshole in the parking lot."

Carrie snorted. "He's all bruised ego. I think he's still smarting because we beat his team with a woman pitching. He's got to find some excuse for his own failure, I guess."

"Yeah, well, prejudice always does." Gina gave her a long look. "Don't underestimate him."

"I won't." Carrie brushed the top of Gina's hand with her fingers. "Promise."

A streak of lightning shot across the sky, a quicksilver flash followed a few seconds later by the distant roll of thunder.

"How far away do you think that is?" Carrie kicked off her shoes and socks and curled a foot underneath her other leg, settling back in the glider.

"If you count seconds, you can estimate the distance. I'd say that's about a mile." Gina turned her glass in her hands, staring at it as if some elusive answers resided in the swirling wine. "Margie and Blake—they made me wish I'd had their guts." Gina's voice trembled. Whatever path she was traveling, the journey was a painful one.

"Did your parents have a problem with you coming out?"

Gina was silent for so long, Carrie wasn't certain she was going to answer.

"Not in so many words," Gina finally said, her voice flat and empty. "Of course, I didn't say anything to anyone, either, for a long time."

"It's not easy," Carrie said. "I was lucky. My parents are radicals—I think I mentioned that. Kind of latter-day hippies. I grew up with all kinds of people around the house and never really worried about what my parents might think. It took me a while to admit to myself I wanted to be with girls, but once I did, I saw the light." Carrie laughed, remembering the exultation accompanying that particular epiphany. The thunder rolled closer, and she started mentally counting the seconds every time she heard it. The twilight shimmered, a false dark as if she were viewing the world through a veil. Her life had been like that, before she'd come to understand her dreams and desires. "Anyhow, by that point, it was kind of an over and done thing."

Gina nodded, her expression distant. "I always knew. I wanted to be like Joe from the time I could think about being like anyone, even though both my sisters were just as tough and just as good at pretty much everything as he was. But they had a girlie side I never had."

"Hey," Carrie said teasingly. "I'm very girlie, in case you hadn't noticed, and I'm very much a lesbian."

Gina cut her a look. "Oh, believe me, I've noticed. I'm pretty much a slave to your girliness."

Carrie caught her breath, torn between laughing and moaning. The heat in Gina's voice struck as potently as a lightning flash. "Good."

Gina leaned imperceptibly closer, her fingertips just touching Carrie's shoulder. Heat lightning coursed along Carrie's skin. Her heart raced and a deep ache kindled in her depths. Carrie sipped her wine to take her mind off the urge to crawl into Gina's lap.

"You're beautiful, if I haven't said that out loud," Gina said. "I think it every time I see you."

"I like the way you look at me," Carrie murmured. "Like I'm all you see."

"You are." Gina traced small circles on Carrie's shoulder, the light touch so erotic Carrie shivered.

"It's going to rain soon," Carrie murmured, as the seconds between the lightning and the thunder disappeared.

"I know. Do you want to go inside?"

Carrie shook her head and emptied her glass.

"No, I want to sit here with you and listen to the rain."

Gina slid closer, her arm curling around Carrie's shoulder.

"I can't think of anything but you. I lie awake at night wanting you."

"But there's something, isn't there." Carrie gave up and leaned into Gina's arms, resting one hand on Gina's taut stomach. "Why did you bring me here tonight?"

"For this." Gina cupped Carrie's face, lifted her chin, and kissed, hard and hungry, a fierce, desperate kiss that burned through Carrie like lightning crashing. Thunder rolled. The storm would be above them in seconds, and she needed to decide if she was going to stand out in the downpour and let the storm rage around her, or run for shelter. She pressed her hand to Gina's shoulder, gently pushed her away, and Gina drew back instantly.

"If you keep that up," Carrie said, "you're going to have to take me to bed."

Gina's fingers tightened on Carrie's jaw. "Would you mind?"

Carrie laughed, hearing the unsteadiness in her voice. "Oh no. I've been thinking about it, imagining it, quite a lot since the last time I saw you."

"The last time you said you weren't ready."

"Oh, I'm ready," Carrie said. "But I'm not sure you are."

"The rain is coming." Gina cradled Carrie against her chest and rested her cheek on the top of Carrie's head. Sheets of water, an advancing army of wild power, tore up the earth. Wind whipped branches from the pines and dashed them across the yard. Thunder boomed, shaking the ground beneath the porch. And always the lightning, feral and unchained. Gina's mouth was close to Carrie's ear, her breath warm in the cool air, her words cloistered on a roll of thunder. A secret passed in the heart of the storm.

"I never told anyone about Emmy," Gina murmured. "I kissed her the first time when we were twelve."

Moving as slowly as she could, Carrie rested her hand lightly on Gina's thigh. The rigid muscles quivered beneath her fingers.

"Her parents were strict with her. They must've known how popular she was going to be, how all the boys were going to want her. They never suspected it was me who touched her first. That she let me."

Gina's voice was low, heavy and dreamlike.

"I worshiped her, would've done anything she wanted. I couldn't believe it was me she wanted, and no one else." Lightning struck in front of the barn, silvering the yard for an instant. A cymbal clash of thunder broke a heartbeat later. Icy slivers of rain blew across the porch, and Carrie shivered.

Gina's arms tightened around her, and Carrie held very still.

"Her parents wouldn't let her date until she was fifteen, and then every boy in school was calling her. She wasn't like some of the other popular girls. Everyone liked her, even the girls who wanted to *be* her. She was junior prom queen, and we all knew she'd be the senior queen too. Her boyfriend was prom king." Gina's voice shook. "But I was the only one who touched her. In that barn right out there the first time. My grandmother was alive then, and she kept cows. We'd come here after school to help clean the barn, and after we'd lie in the hay and she'd let me put my hands on her."

The night turned from gray to black. A light came on over the barn, a shimmering haze, barely visible through the storm. Carrie's world had become the circle of Gina's arms and the beat of Gina's heart beneath her cheek. She pressed to her, as much for solace as to comfort.

"Joe figured it out. He could always tell when I was hiding something. He kept my secret, because Emmy wanted us to be a secret. I was her secret love, and her secret shame."

Carrie stroked Gina's hair and slipped her other hand under Gina's shirt. Her abdomen was tense and cold. So cold. Nothing she could do would take away that old wound. All she could do was let the pain pour down around her like the rain.

"I didn't go to any of the parties on senior weekend because Emmy would be there with Kevin. I hated to see her with him, as if she was his trophy, his prize. But she called me the night of the last party when Kevin got too drunk to drive her home. She called me and I went to get her, and I was angry. Angry that he hadn't taken care of her, and angry that I'd let her go with him. She was crying, and I kissed her. I shouldn't have, but she was mine and I wanted her." Gina shuddered. "We'd always been so careful, but I couldn't think, didn't think, didn't care. All that mattered was that she was mine. And a couple of Kevin's friends saw us."

Carrie held her breath, fighting the nausea building inside her. God, how she wished there was something she could say or do that would make a difference. The past could not be changed, but it could be forgiven. She slid her arm around Gina's waist, held her as tightly as Gina held her.

"Emmy was nearly hysterical when they called us names, laughing and threatening to tell Kevin. To tell everyone. She got behind the wheel of my truck, and I just barely managed to get in the other side before she tore out onto the road. I couldn't calm her down, couldn't stop her crying, and she just kept going faster and faster. I couldn't stop her and the truck rolled and I didn't know until morning when I woke up in the hospital that she was gone."

"I'm so, so sorry," Carrie murmured, squeezing her eyes tight, determined not to cry.

"They never said anything about us, those boys. Maybe they were too drunk to remember, maybe they knew why Emmy had driven off the way she had. That they pushed her until she broke."

"And you never said anything, either, did you," Carrie guessed.

Gina shook her head. "How could I? Emmy died for that secret, and I kept it for her."

"But Joe knows."

"Not about that night. If I'd told him, he would've gone after them. He would've killed them, I think, right then."

"And your family?"

"They knew how close we were, but they didn't want to know all of it. Later, long enough after they could ignore the past, I told them there wouldn't be a husband." Gina laughed harshly. "I still think they hold out hope. It's not so much they're against being gay, they just want a traditional life for me. For them."

Gina sighed and some of the tension ebbed, as if the words had breached a dam she'd tended for years. The thunder was an echo now, and the lightning had spent itself in its fury. The rain had lost its furor too, subsiding into a gentle dance on the tin roof above them. Carrie stroked Gina's cheek, brushing away the tears that might've been only the rain on her face. She kissed her, slowly, as gently as she knew how, brushing her mouth over Gina's until Gina's hands came into her hair and Gina clung to her, desperately vulnerable.

"It's not your fault," Carrie whispered.

"If only I hadn't kissed her—"

"No," Carrie murmured, stroking Gina's face. "It wasn't the kiss, Gina. None of your kisses. It was an accident."

"It should've been me driving. It should have been me who died."

"Neither of you should have," Carrie whispered. "There was no sin, there was no price to pay. You loved each other. There was nothing wrong in that."

"If I'd been stronger, braver—"

Carrie gripped her shoulders. "Gina, you were teenagers, and you did the best you could. You were there for her—you came when she called you. Loving her was not wrong. She wasn't wrong to be afraid. There is no guilt in being afraid. You were both innocent, and what happened that night was an accident."

"I'm sorry," Gina said with a weary sigh. "I'm sorry to put this on you. You don't need to hear my troubles."

Carrie shook her gently. "Don't you say that. How can I know you if you don't share your pain? And since I'm pretty far on the road to falling in love with you, it matters even more."

"You might be making a mistake," Gina said before she kissed her, her mouth urgent and hot.

"That's not for you to decide," Carrie said when she caught her breath.

"The storm's passing," Gina said.

"No." Carrie pulled Gina to her feet. "It's just starting. Take me inside."

CHAPTER TWENTY-THREE

Gina held the screen door for Carrie and reached inside to flick on the kitchen lights. The light from the amber fluted wall sconces bathed the room in muted gold reminiscent of sunset on a hazy August afternoon. Her chest was curiously light, as if her heart had shed a mantle of stone she hadn't realized she'd been carrying. Carrie's comfort, more than she deserved after telling her about Emmy, had soothed an ache so deep inside she no longer noticed it. She wasn't sure she could shed the guilt as easily as she had shed her secrets, and she doubted she'd ever believe that Emmy would forgive her. She'd replayed the night so many times, what she should have done, how the anger she had no right to feel had betrayed Emmy's trust. Emmy had not been at fault. Her fear was real and Gina's rage had come from impotence—impotence and helplessness and jealousy.

Carrie hadn't blamed her, and Carrie was here with her now. Gina stopped in the middle of the kitchen, and Carrie paused, waiting the way she had waited when Gina had made her confession.

"I wanted…needed to tell you about Emmy," Gina said. "You deserved to know before we took things between us any further." She smiled wryly. "And we were headed there fast. I'm glad you know, but I can't promise you there won't be ghosts sometimes."

"I don't want promises, about that or anything else, except…" Carrie reached for Gina's hand.

"Except?" Gina gripped Carrie's hand, probably too hard. Carrie's fingers were cool and steady, a lifeline Gina had never expected.

"I need you to trust me enough to let me see you. I'm not afraid of your shadows."

"All right. I'll try."

"And I want you to leave a light on in the bedroom tonight," Carrie said.

"All right."

"Aren't you going to ask me why?" Carrie's voice teased, but her gaze probed.

Gina cupped Carrie's cheek and kissed her. "I hope it's because you want me to see you, because *I* want to see *you* so much I can hardly breathe."

Carrie covered Gina's hand where it rested on her cheek. "When you put it that way, I most certainly do want your eyes…and everything else…on me." She threaded her arms around Gina's neck and pressed against her body. "Most of all, though, I want you to see *me*, and only me."

Gina caught her breath. She was such an idiot sometimes. "When I've touched you, I've only ever seen you, only ever tasted you, only ever hungered for you. And when I lie down at night, and my body is on fire, you're the one I think of."

"Then you'd better do something about it, right now," Carrie said, an urgent edge to her voice.

Gina kept her arm around Carrie's waist and pulled her through the downstairs to the front staircase, up to the second floor and into her bedroom. The room had been her grandparents' a long time ago, running the entire width of the back of the house, with ceiling-high windows on three sides that let the breeze blow through even on the hottest nights. Gina'd left them open and the recent storm had scrubbed the air clean. She pulled the chain on the brass lamp with its cream-colored silk lampshade and little gold tassels rimming the border. The soft light was enough to see by, but not too bright to shatter the cocoon of quiet stillness surrounding them as they approached the bed.

"Will you let me undress you?" Gina asked.

Wordlessly, Carrie nodded. She'd left her shoes and socks downstairs on the porch and wasn't wearing all that much. She laughed a little self-consciously. "God, I should've been thinking about something a lot sexier than softball when I got dressed. I guess I'm going to have to leave the seductive bra and panties until the next time."

"I've never seen you when you didn't look beautiful. No matter what you're wearing." Gina kissed Carrie's throat and swept her hands down to Carrie's backside, pulling her close so their hips meshed seamlessly, effortlessly. She kissed her again, murmuring, "I think you look so hot in your softball pants, I almost hate to undress you."

"I certainly hope not." Carrie nipped at Gina's lower lip. "Because I want naked. Me. You. So let's get to it."

Laughing, Gina hooked her thumbs in the waistband of Carrie's skintight pants and pushed them down. She caught her breath when her hands skimmed over flesh, and nothing but flesh. Nothing underneath. Her head was suddenly light. She groaned. "I'm out of practice."

"That's good," Carrie whispered, gripping the bottom of her own shirt and tugging it up over her sports bra. "I hope you need lots of practice. Starting now."

Gina pushed Carrie's hands away. "Let me."

Carrie surrendered instantly. Gina's focus was so intense, her features etched with such hunger, Carrie couldn't look away. She didn't even know when she'd gotten naked until Gina bent and brushed her mouth over her breast. The shock of it made her clit tense, somewhere between pleasure and insanity.

Carrie gripped Gina's shoulders. "Oh my God. I'm so totally strung out I'm going to explode."

"Whenever you want." Gina circled Carrie's nipple with her tongue and sucked lightly, letting her teeth graze the tight peak. Carrie trembled, and Gina smiled against the warm, soft flesh, reveling in the taking. She kept her mouth on Carrie's breast and clasped her hips, turning her toward the bed and backing her up slowly. Carrie shuddered as Gina guided her down.

"You still have all your clothes on," Carrie said, her breath tight and urgent.

"In a minute." Gina covered her, letting her weight down gently as she kissed Carrie's throat, her mouth, the angle of her jaw.

Carrie gripped Gina's shoulders so hard she was probably leaving bruises. "I don't think I have a minute."

Laughing, Gina pushed herself up on both arms and settled her hips between Carrie's naked thighs. "You can come whenever you want to, but I've got things I want to do."

Carrie arched, her hair a wild halo of fire on the pillow, her uplifted breasts and softly curved belly an invitation to feast. And Gina intended to feast. She kissed her way down the center of Carrie's body until she reached the delta between her thighs. Lightly at first, then faster and firmer, she tasted her, taunted her, worked her to the edge with kisses and long slick strokes.

"If you don't stop, I'm going to come," Carrie warned, the sheet twisted in her fists.

Gina circled Carrie's hips, holding her still, sucking her gently at the same time she teased her with the tip of her tongue. Almost instantly Carrie spasmed, hips jerking, and Gina pulled her tight to her mouth and kept her there, shuddering as ripples of release coursed through her rigid legs. When Carrie collapsed with a long moan, Gina finally let her rest. Nuzzling her cheek against Carrie's thigh, she closed her eyes. Her heart hammered and her whole body quivered. She'd forgotten the exhilaration of complete satisfaction.

Carrie combed her fingers through Gina's damp hair. She doubted she could move if the house caught fire. "Are you asleep?"

"No," Gina murmured, her voice low and thick as honey. "I'm in heaven."

Carrie laughed. "That's my line, baby."

Gina lifted her head and rested her chin on Carrie's thigh, grinning up at her. "I want to do that again."

"You certainly may," Carrie said, "but not for a few minutes. I need a little more time to recover."

"Oh, that's okay," Gina said. "I'm in no hurry."

"Is that right?" Carrie thrust her hips and turned at the same time, flipping Gina onto her back. She laughed when Gina gave a surprised yelp.

"Hey," Gina complained. "That's some move."

"Twelve years of junior karate," Carrie said smugly. "Second degree junior black belt."

"I'll remember not to spar with you, then."

"I might change your mind. Right now, *you* might not be in a hurry," Carrie said, "but I am. I want your clothes off. Better yet, get up and stand by the side of the bed so I can watch you strip."

Gina hesitated. She'd never played in bed this way—never experienced such lighthearted desire that verged on wanting so much it hurt. But this was different than anything before. This was Carrie. This was now. "Whatever you say."

Carrie stretched out and propped her head on her hand. "That's more like it." She swirled a finger in the air. "Shirt first."

Gina disentangled herself from the sheets and stood up. Carrie was looking right at her from just a foot away. No hiding. She pulled the baseball shirt off over her head, and then the tight tank top she had on underneath it.

"Stop right there." Carrie swung her legs around and sat up on the side of the bed, her face level with Gina's abdomen. She spanned Gina's flanks with her hands, her fingers stroking the muscles in Gina's sides as she leaned forward and ran her tongue slowly around Gina's navel.

"Fuck," Gina gasped, a lightning bolt of arousal slamming into her clit. Her thighs shook as if she'd been running for an hour. She remembered what it felt like to run like that, heart hammering and blood racing. To her complete and utter embarrassment, she whimpered.

Carrie looked up, her smile so satisfied Gina's clit twitched.

"You like that, don't you," Carrie murmured.

"Put your mouth on me again," Gina rasped.

Carrie's smile disappeared, and something hot and feral gleamed in her eyes. Her hands dug into Gina's back and her teeth tugged at the soft skin under Gina's belly button. Gina panted, bracing herself on Carrie's shoulders with both hands. Her nipples tightened, and her sex throbbed. She'd never been taken before. As much as she'd been owned, she'd never been claimed.

"I want you to touch me," Gina said urgently. "Please, Carrie."

"Get your pants off," Carrie ordered, sliding back onto the bed and making room for Gina to lie down. When Gina stumbled down beside her, Carrie leaned over to kiss her as she swept her hand over Gina's breasts, down her belly, and along the length of her thighs.

Gina writhed, wanting her touch everywhere at once, her entire body a live wire. The slightest spark would set her off. "Carrie."

Just that. Carrie.

Gina moaned.

"I'm going to kiss you," Carrie said breathlessly, her mouth against Gina's, "while I make you come the first time."

Carrie's mouth was silk, smooth and sensuous, gliding, pressing, clever and seductive. Gina cleaved to her, one hand in Carrie's hair, the other in the hollow at the base of her spine. Her hips rocked, open and waiting. When Carrie feathered her hand down her abdomen and between her thighs, Gina stiffened, a cry caught strangling in her throat.

Carrie murmured in satisfaction, kissing her breathless, stroking her higher and tighter and winding her up until, with the perfect press of her fingertips, she catapulted her over the edge. Fire blazed behind Gina's closed lids—white lightning seared her brain. She was deaf and blind and drowning.

❖

When Carrie woke, the rain had stopped and the night outside was black and still. She lay curved in the circle of Gina's arms, her cheek on Gina's shoulder, her hand just under Gina's breast. She nuzzled Gina's neck just to feel the softness of her skin and draw her earthy scent, so primal and enticing, deep inside.

She couldn't tell the time, but why should that surprise her? Her internal clock was as thrown off balance as the rest of her. She was in a strange bed with a woman who should have felt like a stranger to her but who, instead, seemed like the final piece of a puzzle she hadn't even realized she was putting together. Gina fit the picture she'd been making of her life as long as she could remember, but she hadn't quite turned the edges and curves the right way to recognize it. She hadn't been searching for the complement but for the contrast, the one so different from her that all her careful rules and regulations and orderly schedules went right out the window. She wanted a woman who pulled her outside her certainties with a grin and a husky laugh, the one who dared her to risk, to walk where all the signs so clearly read danger, deep waters. She didn't know Gina the way she wanted to, but the journey to understanding drew her on with more force than anything she'd ever felt.

Gina kissed her forehead with infinite tenderness. "You want me to take you home?"

"Not unless you need to."

Gina's arms tightened around her. "What I need is to keep you right here and, when I regain a little strength, make you come again."

Carrie laughed. "Baby, you're welcome to try. But I make no promises."

"That's okay, I'm diligent."

"Among many other amazing things," Carrie murmured, kissing the angle of her jaw. She probably ought to worry about how easily she accepted being utterly contented, but she just closed her eyes and went back to sleep.

Her ringing phone woke her the next time. Seven, maybe? Gina was gone, and she smelled coffee. Praise Jesus. And really, was she ever going to be able to tell time without a watch again? She grabbed her phone, squinted at the readout, and thumbed it on. "Need I remind you it's Saturday, and after business hours."

"I'm not calling about work," Presley said with disgusting cheerfulness.

Carrie shut her eyes tightly against the sun blazing right outside the window. God, she hated morning people.

Presley went on, "I took a chance I could entice you with Lila's homemade cinnamon buns. Want to come over for breakfast?"

"Uh," Carrie waffled. Too soon to mention her amazing night? Too many questions, that was for sure. Too new to tarnish with the demands of the day.

"You're not home, are you?"

She must've hesitated too long.

"Not exactly, no."

"Let me guess. You've taken up early morning running."

"Very funny. Not."

Carrie cracked a cautious eye at the sound of footsteps. Gina walked in with two cups of coffee and a raised eyebrow. Carrie frantically motioned her forward and reached for the cup. She took a sip and nearly sighed.

"Gardening?" Presley mused.

"I hate you, you know."

"Everything okay?" Presley said, this time with quiet seriousness.

Carrie glanced at Gina, who slid under the covers next to her. She was wearing a pair of khaki shorts and nothing else. Carrie's mouth went dry and every other part of her instantly overheated. She was suddenly very, very awake.

"Carrie?" Presley said. "Do you need me to send a rescue-me text?"

"When have I ever?" Carrie took another sip of her coffee, enough to get her through the next ten minutes or so, and set it aside. "I'm good. I'll be at the game. Gotta go now. 'Bye."

She swiped off to the sound of Presley's laughter, tossed the phone onto the floor on the pile of clothes, and dragged Gina on top of her. "I think I remember you saying you were planning to make me come again."

"Did I say just once?" Gina murmured, right before she kissed her.

She'd been ready since the instant Gina walked into the room. No, the second she'd opened her eyes. She wrapped her legs around Gina's hips and angled her body until the pressure was exactly where she needed it. Wordlessly, utterly selfishly, she took her pleasure, urging Gina to catch her rhythm, to thrust as she arched, until the pulsing intensity made her explode.

"God," she gasped. "You are so amazingly sexy."

"You got that wrong. It's all you, babe." Gina laughed unsteadily. "You think they'll miss us if we don't make it to the game?"

"How long do we have?"

"A couple of hours."

Carrie found Gina's hand and pushed it between her thighs. "Let's not waste any time."

❖

"You want to ride with me to the game?" Gina said. "Or do you want me to take you to your car?"

Carrie pulled her softball uniform from Gina's dryer and pulled on her pants. Gina was still naked and apparently had no idea how blindingly sexy she was, since she was still forming sentences and Carrie could barely think. Carrie struggled to focus. "Do you have a problem with people seeing us together?"

Gina hesitated.

Carrie tilted her head, studied her. Gina hadn't said very much about how they'd ended up in bed or where it was going, but then, neither had she. They'd been too busy setting a marathon record for awesome sex. She had no complaints. She'd been a willing participant. In fact, she'd been more sexually demanding than she'd ever remembered being in her life. Gina didn't seem to mind. In fact, Gina made it pretty clear she couldn't get enough of her. Being desired like that, *wanted* like that, was exhilarating. Carrie had never felt so sexy.

But…

Gina's careful question reminded her they hadn't established any ground rules.

"Do we have to have the talk?" Carrie asked.

Gina winced. "No. Not if it has anything to do with it was really nice, but now it's over."

"That's definitely not where I was going." Carrie grabbed Gina's hips and tugged her close. "Last night was way better than nice. And I'm not running anywhere except to the game."

"I don't want to go to the game today," Gina said. "I want to take you back to bed, and I want to keep making love to you until I drop or die."

Carrie smiled. "I think I figured that out."

Gina smiled wryly. "If you hadn't, I'm more out of practice than I thought."

"And?" Carrie said.

"No ands. No buts," Gina said. "All I want to know is when I can see you again. When I'll be able to touch you again. I'm going to be crazy for you until I do."

Carrie laced her arms around Gina's neck. "Did you actually think I'd say no?"

Gina visibly relaxed. "I'm feeling a little lucky this morning."

Carrie nipped her chin. "Oh, believe me. You are."

Gina laughed. "I just wasn't sure how long my luck would hold."

Carrie took a long breath. She got it. They were great in bed together. "Why don't you drive me to my car. After all, we've got a tournament to play. We don't want to distract our teams."

Gina didn't argue, and Carrie pushed the doubts aside. The sex was great, and really, what more could she ask for?

Chapter Twenty-four

A half hour later Carrie bumped down the single track behind Gina's truck to the lot adjoining the softball field. When Gina veered right, Carrie turned left to park with the trucks and SUVs lined up behind the Rivers's bleachers. She was just getting out when Presley and Harper pulled in beside her. She grabbed her sports bag and waited by the side of the Mini for them.

"Morning," she called as they walked over to her.

"It's two fifteen," Presley said dryly.

Harper snorted. "*You* might've just gotten out of bed, but the rest of us have been up for quite a while."

Dark shadows circled Harper's eyes. Presley looked almost as tired. Neither of them looked like they'd gotten much sleep.

"Were you in the ER all night?" Carrie asked.

"Most of it," Harper said. "I got home about three after the ER cleared out. Flann was still upstairs in the OR when I left. Glenn, Joe, Abby, and Mari were about finished, so unless things got busy later, they probably got a little sleep."

Carrie winced. The Rivers team was going to be playing with a bedraggled lineup. She'd just have to make sure the Hammers didn't get anything to hit.

"What happened?" Carrie asked as they trooped toward the bench.

Harper sighed. "A carload of teenagers failed to make a curve, sideswiped a pickup headed the opposite way, and rolled into a ditch. Pickup driver managed to stay on the road and was only shaken up. The kids were pretty mangled."

Carrie's heart lurched. She couldn't help but think of Gina's story and struggled not to envision her trapped in a twisted tangle of metal, hurt and bleeding and broken. Even when she pushed the images away, she ached. The community was small, and they all knew each other. Any accident, any tragedy, hit close to home. "Locals?"

Presley shook her head. "Out-of-towners vacationing in Saratoga. They'd come down for one of those weekend rodeos and, unfortunately, found a bar that would sell them beer."

"What a shame," Carrie said. "You need any help with warm-ups, Harp?"

"Nah, I'm good. Lila's breakfast fixed me up." She grinned at Carrie. "Sorry you missed it."

"Uh...thanks," Carrie muttered.

While Harper moved on ahead to get batting practice started, Presley said, "How many guesses do I get about where you spent the night?"

Carrie worked hard not to glance over at the Hammers' side of the field. "I'm not even going to make you guess. I was at Gina's."

"Figured, since I haven't seen you show the slightest interest in anyone else in...oh, forever."

"It hasn't been that long," Carrie protested. Presley snorted, and Carrie grinned. "Okay, maybe it's been a long dry spell, but come on— we did move halfway across the country and just because you met Ms. Right the first damn day is not a fair benchmark!"

Presley's eyebrows rose. "Ms. Right, is it?"

"No." Carrie backpedaled. "No, no, I didn't mean that."

"Uh-huh," Presley said. "Moving on, then. Considering the hour, I guess it was a good night."

"I cannot tell a lie. It was stellar."

Presley bumped shoulders. "Hey, that's terrific. Really. I hope you're having a great time."

"Oh, I am." Carrie ignored the little twinge of apprehension and the rhythmic warning lights flashing red at regular intervals. She *was* having fun. She hadn't felt this excited, this invigorated, this damn glad to be alive in a long time. If it weren't for the tiny matter of the simultaneous sense of being over her head in a raging sea without a life jacket, she would've been 100 percent floating.

"You're good with everything, right?" Presley said.

"I am," Carrie said slowly. "It's early, you know, just casual."

Presley gave her a look. "How long have I known you?"

"Um, six years?"

"Uh-huh. And I won't pretend I know everything about your love life, considering you don't always tell me the good parts." Presley poked her arm playfully. "But I've never known you to look for casual. Casual dating, sure. But not, you know, once you get past that."

"I know." Carrie thought back on the night. She'd simply given in to the powerful attraction, so natural, so damn right, she hadn't considered what might follow. Living hour to hour, day to day, without a game plan wasn't her. "I'm sort of flying without a flight plan right now."

"Wow, that's a powerful statement coming from you, Ms. Little Organization Addict."

"Hey! Am I really that controlling?"

"You're not controlling. Well, you are, but in a good way that's very productive and makes you great at your job. I'm sure it makes you great in lots of other ways too, but I think the heart is one of those things you can't actually control."

"You mean the heart wants what it wants?"

"I think that's it," Presley said.

"I can't say I've ever run up against that before," Carrie said.

"That in itself says a lot, then," Presley observed.

"Maybe." Carrie tossed her duffel behind the bench. "But I can't think about that right now. I've got a game to win. Actually, three games, since we had to forfeit last night."

"So go bring on your A game." Presley gave her a quick hug. "And just enjoy all the rest of it. Don't worry too much, but take care of your heart."

"Yes, to all of the above," Carrie said lightly. As if she could just talk herself into not feeling half-crazy every time she thought of Gina, let alone actually looked at her.

Enough. She would see Gina later. After she helped the Rivers beat Gina's team.

Carrie sat down to put on her cleats. When she bent over to lace her shoes, she tilted her head enough to glance across to the other bench. Gina was standing halfway down the first-base line, her hands in the back pockets of her pants, looking directly across the infield at her. Carrie gasped. Heat washed through her. Staying focused could be a challenge since she had absolutely no control where Gina was concerned. She blew out a breath and concentrated on her shoelaces. Her temperature headed back toward normal. Better. For the next few hours, the only thing she intended to think about was winning.

There. That was a good plan.

❖

Ninety minutes later the Rivers were headed into the bottom of the last inning, up one run. Carrie was facing the top of the order and the Hammers' biggest hitters.

"Are you sure you don't want a relief pitcher in there?" Harper said.

Carrie tossed the ice pack she'd kept on her elbow just as added insurance during their at-bats into the cooler. "Are you kidding me? I'm not letting anyone else finish this one out. Besides, you're going to need Mike and Kiko fresh for the second-half game. If we win this and the next one, we'll head into the doubleheader tomorrow with the advantage."

"One game at a time," Harper said with her usual steady calm. "And I'm going to need your arm tomorrow, especially if it comes down to five games."

"My arm is good. I'd tell you if it wasn't. We've got a lot of the season left, after all. I'm not taking any chances."

"Okay then. You're up." Harper scanned the sky. "No rain today. Let's put this one away so we can get the next one in while we're all still awake."

"You got it."

Carrie threw the first batter out on strikes. Next up to the plate was the brunette who'd pounded the home run on her the night before. She strode into the batter's box looking determined. Carrie decided the brunette would be eager to put another one away and would jump on anything close. Carrie decided on a pitch she rarely used. Sinkers were tough to control. They started out in the strike zone, looking exactly like a fastball coming right down the middle. A home run hitter's dream. At the last second, they dropped below the strike zone, if you threw it right. If she missed the pitch, this batter could hurt her.

Behind the plate, Harper signaled for an off-speed pitch outside. Carrie shook her head. Harper ran through the signals for Carrie's other routine pitches and each time, Carrie shook her off. When Harper finally flashed the signal for a sinker, she nodded and started her windup. The brunette settled into her stance, and Carrie knew she'd go for this pitch. She didn't think when she threw it—she felt it in her muscles and her bones. The ball headed hard and fast straight down the middle of the plate, perfect for a batter to hit squarely and hard. She almost felt the brunette smile when she canted her hips, dropped her shoulders, and swung for the fence. Her momentum as the bat passed over the ball took her nearly all the way around in the box. Strike one. Rattled, the brunette let the next pitch, a fastball, go by. Strike two. The third pitch she swung early on a changeup and missed. Strike three.

The Rivers bench cheered. One more out and the tournament was tied.

Carrie leaned over and rubbed her hand on the powder bag to make sure her grip on the next pitch was firm. The third batter was a power hitter too, but he hadn't been hitting all that well the last few at-bats. He was frustrated, and he was going to swing at almost anything close. And that's all she was going to give him. Something close. He surprised her with her first pitch and let it go by. She'd pitched low and outside and the ump called a ball. She threw the same pitch again, and he couldn't wait this time. He missed it. He connected on the third pitch, another sinker that he just managed to hit at his knees. The ground ball shot past Carrie into the gap between first and second base. Glenn made a diving catch as Carrie raced to cover first. Glenn threw from the ground, an off-speed out of position toss. The batter, a good runner, sprinted down the line. Carrie nudged her foot on the bag and stretched until her shoulder popped. The ball hit her glove. The runner hit the bag.

Carrie raised her glove with the ball in it. The ump called the out.

They were done. The tournament was even, one to one. Now all they needed was the best of two out of three, totally doable.

The Rivers team surged to the infield. Flann grabbed Carrie and swung her around.

"Nice game, sweetheart."

Carrie laughed. "You look like crap!"

"Good thing I'm invincible."

Flann put her down and the team sorted themselves out for the ritual handshake with the losing team. Carrie passed down the line, shaking hands with the Hammers, and slowed as she neared the end. Gina held her hand out, and Carrie took it.

"Nice pitching," Gina said.

"Thanks," Carrie murmured, leaning in a little bit as they drew side by side. "Good luck next game."

"Winner buys dinner tonight?"

Carrie smiled. "That wasn't the bet, but yes."

"Good." Gina nodded and kept walking.

Smiling to herself, Carrie headed back to the bench to ice her arm. She wouldn't pitch the next game unless they were really in trouble.

Flann flopped down beside her. "Nice win."

"Thanks. How are you doing? You must be beat."

Flann stretched, her face drawn and a little pale. "I'm starting to feel it. I'll be good for a couple more hours, though."

"We've got two games tomorrow too," Carrie said. "Maybe you ought to sit this one out."

Flann made a face. "I'll get my second wind when the game starts. I'm not as delicate as some pitchers."

Carrie laughed. "Some of us don't have a God complex."

Flann's brows rose. "Who, me?"

"Yeah, you." Carrie smiled wryly. If she ever needed surgery, she wanted Flann to be the one in the OR. "Harper said things were a mess last night and you were still working when she left. Everybody make it okay?"

"They all made it," Flann said, "but some of them will never be the same. There's only so much a body can take."

Carrie thought of Gina and her ruined knee. How much more had been destroyed that didn't show on the outside? She automatically looked for her, the pressure in her chest easing when she found her leaning against the backstop, drinking from a water bottle and watching the Hammers' pitcher warm up. God, she was good to look at. Even from a distance the thrill was palpable.

"That's the one, huh?" Flann asked.

Carrie glanced at Flann. "Mind reader too?"

Flann laughed. "You know what they say about surgeons—the eye of the eagle, heart of a lion, and hands of a woman."

"No wonder your head is so big." Carrie smiled. "Let's just say she's got my attention."

"Fair enough." Flann rubbed her face. "Blake said some dickhead hassled you after the games a couple times. Tell me or Harp if it happens again, okay?"

"He's just a bad loser, but I will." Carrie scanned the stands. "Are they here?"

"You mean my kid and my sister, presently joined at the hip?" Flann laughed. "They're getting ready to switch over to interning at the vet clinic in a week or so. They're out there this afternoon but should be here soon."

"Good. I'm so glad Blake is doing so well."

"Yeah, me too." Flann stood and stretched. "Time to go kick ass."

Carrie wanted to win. She just wished that didn't mean Gina would lose. But either way, they were having dinner together.

CHAPTER TWENTY-FIVE

Ｈｏw is your shoulder?" Gina said when she caught up to Carrie at the Rivers's bench after the game. She looked pointedly at the ice pack Aced to Carrie's upper arm.

"All ready for tomorrow," Carrie said. "Seriously, though, I'm good. I'll need to ice it a little bit more tonight just to be safe, but that's normal."

Gina automatically grabbed Carrie's duffel bag when Carrie finished zipping it and passed it over to her other hand, where she carried her own.

Smiling, Carrie shook her head.

"What?" Gina asked.

"I kinda feel like we're walking home from school, and you're carrying my books."

"Oh yeah?" Gina grinned. "Is that a problem?"

"You know, it really isn't. I'm pretty sure you know by now I could carry it myself."

Gina chuckled. "Believe me, I'm pretty impressed by everything you can do. I just like doing it."

"I know. I like that." Carrie lifted a shoulder. "You make me feel special."

Gina's chest tightened and she cleared her throat. "Believe me, you are."

"Goes both ways," Carrie said. "I don't let just anyone carry my gear, you know."

"Good." Gina said it a little more forcefully than she meant to, probably more than she had any right to, but she didn't care. She wanted to be the one to make Carrie feel special. She wanted to be the one Carrie looked at with that gut-clenching combination of fire and almost bewildered wonder. She wanted a lot of things, but right now she wanted to watch Carrie's eyes go hazy with need just before she made her come. "So, ah, are you planning to head home and rest up to beat us—or I should say, *try* to beat us tomorrow?"

"I hate to say this," Carrie said, "but I am slightly on the exhausted side." She stopped by the side of her car and gave Gina a look. "I can't imagine why that should be."

Gina tossed Carrie's duffel into the minuscule trunk of her miniscule car, not even trying to keep the smirk off her face. "I think I might have some idea. And it's probably a good idea that you ice your shoulder before you pass out for the night. You'll be pitching tomorrow, won't you?"

"That's the plan."

Gina rested her hip against the car. She ought to let Carrie get home to ice and rest, but damn, she didn't want to let her go. She had nothing to look forward to except a long night of trying to ignore the lust churning up her insides. She blew out a breath. "Good luck."

"Thanks. Same to you guys. It's a great tournament so far."

"It is. Slightly better for us just now being one game up, but we'll be ready for you to come out firing tomorrow."

Carrie ran her finger down the center of Gina's baseball shirt, letting her fingers linger just above the top of her pants. She pressed gently. "I have a feeling you're always ready."

Gina's stomach muscles tensed. "If you don't want to give everybody a show, you'd better not do that again."

Carrie laughed, an altogether evil laugh that sent pounding shock waves straight to the pit of Gina's stomach. "What's the matter? Can't take a little teasing?"

"The way I feel right now?" Gina growled. "No. Not even a little bit." She stepped closer, bracing her hands on the roof and caging Carrie against the side of the car. "Are you going to be upset if I kiss you right now?"

"I think I might be upset if you don't," Carrie murmured.

Gina dipped her head and took Carrie's mouth, the softness of Carrie's lips familiar, but the instant charge of heat flaring in her midsection totally foreign. Carrie's arms came around her waist, trapping her as easily as she'd trapped Carrie. She liked how naturally Carrie set claim to her, and how effortlessly she let herself be claimed. She kept her hands on the top of the car, vaguely aware in the recesses of her still-thinking brain if she touched her, she'd forget where she was and who might be watching. That would never happen again. After a few seconds of searing contact, she gathered the tatters of her willpower and pulled back. Her breath shot in and out of her chest so fast she wasn't sure she was actually breathing. Her legs shook and her stomach swirled. "Every time I look at you, I want to taste you. Every time I do, I want to devour you."

Wide-eyed, Carrie moaned softly and swept both hands up and down Gina's back, her fingers playing over the rigid muscles along her spine. "What do you think about following me to my place, and we'll devour some pizza. Who knows, maybe you'll get lucky."

Gina grinned. "My luck's been good lately."

"So has mine." Carrie pushed Gina away, tracing a finger down the center of her abdomen. "And I'm planning on getting luckier before the night's over."

Gina sucked in a breath. She was barely going to be able to hold together until they were alone. "Before we leave, I'll call and order something to pick up on the way."

"Make sure it's something you want to eat cold," Carrie said. "I'll see you at the house. Thankfully, I've still got a working bathroom."

Gina laughed. "For a few more days."

Carrie kissed her quickly and gave her a little push. "Go."

"I'll see you soon." Gina turned away, her phone already in her hand.

"Drive carefully." Carrie called, watching her for a few more seconds just for the thrill of it. The view from the rear was as hot as the front. She was about to jump in her car when Harper and Presley carried the rest of the gear up to Harper's Jeep.

"Need help?" Carrie called, pretending not to notice the huge grin on Presley's face.

"We got it." Abandoning Harper to stow the gear, Presley hurried around Carrie's car. "I saw that, you know. Who started *that*?"

"No comment."

"Oh, come on. That's just cruel."

"Nope." Carrie couldn't have answered if she wanted to. Gina might have made the first move, but she'd been angling for that kiss and a hell of a lot more since the instant the game had ended and she didn't have to think about team activities. What she had in mind was definitely one-on-one. And soon. God, she was on fire.

"Are you going out for beer and something to eat with us?" Presley said.

"No, I'm beat. Gina's going to grab a pizza, and I'm going to make it an early night."

Presley rolled her eyes. "Oh, sure. If early night means being in bed within the hour, and not alone."

Carrie smirked. "Okay, that might be part of the plan too."

Gina pulled out in her truck, honking the horn to Carrie as she went by. Her window was down, her hair was windblown, and her grin was an invitation to sin. Laughing, Carrie waved.

Presley shook her head. "I gotta say, she's hot."

"Yes, she is," Carrie murmured.

"Okay, I won't keep you since I can see you're just a teeny bit preoccupied with getting home to ice your arm."

"Top of my list," Carrie said, opening her door. "See you tomorrow."

"Save a little for the game tomorrow."

"Don't worry. I'll be ready." She waved to Harper as she backed out and headed for home. Two games to play the next afternoon. They needed to win both to take the tournament. She was looking forward to the challenge, but right now, all she wanted was to get home and get her hands on Gina.

❖

Carrie settled on the back porch with a glass of wine and waited for Gina to arrive. Fifteen minutes later, Gina pulled in and pulled a pizza box from the front seat.

"Beer or wine?" Carrie called, as Gina came up onto the porch.

"Beer would be great." Gina followed Carrie inside, letting the screen door slam shut behind her.

"You can put the pizza on the counter—"

"Done." Gina caught Carrie around the waist from behind, spun her around, and kissed her hard. Carrie automatically backed up until she hit the refrigerator. Gina leaned in to her, her elbows braced on either side of Carrie's shoulders.

"Hi," Gina muttered before kissing her again. "Longest damn three-mile drive in my life."

Carrie arched her neck as Gina kissed along the edge of her jaw and dove into her mouth again. Gina's weight pinned her effortlessly. She couldn't move, didn't want to. The sensation of being captured was as thrilling as the fierceness of Gina's kiss. She laced her arms around Gina's neck and twined her calf around the back of Gina's leg, getting as close to her at every point as she possibly could. Gina's mouth was hot, her lips demanding. Carrie let her take what she needed until she couldn't wait any longer to get her hands on Gina's skin. She grabbed the back of Gina's shirt and tugged it out of her pants, sliding her palms along Gina's sides to the center of her abdomen. Gina groaned.

"Come take a shower with me," Carrie murmured, pushing one hand beneath Gina's waistband. Gina jerked and Carrie pushed lower, stopping with her fingertips just low enough to tease, but not to torture. Too much.

Gina went rigid, a growl rumbling in her throat. "You better stop right there."

"No way," Carrie shot back.

"Then you better be planning to keep going." Gina covered Carrie's hand and lifted her hips into Carrie's palm. Carrie's fingers slid into hot, yielding flesh. Gina closed her eyes and gasped.

"Not yet, baby," Carrie whispered. "I want you naked before I make you come."

"Carrie, come on," Gina said, a note of desperation in her voice.

"Upstairs." Carrie slipped her hand free and Gina stumbled back, breaking their contact with a dazed expression. "I'll take care of you. I promise."

Carrie led her to the staircase, stopping halfway up so she could kiss her again.

"I love the way you taste," Carrie muttered.

"Anytime."

Carrie laughed. "Soon."

They left their clothes in a pile on the bathroom floor and got into the shower together. Carrie soaped her hands, rubbed circles over Gina's chest and belly, and backed her against the shower wall. When she pressed her breasts to Gina's, the slick glide of Gina's skin was as arousing as Gina's fingers inside her. She dug her fingers into Gina's shoulders, straddling her thigh as her sex convulsed. "God. You make me so hot I want to come right now."

"Ride me, then." Gina cupped the back of her neck and kissed her, one hand sliding down her back and over her butt.

Carrie rocked on Gina's leg, their breasts fitting perfectly together. The slick heat pierced her core and she moaned.

"Come on, babe," Gina urged, thrusting hard between Carrie's legs. "Do it for me."

"I'm close," Carrie gasped, shuddering. About to fall. About to shatter.

"Yeah. Now. Come all over me." Gina kissed her harder and deeper.

Carrie threw her head back and wailed. Everything inside her melted at once. Gina's arms tightened around her, holding her up.

"I don't know how that happened," Carrie gasped. "I've never..."

Gina dipped her head and kissed Carrie's breasts. "Good. All mine, then."

Yes, yours. Carrie steadied herself with her hands on Gina's shoulders. "I want to make you come. In bed, like a civilized person."

Gina laughed, ducked her head under the spray, and flipped the wet hair back from her face. She was magnificent. "You want pizza first?"

Carrie laughed. "Hell no. I'm not waiting."

Gina framed her face and kissed her. "I don't think I can."

"Come on." Carrie pushed the shower door open, tugged Gina out, and tossed her a towel. "Race you."

Gina followed Carrie down the hall, leaving a trail of wet footsteps behind. She hastily toweled off on the way and left the towel draped over the back of a wooden chair in Carrie's bedroom.

"Over there." Carrie gave her a shove toward the bed.

Gina grabbed Carrie and pulled her down with her. Carrie landed on top of her, her mouth fused to Gina's, her hand between Gina's legs. One stroke, another, and she was inside her.

Gina's breath stopped in her chest. Her muscles clamped tight and her heart tripped over itself.

"Can you come like this?" Carrie murmured, deep inside her, her teasing strokes short and fast.

"If you stroke my clit," Gina gasped.

"You do it," Carrie ordered and picked up her pace.

Gina was already so close, a few short caresses and she exploded.

Carrie rested her cheek on Gina's shoulder, her face in the curve of Gina's neck. "Oh my God. You are so sexy when you come, I never want to stop."

Gina laughed and rubbed her cheek against the top of Carrie's head. "Like I said, it's all you, babe."

Carrie closed her eyes. "I'm pretty gone on you, Antonelli."

"Ah, Carrie."

Let me see you, Carrie had said.

A surge of panic caught Gina by the throat. She'd gone so long without feeling anything—without even hoping to feel again—she didn't know how to start. Desire, wanting—that came from some primal place she couldn't control. But what Carrie was talking about, what Carrie *deserved*, she wasn't sure she could resurrect. She'd killed that part of herself a long time ago. "I don't want to hurt you."

"I know, and I don't care. It is what it is." Carrie heard the echo of her own words. *The heart wants what it wants.* Even when that road led to heartbreak.

"I wish…"

Carrie pressed her fingers to Gina's mouth. "No. That's not why I said anything. And I don't need you to say anything."

"Don't you?"

Carrie kissed her. "Yes, probably, one day soon. But not tonight."

Gina sat up. "I should let you get some ice on that shoulder."

"First we're eating pizza, and I'm finishing my wine. Plus I owe you a beer."

"Tonight was amazing," Gina said, knowing her words weren't anywhere near enough.

"Yes," Carrie said softly despite the ache in her chest. "It was."

CHAPTER TWENTY-SIX

Stretched out on her back on the dolly under her truck, Gina yanked on the stubborn bolt that refused to loosen. Inventively cursing under her breath, she felt around by her side for a different tool and paused as the crunch of gravel signaled she had a visitor. She scowled. If she'd wanted company she would have answered the phone when it rang, which she hadn't done any of the six times it had annoyed her so far. Turning her head, she regarded the pair of boots lined up next to the truck. She recognized them by the shoelaces. Joe favored red shoelaces.

"Working here," she called.

"You're not answering your phone."

"Like I said, working here."

Joe hunkered down and peered underneath her truck. "You want breakfast?"

"No thanks." He looked tired and Gina sighed. Snapping at her brother wasn't making her feel any better. Working wasn't helping much, either. Every five seconds she thought of Carrie, and the same mix of excitement and apprehension welled up in a tangled knot in her chest. Maybe Joe's company would take her mind off what she didn't want to think about. "You work all night?"

"Nah, midnight to seven. I slept some before I went in last night. Where'd you sleep?"

"Right here." Gina pushed herself out on the dolly and sat up, leaning back against the side of the truck. "Did you just come by to personally invite me to breakfast?"

He turned and sat on the ground next to her, stretching his legs out. "I *called* you about breakfast first. Then when you didn't answer, I figured I'd come around. Haven't seen that much of you lately."

"Busy."

"Uh-huh. Too busy to go out after the games with the team. Too busy for breakfast. What's next, skipping family meals?"

Gina snorted. "Yeah, like that would work. Death and softball are the only two reasons to miss one."

Joe grinned. "So what's going on?"

"Nothing." Okay, so maybe she snapped a little after all. Joe was in one of his niggling get-her-to-talk moods, and if she'd wanted to do that, she would have answered the phone when Carrie called. She would have confessed to Carrie that the idea of getting close to her—really close, like thinking about her every second of every day, and wanting to touch her every time she saw her, and wanting, hell *needing* to tell about all the things she kept locked away inside—was paralyzing her.

Joe nudged her foot with his. "Yeah, that's why you're working on the truck at eight o'clock on a Sunday morning. And not answering your phone. So what is it? Woman troubles?"

The churning in her middle expanded until she couldn't take a deep breath. She'd left Carrie's around eleven after a late meal of beer and cold pizza. At three a.m., she was still staring at the ceiling. At five she gave up. She hadn't wanted to leave Carrie's, and every second that she'd stayed, she'd been torn over wondering if she was being fair. Carrie had been honest and she'd taken a chance revealing how she felt, and Gina wasn't sure she even knew where to start. Blake and Margie, two kids nearly half her age, had more guts than she did.

"Carrie's serious," Gina murmured.

"And you're not?"

Gina stared at the wrench in her hand. She'd scraped her knuckles on the underside of the carriage, and blood streaked the tops of her fingers. She remembered fragments of the accident, mostly in her dreams, but she could never remember seeing Emmy in the wreck next to her. Only pain and flashing lights and the taste of blood in her mouth. She was glad she didn't see her and felt like a coward for not wanting to know. "You know, it was my fault, that night."

"Why?" Joe didn't even need to ask her what she was talking

about. That night was a constant companion, the uninvited guest at every conversation, the secret they both kept.

"She went out with Kevin to some party, and he got wasted. I was so pissed off at him."

"Kevin"—Joe said the name like it was a curse word—"always was an asshole."

"I was pissed at her too. And myself." Gina took a deep breath and told him all of it. Her fury, the kiss and the guys who saw it, the threats, Emmy's panic. When she finished, Joe scrubbed his face with both hands and let out a long breath that sounded like it hurt.

"Fuck, Gina. Why didn't you say something?"

"You're the only one I could've told." She closed her eyes. "And we both know what you would've done."

"Hell—"

"Language," she muttered.

"Fucking hell," Joe said, "I feel like doing it now. Where is the asshole these days, anyhow?"

"Kevin?" Gina grimaced. "He married Chrissy Dominic, remember? Like six months after the accident."

"Yeah, his *girlfriend* dying had a big effect on him, I guess," Joe said.

"Wasn't his fault, not really," Gina said. "He didn't put us in that car. I did."

"That's bullshit," Joe said sharply. "You and Emmy had been together, what, five years by then? She was your girl. She had plenty of time to change her mind about the two of you, and you waited in the fucking dark for her. You didn't do anything wrong."

"It wasn't really like that," Gina said softly, opening her eyes. "We figured when we went away to school, we'd have more freedom, and Emmy would tell her parents eventually."

"Yeah," Joe said with a weary sigh. "I get it. I know it made sense to you then. But damn, Gina. You gotta let it go now. You gotta have a life."

"I'm not sure I can let anybody in, not all the way." Gina met his gaze. "Something's missing inside me, I think."

"I don't believe that, but I'm not the one who needs to." Joe's tone was as unyielding as their father's when he'd settled on a course of action. "This one's on you, sis, and you better decide before it's too late."

❖

Carrie tried Gina's cell one more time and got voice mail again. She disconnected without leaving a message. Gina knew her number. She'd see the missed call. If she'd wanted to call her back, she probably would have by now. Carrie turned her phone over and over in her hands, too restless to spend the next six hours wondering what Gina was doing or second-guessing herself over how dumb she'd been blurting out her feelings when she knew damn well it was way too soon to go there. She just didn't want to pretend she felt anything less than she already did. Maybe she shouldn't have said anything, but sometimes feelings were too big to keep secret. And sometimes secrets like that had a way of coming back to haunt you.

Carrie considered her options. She could call her sister, but seeing as it was still dark in California and Erin liked getting up early about as much as she did, that was out. Mari was working nights in the ER. She'd just be getting ready for bed. She finally called Presley.

"Hey!" Presley said. "You're up bright and early."

"Have any of those cinnamon buns left?"

"Only about half a dozen. Lila baked, remember?" Presley laughed. "You want to come over?"

"It's Sunday morning." *Good one, Carrie. State the obvious.* "I don't want to barge in."

"Harper is out back putting a new roof on the chicken coop. I'm sitting on the porch with my second cup of coffee reading a book. You won't be interrupting anything."

"I'll be there in ten minutes."

"I'll be sitting in the same spot," Presley said.

Carrie grabbed her softball uniform from the dryer and stuffed it into her duffel, tossed her phone and wallet in after, and was out the door in two minutes. When she pulled around back, Presley was exactly where she'd said she would be, in a rocker on the back porch, her feet propped on the railing, tablet in her lap.

"Coffee and cinnamon buns in the kitchen," Presley said, waving her inside.

"Thanks." Carrie helped herself in the familiar kitchen and plopped into the rocker next to Presley. At eight thirty in the morning it was already close to ninety. "This feels a little bit like Phoenix."

"Funny," Presley mused, "Phoenix seems like another planet. This place feels like home to me. Like it's always been home."

"You're right. It does to me too." Carrie broke off a piece of the gooey, deliciously sinful cinnamon bun. In the distance, Harper was banging away at the chicken coop. The young chickens pecked and squawked in the dooryard under Rooster's self-important gaze. "I'm definitely getting chickens. Do you think Harper will build me a chicken coop?"

Presley laughed. "I'm sure we can rustle up a few people to do that, but should I point out that you appear to have your own carpenter at hand?"

Carrie let out a long sigh. "Maybe."

Presley set her coffee cup and tablet on the porch beside her. "What does that mean?"

Carrie picked at her cinnamon bun.

"Hmm," Presley said, "if you're not eating that, there's something very wrong."

"I'm in love with her," Carrie said.

"So is this visit about Gina or about you?"

Carrie caught her breath. "What do you mean?"

"Since you're here before nine, and it's *way* past business hours, and you're not eating, I've come to the brilliant deduction you're not happy."

"I'm not sure it's a good thing."

"Really?" Presley sounded surprised. "Is being in love ever a bad thing?"

Carrie's knee-jerk reaction was to say *sometimes*. But maybe what she really needed to do was separate her feelings from what she was worried Gina would do about them. Somewhere, someone had documented all the neurochemicals and hormones and other bodily things that being emotionally connected released, attempting no doubt to explain away the irrational feeling of being in love, but she knew better. Being in love changed a person. Gina stirred her, awakened things in her, excited and satisfied her. The world seemed a little sharper and brighter and more challenging, as if she'd stripped away a layer of insulation that had been wrapped around her until now. She wouldn't trade that sensation of being more alive, more herself, than she'd ever been before just because she couldn't predict—or control—what might happen.

"Being in love is amazing." Carrie laughed. "As if that's a news flash."

Presley grasped her hand and squeezed. "It's hard to separate the feelings from the expectations. But I say enjoy the experience, because it's special, no matter what comes next."

"Well, I told her, more or less," Carrie said, "so the what comes next is coming fast."

"Did she run screaming from the house?"

"Maybe, metaphorically." Carrie finished off the cinnamon bun and mentally replayed the night before. Again. When they'd finally gotten out of bed they'd attacked the pizza and talked about everything *except* their relationship—the work on her house, the rest of the softball season, a television series they both followed. When Gina left, she hadn't made another date, and so far this morning, she hadn't called or answered her phone. "It's complicated—"

"Isn't it always?" Presley glanced out toward Harper, perched on a ladder in a T-shirt and cut-off jeans, and smiled. "Relationships are always complicated, even when they look simple on the surface." She turned her gaze back to Carrie. "Is this complication something time can fix or something a lot more permanent?"

"I think it's something only Gina can fix," Carrie murmured. "I'm just not sure she believes she can."

❖

When Carrie got to the ball field, Gina's truck wasn't in the parking lot. By the time she finished her warm-up pitches with Harper, Gina was on the field running batting practice with her team. Carrie set the disappointment aside. She had a game to pitch.

The Hammers had come to play after dropping a game the afternoon before. Their hitters were hitting and their fielders seemed to be everywhere at once, scooping up ground balls and making impossible throws, snagging fly balls that ought to have been out of the park and generally shutting down the Rivers's lineup. Carrie pitched all nine innings, going a dozen pitches more than she probably should have, but she'd given up three runs and was one run down. She held them at that but needed a miracle to get the win. Chana Clark, their left fielder, finally saved her when she hit a triple with two runners on base and drove in the winning runs for them. At the end of four games, they were all tied up, two games each.

The teams lined up for the postgame shake before they took a break between games.

"Good luck next game," Carrie said when she reached Gina.

"You too," Gina said. Her gaze lingered on Carrie's, the weight of the words unspoken between them hanging in the air.

No invitation for the winner to buy dinner this time.

Carrie felt the press of the rest of the team moving along the line behind her. She stepped out of the way and backtracked to where Gina stood by her bench.

"Gina," Carrie said.

Gina turned, a quick smile lighting her eyes. "Hey."

"Dinner later?" Carrie paused. "No strings."

"Is that really what you want?" Gina asked.

Carrie didn't care who was listening. "No. Not even a little bit, but if that's what works for now, I'm good with it."

"I'm not so sure I am." Gina shrugged. "The strings part, that is."

"Is that a yes, then?" Carrie grinned when Gina nodded, and just like that, the cloud she'd been wrapped in disappeared. "See you later, then."

Carrie sprinted back to her bench, and Harper tossed her an ice pack. "You're done."

"Maybe—"

"No way. I was counting pitches, and you're over your limit." Harper laughed. "But we needed that win."

"I know. They're on fire today."

"You're sitting out this one and the next couple of games." Harper held up a finger when Carrie started to protest. "No arguing."

"Yes, Coach," Carrie said with a sigh.

"Good." Harper frowned as Abby jumped down from the bleachers and hurried their way with a worried frown creasing her face. "Hey, Abs. Something wrong?"

"Where's Joe? I need to talk to him right away."

"I think he went to fill the water cooler," Carrie said.

"I'll get him," Harper said and jogged away.

"Thanks. I'll be over at the other bench."

Stomach roiling, Carrie watched as Abby signaled to Gina, and Joe sprinted across the field to join them. Seconds later, all three of them ran toward the parking lot. Instinctively, Carrie followed. Something was wrong if Gina was leaving. When she reached the lot, Gina's truck flew past in a cloud of dust. Watching her go, Carrie's heart sank.

She started back to the ball field when the sound of an engine braking hard pulled her around. Gina's truck reversed with a screech and slammed to a halt a few feet away. Carrie ran through the swirling dust and bits of shredded grass and yanked open the passenger door.

"Gina?"

Gina held out a shaking hand. "Can you come? It's my dad."

CHAPTER TWENTY-SEVEN

As soon as Carrie slammed the door, Gina floored the gas and fishtailed the truck across the dirt track toward the highway. Carrie grabbed for her seat belt.

"Do you want me to drive?" Carrie asked quietly.

Gina shot her a look, glanced down at the speedometer and, bracing both hands on the wheel, sucked in a long breath. "Sorry. No." She eased off on the gas, staring straight ahead. "Sorry. You must think I'm crazy."

"No, of course not. I'm glad I'm here." Carrie leaned as close as she could and settled her hand on Gina's thigh. "What happened?"

Gina briefly covered Carrie's hand before gripping the wheel with white-knuckled hands.

"Mari was on call," Gina said, her voice flat and, if Carrie hadn't known better, emotionless. Nothing could be less true. She was nothing but emotion—her body vibrated with pent-up tension. "He collapsed at the office. Thankfully, one of our crew was right there picking up his check, and he called 9-1-1." She grimaced. "That's all I know."

"He's got the best people taking care of him now." Carrie swallowed back the platitudes and other reassurances she knew wouldn't help, as much as she craved some way to comfort her.

"That's what I keep telling myself." Gina's jaw tightened. She took the corner onto the main road into town on two wheels and instantly slowed again. "Damn it. This is our fault."

"Whose fault?"

"Mine, Joe's." Gina bit off the words as if they had a bitter taste.

"My dad told us he had to go in for tests. Some kind of irregularity with his heart. We didn't push him and now this happens."

"He couldn't be in a better place right now." Carrie didn't argue. Even trying to rationalize with her was pointless and, more importantly, not what Gina needed. Right now, Gina just needed help holding her fear at bay. Carrie rubbed her palm up and down Gina's thigh, fighting her own sense of helplessness. She wanted to do more than comfort her—she wanted to stand between Gina and anything that threatened to hurt her. She'd never felt like much of a warrior, but she was ready to go to battle now. "Let's trust Abby and Mari and the others, okay?"

Gina turned onto the road up to the hospital and glanced quickly at Carrie. "I trust you."

Carrie smiled and forced a calm she didn't feel. "Then trust me on this one. Absolutely everything that needs to be done will be done."

Gina pulled in to the ER lot and braked so quickly, Carrie rocked forward against her seat belt. Gina grabbed her hand. "Are you okay?"

"Yes, fine. Where do you want me to wait?" Carrie said.

Gina met her gaze, and nothing shielded the pain and uncertainty riding her. "I want you to come with me. Can you?"

Carrie released her seat belt. "Absolutely."

Gina jumped out and Carrie hurried to join her. Gina grasped her hand again, and they ran across the lot to the double doors of the ER. When they hurried inside, Joe, standing in the hall outside the waiting room where he could watch the entrance and corridor to the main treatment area, was the first person Carrie saw.

"Anything?" Gina called.

Joe shook his head, his gaze taking them both in, lingering for a second on their joined hands. His grim expression lightened a little. "Abby's back there now. They wouldn't let me go back." He ran a hand through his hair, making the sweat-dampened locks curl along the back of his neck in an unintentionally attractive fashion. "I understand why they're keeping me out, but it's making me crazy."

Gina released Carrie's hand and squeezed Joe's arm. His distress seemed to have the opposite effect on hers, and the rigid set of her shoulders softened. "Abby and Mari are back there. They'll handle it."

"Yeah, I know."

A tall woman in a pale blue shirt and casual dark pants appeared beside Joe. Carrie didn't need an introduction to know who she was. Carrie's stomach fluttered. Gina's mother was nearly Joe's height, her dark shoulder-length hair shot through with silver and worn loose, her face strong featured, her eyes sharp and penetrating. Her focus landed on Gina and Carrie and stayed there, as commanding as if she'd laid a hand on Carrie's shoulder.

Gina said, "Mom, this is Carrie."

Gina's mother nodded. "The picnic girl."

Carrie stepped forward and held out her hand. She'd faced worse appraisals and had every reason to be sure of herself now. She was there for Gina. "Yes, among other things. I'm Carrie Longmire. I'm very happy to meet you, although I wish it wasn't under these circumstances."

"We can't always pick our times, can we?" Gina's mother's hand was firm and steady. "I'm Jeanne Antonelli. Gina should have brought you to dinner before this."

"Thank you," Carrie said softly, "I definitely enjoyed the chicken."

"We'll talk about that," Jeanne said.

"Mom!" A nearly identical version of Gina with longer hair and a fuller body came charging through the ER entrance toward them. "What's happening?"

"Your father had an episode at the office," Jeanne said to Gina's sister. "We don't know yet exactly what it is." She looked sharply from Joe to Gina. "Do we?"

Joe straightened, but Gina spoke first. "He didn't say anything to you, did he?"

Gina's mother's eyes narrowed. "No, but I knew there was something. He told you?"

Carrie backed up a little bit, separating herself to give them privacy, although none of them appeared to care that she was there. Gina had brought her, and apparently, that was enough.

"He said he had to go in for some tests soon," Gina said. "He didn't let on how serious it was, or maybe he didn't know."

Joe finally found his voice. "And he said he was going to tell you."

Jeanne drew in a breath and nodded once. "Well, I'll take that up with him a little bit later."

The Gina look-alike finally noticed Carrie and smiled, a question in her eyes. "Hi, I'm Angie."

"Carrie," Carrie said, holding out her hand. "I'm—"

"She's with me," Gina said.

She's with me.

Those seemed to be the magic words, as Angie immediately turned to Joe and peppered him with questions. Gina swayed and braced her arm against the wall. Carrie quickly moved to her side and stroked her back. Out of the corner of her eye, she saw Gina's mother and sister watching her. She didn't move her hand.

"Hey," she said quietly, "you could use something to eat and drink. Probably everyone else can too."

Gina, dark circles already forming under her eyes, shook her head. "I don't think I could eat anything."

"Then at least have something to drink. Why don't you get your mother to sit awhile, and I'll go to the cafeteria and find some sandwiches and drinks."

"You're not leaving yet, are you?"

"No. Not as long as you need me."

Gina's smile was grim. "I don't think you have any idea what that might mean."

"Oh, I think I do." Carrie gestured toward the waiting room. "Go ahead. I'll be right back."

Joe, standing nearby, must've overheard, because he said quickly, "I'll go with you." He glanced at Gina. "Text me if Abby comes back."

"Okay."

When they were out of earshot of the family, Carrie said, "How serious is it, do you think?"

Joe grimaced. "I don't have any idea. When my father told me and Gina he needed some tests, he pretty much downplayed the situation, and we didn't push."

Carrie squeezed his arm. "Hey, parents are adults, remember. And they never listen to their kids, even when we're adults too."

He sighed. "Oh yeah, I know. But it's hard not to beat yourself up."

"Believe me, I understand. I would probably do the same thing in your place."

"It's probably none of my business—no, as a matter of fact, it's definitely none of my business—but I'm glad you're here with Gina."

"I am too."

"She told you, didn't she."

"Joe," Carrie said gently, mindful of protecting Gina's privacy, "you can trust your sister. She's a lot stronger than you might think."

"Sorry," he muttered. "I'm meddling, and I shouldn't be, but I love her, you know."

"Yes, well, she's very special."

He shot her a look and a little of the tension left his face. "That's real good, then."

Yes, Carrie thought, *it is.*

When Carrie and Joe got back with the sandwiches, Abby still hadn't come out with a progress report. Carrie finally coaxed Gina to have something to eat, even if she insisted she wasn't hungry. She could tell from Gina's mother's expression that had won her some points. She wasn't sure if she needed them, but she'd take then anyhow. Just as they were all finishing, Abby walked in and everyone leapt to their feet.

"He's stable," Abby said instantly, addressing Gina's mother but including everyone who gathered around in her gaze. "He most likely had a brief period of cardiac arrhythmia—irregular heartbeat—that triggered an episode of angina. Not a full heart attack, but the next step to it. The cardiologist is with him now, and we're going to admit him for observation. He's probably going to need further treatment, most likely the placement of cardiac stents."

Gina's mother stood tall and straight, her eyes laser sharp on Abby's. "And he'll be all right after that?"

"The procedure has a very high success rate, but I'll leave that to the cardiologist to discuss with you." She glanced at Joe for the first time. "It's Warren Chu. I think you know him, and he's one of the best."

Joe looked relieved. "I do. That's good."

"You can see him when he gets upstairs," Abby said, "probably in about forty-five minutes."

Gina squeezed Carrie's hand. "You don't have to wait."

"Will you call me after you get home?"

Gina nodded. "I will."

"I'll be waiting."

❖

Carrie's phone was ringing as she pulled in behind her house. She thought it was Gina and grabbed her phone. "Hello?"

"Hey," Presley said. "How are things at the hospital?"

"All right, I think." Carrie filled her in on what had happened.

"How are you?"

"Other than exhausted, I'm okay. I'm worried, but Abby was very positive. And Gina's okay."

"That's great."

"So?" Carrie said. "What happened at the game?"

"I'll just give it to you quick. We lost."

"Oh, well." The tournament seemed very long ago and not nearly as important as the last few hours. "I lost my bet, and I'll have to take Gina out to dinner."

Presley laughed. "And somehow, I don't think that's going to be a hardship."

"You know what?" Carrie laughed. "You're right."

Carrie walked through the house as she talked, and by the time she reached the bedroom and said good-bye, all she wanted was a shower and to close her eyes for a few minutes. When the sound of a vehicle pulling into her yard woke her, it was dark. Carrie sat up and checked the time.

Eight thirty. The days were getting shorter, but the little pang of disappointment that always followed the realization summer was ending quickly vanished when she looked out the window. Gina was getting out of her truck. Carrie had fallen asleep in a tank top and boxers after her shower, and right now she didn't care she wasn't at her sexiest best. She raced downstairs and out the door to the porch. When Gina saw her, she took the stairs two at a time and pulled Carrie into her arms. When Gina kissed her, Carrie shuddered under the surge of desire that crashed through her. Gina's mouth was firm and demanding, her hands possessive as they swept beneath her tank to cup her breasts. Carrie clutched her shoulders to steady herself under the onslaught.

When Gina finally pulled back, she said hoarsely, "I thought I'd go completely crazy before I finally got here. I'm sorry I didn't call. I just needed to see you so bad."

Carrie grabbed her hand. "Shut up and come upstairs."

As soon as she reached the bedroom, Carrie yanked off her tank top and kicked off her bottoms. Gina was right behind her. Naked and panther sleek, Gina grabbed her and tumbled her onto the bed. Gina's body covered hers, her mouth and her hands everywhere. Carrie wrapped her legs around Gina's hips.

"Don't stop touching me," Carrie urged. "I want you. I want you to take me."

Gina did, filling her, driving her up and over, hard and fast. When Carrie came, the sharp release was almost a shock and she cried out in surprise.

"Carrie," Gina murmured, her lips against Carrie's throat. "Carrie."

"Don't worry." Carrie kissed her neck, slid her thigh between Gina's, and dragged her as close as she could. "I'm real and I'm right here."

"*Yes.*" Gina braced herself on her arms, her mouth on Carrie's breast, and thrust against Carrie's leg until she stiffened with a deep groan.

Carrie wrapped her arms around her and kissed her sweat-dampened cheek. "You make me feel like a god when you come."

Gina laughed weakly. "I think you might be. I can't even think when you're touching me. All I can do is feel."

"I think that's how it's supposed to be."

Gina kissed Carrie's throat. "So do I."

"Are you all right?" Carrie said.

"A lot better now."

"Did you see your dad?"

"Yeah. He's already complaining."

Carrie smiled in the dark. "That's good news, then."

"Thanks for being there."

"Of course."

"You know what you said, this afternoon?" Gina said slowly.

"Which part?"

"About us getting together tonight. With no strings?"

Carrie's heart pounded. "I remember."

"That's not gonna work for me," Gina said.

The hammering in Carrie's chest got even harder. "Oh? Why not?"

Gina rolled onto her side and wrapped her arm around Carrie's middle. "Because I'm already all tangled up where you're concerned, and I want everything that goes with being with you. I want you."

"You already have me. Remember when I told you I was on the way to falling in love with you?"

"I remember," Gina said in a hushed whisper.

"I'm done falling, and I've landed," Carrie said. "And I love you, with all the strings attached."

"That's exactly what I need," Gina said, "because I love you too."

EPILOGUE

You look great," Gina said, leaning against the bedroom door, observing Carrie finish putting on her makeup. She'd watched her do it a dozen times now and still hadn't gotten over the fascination of her small, precise movements and all the subtle ways she accentuated and enhanced and highlighted. Nothing to her way of thinking was needed to make Carrie beautiful, but the process was like an exotic and private dance, and one that gave her secret pleasure to know she and she alone got to share in.

Carrie's eyes met hers in the mirror and she smiled softly. "Are you watching me?"

"You know I am."

Carrie's cheeks colored faintly as she chose another of the mysterious little vials on the dressing table they'd resurrected from the attic and moved down to the bedroom. Carrie had only planned to stay a few days while Gina tore out the plumbing at Carrie's, and a few days had become three weeks.

Neither of them mentioned the time passing, and now the bedroom seemed like theirs.

"I don't think I'll ever get tired of you watching me," Carrie said softly.

"Good thing about that, because I'm never going to stop."

Carrie put down the comb she'd just picked up. "You need to stop watching me right now."

"Why is that?"

"Because we have a wedding to get to in eighty-seven minutes, and I don't want to be out of sorts all day."

Gina laughed. The thrill of Carrie's desire rushed over her, as fresh and powerful as the first time they'd touched. "Sixty seconds."

"Don't brag, and I'm not that easy."

"Just to get you through the day."

Carrie pivoted quickly and tossed a hairbrush at Gina's head.

Gina caught it out of the air. "Nice arm."

"No kidding." Carrie cocked an eyebrow. "I notice you haven't bothered to button your shirt. Finish buttoning and stop trying to seduce me."

Gina strode across the room, bent over, and kissed her carefully. She'd learned the proper timing to messing up the makeup, and this was definitely not it just yet. "You don't mean that."

Carrie cupped her cheek. "No, I don't. But you'll just have to hold on to it until tonight."

Gina knelt by Carrie's chair and draped an arm around Carrie's shoulders. "Will you think about me today?"

"I think about you every minute of every day, and today will be no different." Carrie tilted her head. "Well, almost every minute, except when I'm helping to calm Abby down—every bride gets the jitters."

"Of course."

Carrie leaned an elbow on Gina's shoulder and played with a lock of dark hair. "You know, it's been two weeks since I got the permits for the ER extension straightened out, and you haven't spent much time on-site. You don't have to finish Harper's house yourself."

"Harper's house?" Gina said softly.

Carrie blushed. "I haven't actually lived there much, so I still think of it that way most times."

"About that," Gina said.

"What?"

"We've only got a couple more weeks, so I'll finish the job at Harper's with my crew. The ER project is going to run into full winter, so I'll pick that up as soon as I'm done. But..." Gina took Carrie's hand. "I'd really like it if you moved in here with me."

Carrie caught her lip between her teeth. "I don't suppose Harper would have any trouble renting or selling the other place."

"I'm sure she wouldn't."

"You know, if I stay, it's forever."

Gina kissed her. "That's what I'm counting on."

Carrie kissed her back, and whispered, "I already love this place almost as much as I love you. So forever is just the beginning."

About the Author

Radclyffe has written over fifty romance and romantic intrigue novels, dozens of short stories, and, writing as L.L. Raand, has authored a paranormal romance series, The Midnight Hunters.

She is an eight-time Lambda Literary Award finalist in romance, mystery, and erotica—winning in both romance (*Distant Shores, Silent Thunder*) and erotica (*Erotic Interludes 2: Stolen Moments* edited with Stacia Seaman and *In Deep Waters 2: Cruising the Strip* written with Karin Kallmaker). A member of the Saints and Sinners Literary Hall of Fame, she is also an RWA/FF&P Prism Award winner for *Secrets in the Stone*, an RWA FTHRW Lories and RWA HODRW winner for *Firestorm*, an RWA Bean Pot winner for *Crossroads*, an RWA Laurel Wreath winner for *Blood Hunt*, and the 2016 Book Buyers Best award winner for *Price of Honor*. In 2014 she was awarded the Dr. James Duggins Outstanding Mid-Career Novelist Award by the Lambda Literary Foundation. She is a featured author in the 2015 documentary film *Love Between the Covers*, from Blueberry Hill Productions.

She is also the president of Bold Strokes Books, one of the world's largest independent LGBTQ publishing companies.

Find her at facebook.com/Radclyffe.BSB, follow her on Twitter @RadclyffeBSB, and visit her website at Radfic.com.

Books Available From Bold Strokes Books

Change in Time by Robyn Nyx. Working in the past is hell on your future. The Extractor series: Book Two. (978-162639-880-1)

Love After Hours by Radclyffe. When Gina Antonelli agrees to renovate Carrie Longmire's new house, she doesn't welcome Carrie's overtures at friendship or her own unexpected attraction. A Rivers Community Novel. (978-163555-090-0)

Nantucket Rose by CF Frizzell. Maggie Jordan can't wait to convert a historic Nantucket home into a B&B, but doesn't expect to fall for mariner Ellis Chilton, who has more claim to the house than Maggie realizes. (978-163555-056-6)

Picture Perfect by Lisa Moreau. Falling in love wasn't supposed to be part of the stakes for Olive and Gabby, rival photographers in the competition of a lifetime. (978-162639-975-4)

Set the Stage by Karis Walsh. Actress Emilie Danvers takes the stage again in Ashland, Oregon, little realizing that landscaper Arden Philips is about to offer her a very personal romantic lead role. (978-163555-087-0)

Strike a Match by Fiona Riley. When their attempts at matchmaking fizzle out, firefighter Sasha and reluctant millionairess Abby find themselves turning to each other to strike a perfect match. (978-162639-999-0)

The Price of Cash by Ashley Bartlett. Cash Braddock is doing her best to keep her business afloat, stay out of jail, and avoid Detective Kallen. It's not working. (978-162639-708-8)

Under Her Wing by Ronica Black. At Angel's Wings Rescue, dogs are usually the ones saved, but when quiet Kassandra Haden meets outspoken owner Jayden Beaumont, the two stubborn women just might end up saving each other. (978-163555-077-1)

Captured Soul by Laydin Michaels. Can Kadence Munroe save the woman she loves from a twisted killer, or will she lose her to a collector of souls? (978-162639-915-0)

Underwater Vibes by Mickey Brent. When Hélène, a translator in Brussels, Belgium, meets Sylvie, a young Greek photographer and swim coach, unsettling feelings hijack Hélène's mind and body—even her poems. (978-163555-002-3)

A Date to Die by Anne Laughlin. Someone is killing people close to Detective Kay Adler, who must look to her own troubled past for a suspect. There she finds more than one person seeking revenge against her. (978-163555-023-8)

Dawn's New Day by TJ Thomas. Can Dawn Oliver and Cam Cooper, two women who have loved and lost, open their hearts to love again? (978-163555-072-6)

Definite Possibility by Maggie Cummings. Sam Miller is just out for good times, but Lucy Weston makes her realize happily ever after is a definite possibility. (978-162639-909-9)

Eyes Like Those by Melissa Brayden. Isabel Chase and Taylor Andrews struggle between love and ambition from the writers' room on one of Hollywood's hottest TV shows. (978-163555-012-2)

Heart's Orders by Jaycie Morrison. Helen Tucker and Tee Owens escape hardscrabble lives to careers in the Women's Army Corps, but more than their hearts are at risk as friendship blossoms into love. (978-163555-073-3)

Hiding Out by Kay Bigelow. Treat Dandridge is unaware that her life is in danger from the murderer who is hunting the woman she's falling in love with, Mickey Heiden. (978-162639-983-9)

Omnipotence Enough by Sophia Kell Hagin. Can the tiny tool that abducted war veteran Jamie Gwynmorgan accidentally acquires help her escape an unknown enemy to reclaim her stolen life and the woman she deeply loves? (978-163555-037-5)

Summer's Cove by Aurora Rey. Emerson Lange moved to Provincetown to live in the moment, but when she meets Darcy Belo and her son Liam, her quest for summer romance becomes a family affair. (978-162639-971-6)

The Road to Wings by Julie Tizard. Lieutenant Casey Tompkins, Air Force student pilot, has to fly with the toughest instructor, Captain Kathryn "Hard Ass" Hardesty, fly a supersonic jet, and deal with a growing forbidden attraction. (978-162639-988-4)

Beauty and the Boss by Ali Vali. Ellis Renois is at the top of the fashion world, but she never expects her summer assistant Charlotte Hamner to tear her heart and her business apart like sharp scissors through cheap material. (978-162639-919-8)

Fury's Choice by Brey Willows. When gods walk amongst humans, can two women find a balance between love and faith? (978-162639-869-6)

Lessons in Desire by MJ Williamz. Can a summer love stand a four-month hiatus and still burn hot? (978-163555-019-1)

Lightning Chasers by Cass Sellars. For Sydney and Parker, being a couple was never what they had planned. Now they have to fight corruption, murder, and enemies hiding in plain sight just to hold on to each other. Lightning Series, Book Two. (978-162639-965-5)

Summer Fling by Jean Copeland. Still jaded from a breakup years earlier, Kate struggles to trust falling in love again when a summer fling with sexy young singer Jordan rocks her off her feet. (978-162639-981-5)

Take Me There by Julie Cannon. Adrienne and Sloan know it would be career suicide to mix business with pleasure, however tempting it is. But what's the harm? They're both consenting adults. Who would know? (978-162639-917-4)

Unchained Memories by Dena Blake. Can a woman give herself completely when she's left a piece of herself behind? (978-162639-993-8)